She's Leaving Home

JOAN BAKEWELL

virago

VIRAGO

First published in Great Britain in 2011 by Virago Press
This paperback edition published in 2012 by Virago Press

Copyright © Joan Bakewell 2011

The moral right of the author has been asserted.

*All characters and events in this publication, other than those
clearly in the public domain, are fictitious and any resemblance
to real persons, living or dead, is purely coincidental.*

All rights reserved.
No part of this publication may be reproduced, stored in a
retrieval system, or transmitted in any form or by any means, without
the prior permission in writing of the publisher, nor be otherwise circulated
in any form of binding or cover other than that in which it is published
and without a similar condition including this condition being
imposed on the subsequent purchaser.

A CIP catalogue record for this book
is available from the British Library.

ISBN 978-1-84408-670-2

Typeset in Palatino by M Rules
Printed and bound in Great Britain by
Clays Ltd, St Ives plc

Papers used by Virago are from well-managed forests
and other responsible sources.

MIX
Paper from
responsible sources
FSC® C104740

Virago Press
An imprint of
Little, Brown Book Group
100 Victoria Embankment
London EC4Y 0DY

An Hachette UK Company
www.hachette.co.uk

www.virago.co.uk

To my sister, Susan

Chapter 1

They had agreed to meet in the foyer; funny word, 'foyer'. Sounded to Martha a bit French. Like that film star Charles Boyer. She didn't know how to pronounce him either.

Martha loved these forbidden visits. She stood on the gaudy threshold, the night dark with fog behind her, and drank it all in. The Grande was the town's prime cinema. Its owner – the dilapidated Mr Vernon – had insisted on the final 'e' to add tone to the place. It had given Staveley, a drab little town on the outskirts of one of the north's most imperial cities, to which it played second fiddle in so many ways, a bit of glamour. About thirty years ago, Mr Vernon had rounded up the necessary finance from his Masonic Lodge colleagues and, through the same business contacts, acquired a corner site where the through-roads travelling north and south converged into Staveley's main square, the hub of the town's activities. The result had surprised even him. The Grande's gleaming white tiles towered storeys high over the bus station and the beetling rows of shops that edged past it and up the hill. In front, the broad space of pavement accommodated a clump of dusty trees, trees that thinned out around the square's perimeter pavements. It was the trees that had once given Staveley some sense of gentility, but by the late 1950s industrial decline had blighted that claim.

Martha had arrived in her school gaberdine: a faded and crumpled navy coat that scarcely covered her wrists and was embarrassingly short about her knees. She had left school the previous term but her mother insisted there was a good deal of wear in it, even though they both knew she had grown out of it and looked ridiculous. Underneath her coat she wore a fawn tweed skirt and a favourite knitted sweater she loved for its poppy-red colour and cable-stitched pattern. It was just a pity that her aunt's arthritic fingers had let slip a stitch or two when she knitted it. What had promised to be a show-off garment among her friends had become an embarrassment. She ached to break free and make her own choices. But it wasn't easy. On the last day of school she had cut off her plaits with the kitchen scissors and now her coarse black hair was all over the place. She stood by the changing pink and green lights of the Grande's floodlit alcove hoping their peachy bloom would cast its spell.

A queue was forming at the box office, held back by a crimson rope slung between two brass poles. It was early evening and women with aching legs and shopping baskets huddled close, pointedly ignoring a cluster of lads in draped jackets and narrowing trousers. The film was proving popular with all classes. 'An electrifying adult experience' the poster promised. Sex in films was getting bolder and bolder. A nervous excitement seemed to flutter along the queue.

Martha had come to know the staff of the Grande ever since her father had first brought her to the cinema and she'd been ushered into the plush seats, proudly knowing that it was her dad behind the sprockety sound and smoky white light showing the picture. And then, just over a year ago when she had had her fifteenth birthday and was still in knee-high white socks, he smuggled her into his projection box. She was his only and adored child and she knew he wanted her to share his passion for film. He had sat her on the high stool by the porthole that looked out over the auditorium where, spellbound, she watched the worlds of gunmen and hoodlums, cowboys riding the big country and glamorous women in slinky gowns sipping drinks from wide glasses. But the films were changing. The times were changing. And so was she.

As she waited to be collected she looked around her with the keen attention that went with growing up. There was the cheerful bulk of Josie fitting tightly inside the crisp little box office booth, her red nails chattering on the chrome keys that delivered the tickets. Across the once elegantly patterned carpet, now washed out with frequent efforts to remove the mud from wet shoes, was the sweet counter, where a lad called Frankie doled out viciously bright sweets from tall jars, pausing from time to time to run a comb through his quiff of black

3

hair. Martha was on smiling terms with all the thirty or so who worked there. All of them loved the Grande, worshipping at its temple, as though just being within its golden walls bestowed glamour and status on their own meagre lives. They arrived from the plain terraced houses and the little semi-detacheds ribboning their way towards the countryside to be daily astonished at working within the embrace of the fabulous building. Gilding was everywhere. The walls glistened with pink paint suffused with gold that swirled into plaster cascades. Inside the high, arching auditorium, plush velvet seating glowed within a magical array of soft lights drifting from peacock to jade, from rose to aquamarine. It was fitting it should be so: film was, after all, the greatest story-telling venture there had ever been. Theirs was a calling worthy of the times. Her father Eddie was one of them.

At six thirty the newsreel was running; it showed people queuing outside bookshops for *Lady Chatterley's Lover*, that scandalous book that had just won the right to be published. The book had been a shock for the nation; there was a sense it wouldn't be the last. The usherettes, Florrie and Ethel, smoothed their black satin dresses and exchanged meaningful looks, neither quite sure what meaning the other meant to convey. Florrie had already bought a copy for herself, but Ethel had declared that no copy would ever enter her home – she had the morals of teenage daughters to safeguard. Or, as she called them, 'mortals'.

*

4

Eddie left Bert in charge of the projection box and came to fetch his daughter.

'Had your tea, have you?' A formality: he knew she had.

'Yes, bit of a rush ... told Mum I was going round to Marjory's.'

Eddie grinned. He enjoyed a sense of conspiracy behind his wife's back. They both did. Whenever they were alone together there was a third presence: Beattie. They made a tight threesome.

They grinned together, his warmth and approval cancelling her worries about gaberdines and flying hair. He was a striking man to look at and it made her proud. Tall and thin, and ungainly in a louche sort of way, he walked with a limp from a war injury but managed to turn it to attractive effect. His hair was thinning, still dark and elegantly slicked back. His eyebrows, arched and mobile, determined the mood of his face: at work they could be quizzical or open-hearted; away from the Grande they were still, inclining to a frown. When cinema colleagues called him Gary Cooper he was quietly pleased. Nowadays he got no such attention at home. He glanced at the queue extending outside under the floodlit canopy. The fog was in retreat, the brittle lights of the square winking feebly through the dark of a late November afternoon.

'They seem to like it, don't they, this film? The fuss in the papers'll have helped.' He wanted her to share his favourites: cowboys, girls dancing, couples being witty and funny men falling over. But this film was different and perhaps not quite suitable for a young girl. Was he making a mistake? Martha was at that age when girls became a mystery to their fathers, a mystery and an alarm. They shared secrets to do with blood and pain with their mothers, and shut bathroom doors with a new defiance. Like all the men of his generation he had never wanted to understand about women's bodies. It was enough to respond to their shape, and the strange muskiness of their allure. Martha was moving towards that destiny and he wanted to be kept ignorant of it.

This latest film was said to be outspoken and daring. He knew what that meant. Ethel, he had heard, wouldn't let even her eldest daughter see it. Well, it was too late now. He offered an explanation Martha was too excited to heed. 'It's not my sort of thing at all, you know that ... and an X too. I'm not sure you should be here.' He felt suddenly uneasy. She gave him a wry smile, 'Oh, Dad!', and hugged his sleeve disbelievingly. It released the pungent smell that lingered in his clothes from the pipe he smoked. She loved that smell: she had known it since her early years when he would throw her into the air and catch her, laughing, back into his arms.

'Hello there, young Martha.'

Bert, Eddie's colleague on the current shift, was shuffling around getting the big picture ready to follow the advertising slides. He was a gentle man in a long drooping cardigan of tan-shaded wool. He continued to treat Martha as a little girl, digging deep into the cardigan pockets for a silver-wrapped sweet. Sometimes the sweets were fluffy and only appetising once Martha had picked the woollen shreds away. But Martha was getting

6

older and they no longer seemed appetising at all. Bert, like the Grande itself, was slow to adapt.

'I hear more rumours, eh?' Eddie was tapping tobacco into his pipe while Bert fetched the next can of film. 'Something's brewing and it isn't tea.'

The two men kept themselves apart from the cheekier scandals and tiffs that occupied the staff who worked below. In their eyrie at the top of the building they breathed a purer air, figuratively speaking that is, for in truth the little room was often dense with smoke and saucers of old stubs stowed on what little table space there was, set away from the machinery. Daisy came once a week to clean: it was a men's place, after all. Daisy wasn't in on the secret of Martha's illegal visits.

Bert was not alarmed. 'I'll worry when the films stop arriving. Till then we're in work, you and me.'

'Or if the punters stop coming. What if they give up on us? They like the sort of stuff the television's dishing up for them, don't they? And you don't get wet waiting in the queue.'

Bert was not to be unsettled. 'Well, there you are, you said it. They're queuing out into the square right now, aren't they? If you get the right film, they'll always come. I've always said that. Look at *Spartacus*, they loved that.'

'You say the right film, but I don't know what that is any more. They're going more and more for this kitchen-sink stuff, aren't they? All about lives of people like us. Well, some of them – it's not what I want to see. And I can't believe many do. People want glamour,' said Eddie, adding quietly, 'I know I do.'

'Yes, but look at young Martha there ... eyes glued. Her generation'll go for this kind of thing.'

Eddie and Bert were lighting up at the back of the room, glancing across at Martha on her special seat.

Martha had come to side with her father. He at least talked to her. Not about his feelings at all; even she knew that a man couldn't do that and retain his self-respect. But they both loved to talk about the daily routines and domestic trivia, and always about the cinema.

Martha was utterly at home in the projection box. She was impressed by her father's place in the world and delighted when he explained how things worked. She saw him take the reels of film from the big shiny cans and mount them on one of two huge projectors. With the two thousand feet of film running out every twenty minutes it needed six projectionists in all, working two at a time, to keep the film running smoothly. Eddie had shown her how you could insert a penny within an inch of the reel's end – not something you were supposed to do – and when the penny was released and pinged on the alu-minium lid you knew the reel would soon need to be changed. From her seat by one of the two portholes she could look down over the broad spread of the dress circle and beyond it to the even wider expanse of the stalls. When the film was a popular one, the place was seething with people, humming with pleasure and jokes. And she felt privileged and above it all, special. She could even see, tucked away behind the illuminated parapet that separated it from the front rows of the audience, the mighty Compton organ, stowed away in all its glory for the rare occasions when it was still featured as part of the programme. From her perch high up, its surface looked pristine: the pink-tinted mirror-glass etched with sun and clouds enclosing the entire bulk of the instrument. And when the moment came for it to rise the music would roll out in great swelling crescendos, and Derek the organist would slowly come into view, sitting like a spider within his glistening web, waving his red silk scarf towards the audience. For Martha, the tingle of actual performance could carry as much thrill as the most lavish film extravaganza. But she knew that most people didn't think that any more.

Martha was engrossed in today's film. She had cast off the gaberdine, fingering the poppy-coloured cable stitching with a twinge of vanity, and taken her perch on her usual stool. She did so with easy confidence, thanking Bert, who helped her there. But what was to follow would shift that confidence. She would become self-conscious and embarrassed in a way she had never known. It would change the way she felt about the world, and about herself. Years later when she was asked how the 1960s got going, she would remember this moment.

What was happening on the screen was something she hadn't ever seen before: a young man, dressed like a manager type in a suit and tie, was leaning a girl against a wall and putting his hand up her skirt. She was wriggling half in protest, half laughing at the fun of it. Soon he was pulling her knickers down over her suspenders. Then she scrambled to take off her blouse. The camera angle was very close to them, making them both look awkward and ungainly. In romantic films there were

9

gentle caresses and sweeping music, not this brutal, unlovely clawing. But that was what gripped the attention – the rawness of it, and how the actors were really at it. The tension was conveying itself to her, to Martha. She felt a heat in her body and her hands began to sweat. She wanted to wriggle, to release the tension, to be outside the film experience, not drawn into it. She struggled to stay motionless so her father wouldn't notice her embarrassment. She dreaded catching his eye, so she kept her gaze fixed, her eyes bulging, as she focused on the bodies tumbling over each other on to an awkward, narrow sofa. Now the man grabbed at the girl, pulling her to him and reaching to undo the fastening of her bra. They weren't speaking, just making breathy exclamations.

Ping! The penny flew from its place. Eddie put down his pipe and went to fetch the next reel. He noticed that the film dialogue had stopped and that there was a lot of rustling on the soundtrack. He dipped his head to look through the second of the projection box portholes, aware of Martha's stillness. As Bert had said, this stuff engrossed young people. For a moment he caught the sight of flesh and struggle. The scene was in the shadows but light coming from a window framed the whiteness of thighs in close-up. He glanced across at Martha in her engrossment. He felt a sort of guilt watching his daughter watch sex, but he didn't turn away. And as he watched he had a sense too of her moving away from him, in the way a reverse zoom of the camera put people at a distance. She was still the same, still in focus, but realigned.

The reel would run out soon so he had to move briskly to heft the next one into its place on the other projector. It was a moment for effective professional action. No time for thought or sensation. Anyway it wasn't Eddie's style. But later that night he was seized by a mysterious sense of apprehension.

On the news, Harold Macmillan was allowing American nuclear submarines to use Holy Loch.

Chapter 2

He caught sight of it first out of the corner of his eye – a dark blurred smudge on the white surface. It was at eye height, a long horizontal mark that shouldn't be there. He paused, squinting to make out what it was. He knew he would soon need glasses. The trees around the square were coming into bud, their bright enamel green touching the drabness of the surroundings with a hazy sense of hope. Perhaps a swirl of March winds had scooped up what remained of last autumn's leaves and dashed them against the white front of the building. It marred the start of his working day. Each time he cycled round the corner into Staveley's central square and came face to face with the Grande's façade he still saw it as a place of beauty. The tensions in his brow and neck eased. He loved his work. More than that, he sank his soul into it. He knew without asking that the others who worked there felt the same. And his daughter too. Earlier that week Martha had sat on the stool in the projection box and shuddered with terror at George Sanders and Barbara Shelley in *Village of the Damned*. Bert, his fellow projectionist, thought it was ill-advised exposing a sixteen-year-old to horror stories about weird children, but he stayed silent. Wiser not to interfere: families had their own ways.

Eddie would make sure the mark on the façade was cleaned later. He would mention it to Sid, who often hovered around until the day's shows began. Sid claimed he liked to get an eyeful of the customers coming to the first showing of the afternoon, keen that their muddy shoes didn't mark the once bold pink and green zigzags of the foyer carpet. As maintenance man his responsibilities didn't run to the furnishings. It was Daisy who flicked her feather duster across the swirling pink and gold. But Sid shared her pride in how glamorous it all looked and he loved to see its bustling customers relax into smiles and pleasure as they came through its doors. So long as they didn't bring in the dirt.

Eddie wheeled his bicycle down the side alley and propped it against the back wall of the building. Here the red bricks were rough and the grouting blackened from the factory smoke perpetually in the air. Sometimes young couples crept round here to kiss and cuddle, so the gravel up against the wall was churned and scuffed. But the wider public never came this way so it didn't matter that it was as humdrum as the rest of Staveley.

He took off his cycle clips, wrapped them in a crumpled brown paper bag he kept for the purpose and tucked them away in the pouch strapped on the back of the saddle. He smoothed his hand across his thinning hair, as he did when he was worried. That smudge was bothering him. His routine took him round to the front again and he paused to examine it. It was worse than he imagined. It was a crack across two of the white ceramic tiles that covered the towering building to the top. Eddie felt across it with sensitive fingertips. He kept his nails neat and clean out of respect for the film footage he had to handle. The crack wasn't merely a chip but a full-depth wound to the surface of the Grande. Mr Vernon would have to be told.

Eddie was turning up early because of the meeting. Months of rumours were reaching their climax. The meeting had been called by the younger Mr Vernon – whom Eddie called, without in any way meaning to be disrespectful, Mr Colin. Mr Colin managed the Grande for his father, who had years ago recruited Eddie as a trainee projectionist. There had been an advertisement in the local paper and Eddie had a no-hope job in a local radio shop at the time. The elder Mr Vernon, then tall and severely proper, had conducted a perfunctory interview asking about his family, his responsibilities (Beattie had just given birth to a baby girl) and insisting that punctuality was essential for such an exact function as the showing of films. By way of concluding he drew his bulk to an even greater height, puffing himself out, it seemed to Eddie, like some large aggressive crow, threatening to pop the buttons on his double-breasted navy suit. From this magisterial height he delivered a homily about the responsibilities of the job, the nature of cinema as the conduit of pleasure and happiness to thousands, and Eddie's

14

role as the final link in a chain that led all the way back to Louis B. Mayer of MGM. Eddie was awed.

In the years since, Mr Vernon had grown in bulk, the suits bulging ever larger, his breath short and his face red. He was gradually ceding power to his son and heir Mr Colin. Unlike his father, Mr Colin lacked any severity, crow-like or otherwise. He was more of a worm, waiting apprehensively for his father to pick at his shortcomings. His long neck stretched into his small head poking forward in a wormlike way. As a boy he had had an obsessive interest in animals, which might in another family have drawn him into farm or even zoo work. But he had made no choices about his life. His parents had been firm: 'You are part of the business, Col, you can always have animals as a hobby.' So Colin and his pale wife Phoebe kept a border collie and two rabbits in a hutch in their garden. To the best of his worm-like ability he now sought to replicate his father's behaviour in preparing to address the employees of the Grande.

On his way through the blue side door, Eddie met Florrie, who had been summoned long before her usherette shift was due.

'Summat's up!'

Florrie relished a crisis. He gave her a wry smile and a cheery 'Says who?', not staying for an answer as she bustled off into the little cloakroom that was the women's domain – coat hangers, gas ring, couple of shabby chairs and a pile of out-of-date *Picturegoer* magazines. Eddie could sense the unease of others almost before they were aware themselves that something troubled them. It came from long years of marriage to Beattie, whose moods seemed finely tuned to get under his skin. He had learned to remark tell-tale signs that something troubled her: a slight sweat along her brow, a certain grimness in the line of her mouth. And he was ahead of her in identifying how she would respond. It was a nuanced and fretting way to live. Until now, the Grande wasn't like that at all. It was his great escape, a place where even worries carried their own drama. But he could sense everyone's anxiety.

He leapt up the shabby stairs steps two at a time and found Bert already in the projection box. 'Florrie reckons it's bad. She's such a worrier, that woman. Trouble gives her real pleasure.'

Eddie's arrival provoked a small response of friendship and the perfunctory nod that was Bert's regular greeting. He said little in response to Eddie's words. If there was trouble, Bert's policy was to stay silent; that way everyone believed he shared their point of view. Eddie made that assumption now and it comforted him.

Of all the projectionists, Bert was his ally. The rest were noisy, drinking types who filled in their football coupons between reel changes. Bert was small and of a ginger presence: hair ginger, skin white but ginger freckled and his clothing almost to match – a series of gingerish tweeds and tan-coloured cardies. His body was broad, thickset, sturdy, graced by delicate extremities – neat hands with tapering fingers and manicured nails; small feet clad in his trademark tan suede shoes. His hobby was ballroom dancing, where he deployed his considerable weight like a cartoon elephant – Dumbo,

16

even. He had silver cups displayed in a cabinet at home. Bert had a warm heart but kept its glow strictly within limits.

Young Mr Colin seemed in thoughtful mood as he surveyed the staff filing into the front seats of the stalls. He had a stark white handkerchief folded into his top pocket and had given his shoes an extra polish. He was resolutely trying not to pick at his fingernails as he confronted the full complement of his thirty workers. They were rarely all together like this, and those from the kitchens and the Palm Court café, the waitresses and chefs, eyed the house staff with open curiosity.

The usherettes were a self-absorbed bunch, bundling together, twittering like a flock of finches newly landed on the plush seating. They were known collectively as 'the girls' and frequently given little pats and squeezes by the men to acknowledge their girlishness. The sexual content of these gestures was minimal, merely a routine expression of a bar-room ethic about what women were for. The two oldest among them, Ethel and Florrie, accepted the attention with a jaundiced grace. Ethel was, after all, in her early forties and the mother of schoolchildren with whom she left a door key to let themselves in whenever she was working. No one commented but several disapproved. Florrie shared her spinster life with an ageing mother and a cage of budgerigars. She was much taken with cheap scent which clouded wherever she moved. Everyone always knew when she was approaching. The two of them stood together, apart from the others, smoothing their black satin uniforms.

Josie, box office manageress, was acknowledged as the Grande's grande dame even though still in her thirties. Hers was a buxom presence of unashamed physicality: her large breasts wedged against the ticket machine, swathed in coloured silks; her large laugh ringing out from her gilded cubicle as she greeted her extensive following of friends. Her eyelids were blue, though her eyes were green, which Eddie thought gave her a witchy look; long swinging earrings added to the gypsy style. Her all-time favourite film had been *Madonna of the Seven Moons*, and she was known to have taken up the banjo recently after seeing *Some Like It Hot*. Eddie was impressed by her confidence, the scale of her and her sense of freedom. More importantly, she always showed him personal generosity without threatening him with any sexual intrusion. Her warmth was motherly, and he was grateful for it. She and the other box office staff approached the meeting with gravitas, knowing what they knew about the Grande's falling audience numbers.

Bert and Eddie arrived, tacitly acknowledging a professional esteem not accorded to the others. They, after all, were the essence of the business; they were the showmen, the performers almost, threading the magic of film through their projectors and into the hearts of eager audiences. The keepers of the flame. There was a sense that once they arrived the meeting was formally convened. Lumbering in after the others came Gerald, the commissionaire, already dressed in his bulky maroon uniform with its silver epaulettes. As an ex-army sergeant he carried his military bearing into the foyer, marshalling queues with precision and authority. He had taken up the job reluctantly when, like thousands demobbed after the war, he'd had little choice. He had no interest in the films themselves apart from a surprising admiration for the diminutive James Cagney. He was uneasily aware he had authority without power and crawled obsequiously to Mr Colin whenever he turned up. Mr Colin winced at the attention but recognised it went with being of the employer class. Frankie, uneasy outside his sweet kiosk, lingered at the back.

Finally Sid idled in, hanging back as was proper for the maintenance man, his stained hands dug firmly into the pockets of his brown overall. He knew every corner of the Grande and, unbeknown to Eddie, had already noted the cracked tiles on the front. The building itself was his love; he was less sure about the people, deeply absorbed in the silly matter of film, transient, flimsy stuff, whereas heating pipes and boilers spoke of larger, solid interests. Daisy shuffled in beside him, her day's cleaning already done, carpets and curtains savaged for dust. She wasn't worried about Mr Colin's announcement, whatever it was: the world always needed cleaners. She reached in her pocket for her lighter and a Park Drive.

Mr Colin leant against the illuminated glass barrier that fenced off the cinema's organ, surveying them all. His expression was solemn as he imagined his father's might be. His voice was lighter but that could be counted an advantage: his father's gruff words were sometimes blurred by lunchtime drinking. He flexed his long neck, looking around to make sure they were all gathered. Surreptitiously he took the square white handkerchief from his pocket and wiped his hands. And then he delivered the word.

'Bingo! I have to tell you all that there has been a bid from a major chain of bingo establishments to take over the Grande.'

Bingo – the oncoming tide of change they all feared. Film was what they lived by and for: it had put their lives if not into the mainstream, then into one of the meandering tributaries of Hollywood glamour; they glittered with the distant stardust of a golden land and golden creatures. They brought to the drab and dismal citizens of this northern town truths about other lives, distant and strange places, weird and thrilling adventures. How would they do without it? Eddie, who in the desert of his private life drew so deeply on the films he handled, felt a wave of panic.

Mr Colin paused to let the announcement sink in. He had seen enough films to acquire a sense of dramatic timing. The pacing of his announcement owed more to the style of Humphrey Bogart than the clumsy language of his father.

'So my father asked me to break the news to you. Hmm.'

He coughed and allowed himself a bleak smile.

'There is both good news and bad.'

He paused, measuring his audience: there had been a general intake of breath and a small outbreak of tutting.

'First, the good news is that we have turned the offer down.'

Sighs and tuttings turned to grateful groans of relief.

' . . . but the other news is that we are going to have to find ways to survive when people aren't coming to see films in the numbers they once did. Hmm.'

The involuntary syllable was a little reward he gave himself for ploughing on.

'Our chain, as you know, is small – only the Grande here, plus the one along the Commercial Road and the other in Prince Albert Street.'

By now he had his listeners in the palm of his hand.

'It is a struggle against the big boys – the Gaumonts and the ABCs. You know the problems: we can't get the lead releases, they come to us late. So we want to make ours a special place to come. Hmm.'

Someone turned and nodded at Daisy and Sid. They were being given the credit for how nice the place always looked.

'There is one other thing – hmm.'

They turned back to Mr Colin who they thought had finished.

'Yes, just one change. The organ – hmm. The organ won't be performing any more. It is, after all, more to do with the war than today. So Derek, hmm, after years of sterling work has agreed to retire. There will be no more Sunday recitals. We must – what is it they say? – hmm, move with the times.'

He could see they weren't impressed.

'But' – Mr Colin waved a limp hand – 'we shall be holding a farewell organ concert in his honour.'

There was a buzz of approval at this and Mr Colin took the chance to make his getaway. He was keen to be back in his office upstairs. It was safer up there, on the phone to his distributors. *Breakfast at Tiffany's* would be his as soon as the majors let it go.

*

21

In the pub next door the hubbub of talk was more intense than usual. Eddie bought his round but remained quiet. He was sick at heart. The moment he had seen the cracked tile he had felt a quiver of alarm. Then he had watched Mr Colin giving his speech, knowing from now on things would be different. He had trouble enough dealing with things as they were without the new complexities that lay ahead. He had made this place his nest, his home. His arrival on his bicycle each day brought him from his confused unhappiness at home into the chatter and familiarity of this, his real family.

'So Martha'll still be sneaking in for her private viewing' – Eddie knew that Bert privately relished the sense of conspiracy – 'but what'll Beattie say, eh? She always turns up for those Sunday recitals. Derek was a friend, after all, and they were her favourite, eh? She's sure to be disappointed.'

Bert, like others at the Grande, held Beattie in a certain awe: perhaps it was her height or the stylish way she presented herself. She was, after all, a woman now in her forties, but she had not given up the struggle and traces of an earlier glamour clung to her.

Eddie thought it a shame that his wife preferred the hackneyed old organ music to the films themselves. He wondered many a time whether it was a genuinely felt preference or a deliberate contradiction of the very things he loved most. It was all part of the conundrum of their marriage.

'Oh, she'll accept it. She'll accept it. That's what she does.'

*

Later that day Eddie took a moment to cross the square and stand against the row of shabby shops opposite to gaze up at the Grande before going inside. The sharp breeze of the March day caught at his nostrils and cleared them of the bruising smoke of the pub. He enjoyed being alone. Passers-by moved to avoid his bulk, broad shouldered and tall, his trilby on the back of his head and his trench coat open and flapping in the wind. His eyes went upward and upward to the castellated roof line: it was as much a thing of beauty as any cathedral, the long narrow windows giving the pale tiles a hint of Moorish elegance. The Grande was an appropriate name, he thought again. Apart from the red-brick church two streets away, this was as grand a building as any of its Staveley customers were likely to enter.

He thought fondly of the Grande's local clientele: clerks and bus drivers, shopkeepers, municipal gardeners, coopers who worked at the local brewery and lived in a cluster of terrace houses alongside. There were nurses who took a bus to the city hospital and warehousemen from the nearby factory. Mothers in pairs, sometimes with children in tow, the children jumping and noisy with excitement. One or two teachers had become regulars, asking about the chances of seeing foreign films. Sometimes the vicar from All Saints turned up with his wife. Eddie leant against the crates outside the greengrocers and lit his pipe: for a moment, cupping it in the palm, he felt like the lonely hero of one of those films that featured tough men with soft hearts. The moment passed. He put his pipe in his pocket.

In the projection box Bert already had the cans of film

23

down from the shelves and was mounting the first reel of the first movie. It was the usual double bill, plus newsreel, cartoon and advertisements. The newsreel that night showed the Russians launching a dog into space and its safe return; the Campaign for Nuclear Disarmament – CND – had a sit-down at the Ministry of Defence.

Between two o'clock and ten thirty there would be three showings; taking it turn and turn about they would manage the projectors. Then he would head home.

Chapter 3

It was a dour day: the sky a heavy spread of dirty cotton wool pressing down on the rooftops. Martha could see a line of red chimneypots from where she was sitting. Other than the leaden sky there was little else to be seen from the attic window of the college classroom, but rather than turn away, she looked harder. The chimneypots were aligned along the row of buildings with a certain decorative panache. Wasn't it remarkable, Martha thought, that someone had taken the trouble, even been inspired to make fancy chimneypots where no one could see them and enjoy them. I shall enjoy them, she thought; I shall make an effort to notice how they are shaped, how they have an oblique curve halfway up as though making an awkward move in an ancient dance. Then whoever put them there will have their work appreciated. Some dead architect would not have lived in vain, not while someone like me was enjoying his work. She wondered how one became an architect, how one became anything, anything at all. Even if all one left behind was a row of chimneys, at least that was an achievement.

She turned back to the typewriter and the jarring routine of the exercise. There was no consolation in it. The machine clattered away beneath her fingertips: 'Not too fast, pace yourselves, keep the rhythm,' Miss Saward was saying, as though she was conducting an orchestra, an orchestra of drab young women signed up to a dull destiny at the desks of severe male employers. Wouldn't it be better to be a chimneypot perched precariously above the droning traffic, dancing away in a shimmying chorus line of others like yourself? Martha looked around her. Who among the grim rows of trainees was anything like herself? She had few friends. Marjory who lived three doors along filled the gap of someone to go out with, but was dim and dull, not any kind of sympathetic spirit. Who, were she to mention her fondness for the chimneypots, wouldn't stare with widening eyes as though she had taken leave of her senses? She would try it.

'Pssst.' The clattering keys drowned her voice. 'Pssst, Jackie!'

The girl at the desk beside hers, a sparrow-like creature in brown feathery clothes, looked up alarmed, and frowned.

'What?'

'Look . . . look out there.'

'Err, what at?'

'Chimneypots . . . those red chimneypots. They're dancing.'

Jackie's eyebrows flexed with irritation and with a sharp move of her neck she grabbed a quick look for politeness' sake, then turned without comment back to the safety of her keyboard. Martha felt even more isolated and alone, bored by the rhythm of the typing lesson and appalled at the idea she would be doing this for a living. Living? Huh! She stabbed at the keys with a vigour that brought Miss Saward to her side.

'I hope your mind is on your speed, Martha.'

Outside in the drizzle of the late afternoon, she hesitated to take the bus home. From the start of the secretarial course she had told her mother that the lessons finished an hour later than they in fact did. It was an hour stolen just for herself and she got a little thrill from the idea of being not quite honest. The problem was how to spend it. Whenever she thought of things to do in her imagination they were bright and lively, surrounded by chatter and bright lights. But when it came to it, she wasn't sure how to get started. She was simply standing in the wet and letting the buses go by.

She began to walk, pretending to herself that this was exactly what she wanted. But the misty rain began to settle on her headscarf and the shoulders of her gaberdine. She tried telling herself it nourished the gardens, and was already bringing on the daffodils in the municipal parks and the crocuses under the single garden tree at home. Loving the actual feel of it was harder. It loosened the lotion she used to fix her unruly hair and now dank strands of it were hanging down, dripping against her cheek. She felt the misery of looking unattractive.

She walked along the High Street, slowing her steps to take in the windows of dress shops, their sensible clothes hanging awkwardly on lumpy hangers; she paused at the radio and television shop, where the lids of walnut radiograms were open to show the turntables within.

The thought of music cheered her up. It was the one thing they all talked about at the youth club. Clive had said he would bring his records along. Clive had a good job in the town hall and could afford records. He bought them systematically, a new one each Friday. He liked jazz most – Chris Barber, Humphrey Lyttelton – but he had some skiffle that she enjoyed, all jumpy and jolly. She brightened at the thought of it and began to hum. Further along the High Street, its windows misted with steam, was the coffee bar, a place where all sorts of young people gathered. She wished she were one of them. They were different in a way that she envied and mistrusted.

Clive had arrived in her life the previous autumn without anyone really noticing. His was a pale anony-mous presence, gentle and unaggressive. He wore neutral colours – fawn, beige, tan – which shaded into the waxy paleness of his complexion and the straw-like neutrality of his hair. He was like the echo of a man you saw in ghost films standing behind the flesh and blood hero. But there was nothing heroic about Clive. They had met at a table-tennis championship at the club. They were both timid players, soon out of the contest and watching the flash and flair of the others. As no one bothered speaking to them they took refuge in each other. It had been an awkward beginning. Clive began to phone and check whether she would be going along as usual each Wednesday. As it was her regular intent, she suspected him of a subtle ruse to get closer and his phone call as a major initiative in their friendship. There was no question of asking Clive to step inside the front door. The family cherished its privacy too much for that. As the same time it was important to show they were as happy a family as any other. In the event Beattie rose, as if naturally, to the occasion, calling out a modest greeting from the back of the house.

It was her mother who, a week or two later, first referred to Clive as 'your boyfriend', a designation Martha felt was overhasty if not entirely misjudged. But it was what her mother seemed to want. It even raised in Martha the tentative hope that her mother might be softening her disapproval.

Clive proceeded to fulfil whatever expectations her mother had. His very opacity seemed to recommend him to her: as the autumn weeks had gone by and he called each Wednesday evening, Beattie told Martha she could invite him into the hall of their house where the temperature, without actually being warm, was a few degrees higher than the chill November air on the doorstep. He waited there at the foot of the stairs for Martha to complete her preparations. On each occasion her mother would stretch her head round the living-room door and greet him with surprising gaiety.

'Good evening, Clive.'

His response: 'Good evening, Mrs Clayton. Are you well?'

Beattie enjoyed the sound of his uncomplicated voice, so direct and amiable. But she chose not to reply. She had grown to feel herself judged by Martha and Eddie, sensing their displeasure whenever she made some modest request. It was her job, after all, to keep the home spotless and tidy for them. Was it too much to ask that they cleared their magazines away? And Martha's refusal to keep her room tidy and her clothes properly hung smacked of youthful rebellion. Beattie always hoped that family would be based on shared principles, but where were they now? Perhaps they had never been spelled out. But did people do that? Wasn't there meant to be a tacit agreement? Well, she no longer felt anyone was about to agree with her. Except possibly Clive.

And so it was that Clive felt himself growing to be an established part of the household. Buoyed by Beattie's mild encouragement, he ventured further intimacy with Martha. As they walked along the street he reached for her hand and drew her arm through his. The gesture struck Martha as so antique as to be almost laughable. But she went along with it for the sake of the temporary harmony her liaison had brought to the household at number 26 Galton Road.

As weeks turned to months the realisation arose in her mind that others considered she was on some path of involvement with Clive which would lead to engagement and marriage. It was how others seemed to move from friendship to courtship, accepting the ritual of their tribe and being happy to embark on it. Clive appeared to share such expectations. The regular involvement suddenly seemed to have her held fast in a net of obligations. She was aware she owed a good deal to Clive. Without his whispering presence at her side, the youth club would have been too much to bear. She would have been left standing alone, unsure what to do. Clive provided her with something to do. She must, it seemed, be somehow in his debt.

There were other things to be thankful for too. He pleased her mother. He seemed to prompt this brooding woman into episodes of natural warmth. Martha could remember a time when Beattie sparkled with jokes and teases, playing silly games without being self-conscious – more fun, it seemed, than other mothers.

Whatever had driven her mother into her silences seemed to wake up to the deep ordinariness of this young man. It was a consideration that carried weight in Clive's favour.

Beattie stiffened as she heard Martha lift the latch on the back door. She was at the sink in the long dark kitchen, preparing their high tea.

Beattie was in her domain, the home she cherished, polished, titivated with obsessive care. It had come to dominate her days. Once she and Eddie had found a house they could afford to rent, she had taken possession and begun to shape it to her taste. It gave her authority. Staveley's shops and the austerity of the years after the war did not offer much choice. She worried about tray cloths and matching china, about fluff under the beds and the lining of curtains. She began to rearrange the china objects that accumulate with years – ash trays, small animals, trinket boxes. It became an absorbing task and one where she brooked no challenge. Eddie and Martha going about their lives simply took her efforts for granted and rarely noticed the precision of her activities, the shine on the brass ornaments, the way a bedspread was folded. All they did was mess things up. They got in the way, seeming to take malicious delight in untidiness. At times it was as if they were out to thwart her.

But at least when they were out of the house – at school, at work – it was entirely hers. She had spent the morning wrapped in her faded floral overall for the daily room-by-room clean, then in the afternoon changed into more genteel attire, a pale turquoise wool dress and white apron to take on less strenuous tasks. Today it had been taking from the cabinet then washing and polishing the modest collection of antique Bristol blue glass left her by her grandmother. Pretty, she thought, but inconsequential. One day they must make a point of drinking from the glasses.

When she was alone she blossomed, the heroine of her own story, moving through rooms and spaces with dramatic authority, the kind of authority and drama that she'd had as a young woman at the factory.

Beattie had a dull sense she was not as she had once been. The tall glamour of her youth was turning to a gaunt angularity; porcelain skin was now traced with tiny wrinkles; once luscious blonde hair had lost its gloss. Beattie did not feel rewarded. She felt invisible. It never occurred to her that her silences made any kind of impression.

'I'm back,' called her daughter. She began to take off her gaberdine and shake from it the drops of clinging rain. They speckled the linoleum floor.

'I scrubbed that floor this morning!'

'I don't think the rain's dirty, Mum. Just water, that's all.'

'Well, hang your coat where it can dry.'

The noise of water gushing from the tap into the saucepan masked the possibility of further talk. Martha hung her coat on the mahogany hall stand, then moved into the living room at the back of the house and stood, as was her father's habit, with her back towards the glowing coal fire. She liked the thought of copying him, doing as he did. She wasn't keen to copy her silent moody mother. Standing there flexing her calves with the heels of her shoes on the fender, she let the dull embers warm her thighs and her hips. It felt good.

They ate their tea in a neutral silence. Boiled cabbage and thick slices of gammon with mustard hot enough to bring tears to her eyes. Beattie had yet to try the new cooking with stuff such as garlic and aubergine that was cropping up in the magazines.

Martha had become expert in Beattie's silences. They were of an infinite variety and domestic harmony depended on reading them accurately. Tonight's silence began as one of exhaustion and a weariness of spirit, but when her mother passed the little gilt tray with the salt and pepper Martha sensed something shifting.

It came with an unpractised smile as she spooned custard on to the last of her jam roly-poly.

'The Johnsons have asked us to a party in a couple of weeks' time: the Saturday. They've been married twenty years and think there's something to celebrate.'

The Johnsons lived along the street, and were a noisy clumsy family always falling over the bikes and hula-hoops that littered their drive, and laughing as they stumbled.

'What did you tell them? Do you feel like going?'

'It's not about me feeling like it; my feelings don't come into it. But I think we should show a little neighbour-liness, don't you? Your dad chats to Mr Johnson when he's washing his car at the weekend. He'll like to go.'

Such a degree of engagement on her part felt like the sun coming out from behind a cloud.

'Yes, yes, I think he will.' Martha paused. 'I was plan-ning to go to the youth club dance with Clive.' It was nothing special: they would be dancing to records people brought along. Clive's offer to bring along Django Reinhardt had been quickly trumped by some-one else's promise of Buddy Holly. 'But it doesn't matter ... I'm not that keen.'

Her mother poured herself a cup of tea and ran her tongue over her teeth thoughtfully.

'Well, I don't think we can take Clive with us. He doesn't really belong yet, does he? Not in any family sense. It would be to impose on the Johnsons if we simply brought him along too.'

'Yes, I'm sure he'll understand.'

Clive always, in his opaque way, understood. It was one of his more maddening habits: Martha wanted to rage at his compliance but it would be like punching jelly.

Martha waited up for her father. She knew the job at the cinema didn't finish until around eleven o'clock and that Eddie would arrive still exhilarated by whatever film had been showing. It was his way to tip Martha off to the ones he reckoned she and her friend Marjory might like to see; Marjory's taste ran to exploits of colonial derring-do: *The Stranglers of Bombay* and *O'Rourke of the Royal Mounted*, colourful and full of shouting and patriotism. But Eddie was keen Martha should share his own enthusiasms; he wanted to educate her taste to his. It was his love of the macabre that had first led him to invite her to his projection box when X films were showing: they talked of *The Mummy* and *House of Wax* for days.

Martha could love almost any film: images piled on images, each one filling her mind with dreams of the way her own life might go. More recently there'd been a crop of films about ordinary life in Britain, people in offices and suburbs just like hers; the films were usually black and white. She was quite clear she didn't want her life to be like theirs: pregnancy, an indifferent husband. And then there was sex. She found that exciting, it brought embarrassment. What she relished most were tales of escape: not *Wages of Fear* stuff but people exchanging dull lives for something better. She wondered whether her mother had ever felt like that: she had on occasion talked of having a high old time during the war. But it was harder for women, Martha thought.

Chapter 4

Martha heard her father's key turn in the front door lock and went into the kitchen to put the kettle on.

She put a hunk of cheese and some cream crackers on a plate, set it on the tray with the mug of dark orange-coloured tea and took it in to the back room. Together they huddled over the collapsing coals of the fire. It was late, not worth stoking it.

'Good film, was it?'

'Absolute winner.'

Bad news about the Grande could wait.

'Hitchcock: one of the best. There's a scene where Cary Grant is being chased and he's miles from anywhere, miles of cornfields all around, then suddenly in the corner of the screen you see a small plane crop-spraying, and then ... Oh, but I won't spoil it. You really must see it. Get Clive to go.'

She gave him a deprecating smile.

'OK, not Clive. Drag Marjory along then.'

The embers fell in the fireplace. He loved this time with Martha. As Beattie had withdrawn into herself, he'd pulled back too. Hard to credit that when she and Eddie were young they had once talked non-stop as if to tell each other everything. In those days they had laughed a good deal, never taking their eyes from each other. Or their hands. They even played a game together: 'I love you because ...' Each vying to make a more fantastical and flattering list. Then they had laughed and tumbled together. The memory of it made him blush. Slowly the smiles had departed and an inertia broken by occasional sallies of aggression had become the pattern of their days.

Sometimes the earlier image of her was strong and assertive in his mind, her outline clear. Eddie saw her blonde hair fading to grey, still holding traces of its girl-hood bounce, but now only in Beattie's bouts of sudden rage did Eddie recognise the energy of the woman he had married. He came to assume it was he who must be responsible, that the burden of her disappointment rested on his shoulders. And he had lost the way of speaking intimately. Even when, out of habit, he enfolded her in his arms before sleep, he never spoke tenderly. And now it was too late. And from the shadows of this sorrow he sometimes confided in his daughter. He still felt uneasy about it though: it somehow demeaned the family.

'Ma in bed?'

'Of course.'

'Anything to report?'

The sort of query a doctor makes, checking out on a patient with a routine but unyielding affliction.

Martha paused. She usually recounted the degrees of

her mother's silence. But tonight there was real news. She grinned.

'The Johnsons are having a party in two weeks' time, the Saturday, a wedding anniversary. And we're invited. What about that?'

He grinned back at her.

'I like Fred Johnson, he's a great chatterer.' He bit hard into the lump of cheese – waved a cracker at her. 'Thanks.'

'Oh, I forgot: piccalilli?'

Martha wanted the snack to be perfect. He shook his head.

'It's fine, fine. Don't fuss, love.'

He spoke with his mouth full, spraying flaky crumbs.

'Always going on about his home decorating is Fred. He's got some lovely tools; very proud of them.'

'I bet they go in for brighter stuff than this.'

Martha looked round scornfully at the dark furniture and drab walls. Dated, depressing. No wonder her mother sulked.

'Oh, this is OK. Anyway, has she said yes?'

'She said you'd like it – and that's why we should go.'

He gave a wry grin. 'It'll be good to get her out of the house: cheer her up a bit.'

The exciting thing for Martha about the Johnsons' party was that it was Easter and their daughter, Enid, was home from the university. Enid was nineteen and glowing with the knowledge of exotic worlds. University: it was rare in either of their families for a girl to have such aspirations. What must it be like? She was studying

French and spoke it easily and without embarrassment. Martha had heard her: it sounded sophisticated, as easy and casual as in French films. Dad's cinema didn't show French films but there was a small one called the Pigalle that did. Martha looked up its programmes in the *Advertiser* and went along. Clive went too but without much enthusiasm. He preferred *Doctor in the House*. The Pigalle audience was younger than at the Grande. They wore different clothes and seemed to be sharing private jokes. Martha would have liked to have talked to them. But when she went along with Clive there was no chance. People left couples alone, and she and Clive were a couple, weren't they? She wanted to break out and say, 'We're not permanent, you know, it's not final. I can make new friends ... ' But they were often in couples too, couples who were enjoying being together, nuzzling close, making little whispering sounds and smiling a lot. Smiling was something Martha didn't do easily. It wasn't within the code of the house. Dad would come breezing in from work, discarding his coat here, his newspaper there, straining to bring some cheeriness with him, but the air was soon stiff with hovering unhappiness and his laughter rang false. Only by the late night fire would they smile together, almost conspiratorially. She would like it if she found something, or even someone, to make her laugh. That would be great. She might even do more than smile; she might laugh aloud, great guffawing laughter that you heard at funny films. Even then she only smiled. Perhaps Enid would make her laugh.

Chapter 5

Beattie was a long while getting ready.

She found herself strangely energised by the invitation. There was something dramatic about going out, dressing up, drawing a bit on her old self. She had to admit – just to herself – to suppressed excitement.

Ever since returning from the hairdresser's in the afternoon, she had remained in the bedroom, only popping her head round the door to demand, 'If you're making a pot of tea I hope you haven't forgotten I'd like a cup too.'

When Eddie went up at the last minute, as men do, to put on something better than his gardening corduroys, he was taken unawares. Beattie had dressed herself in a dark red dress of heavy silk trimmed with startlingly white cuffs and collar. She had fine stockings and black suede court shoes Eddie hadn't seen before. They weren't new so perhaps, he thought, they had been lurking at the back of the wardrobe. If so, they had dusted down a treat and she looked almost elegant. For a moment a pang of yearning seized him. It seemed sad that she only needed a small treat to release something of the young girl again.

'Well, this is a turnout and no mistake.'

His words were clumsy but his smile was honest.

'Oh, I know how to turn it on, remember, when the occasion arises.' She couldn't check the trace of peevishness in her voice. Then she adjusted her newly set waves in the dressing table mirror before descending the stairs in a style that put Eddie in mind of Gloria Swanson.

'You look really great, Mum, really great.' Martha, waiting in the hall, frowned at the vision that took her by surprise. She felt bewildered and somehow caught out.

'I wish I could say as much for you, young lady.' Still the sourness. 'Why are you wearing trousers, I wonder. Not very respectful to Mr and Mrs Johnson.'

Martha was already uneasy about how she was dressed. Beattie still had a grip on what her daughter wore, making Martha's clothes on the home sewing machine or whenever they bought her clothes from department stores only paying up for little-girl styles. Martha had confided her problem to a girl at the typing college who was thought to be very up-to-the-minute. 'Don't worry: you can borrow something of mine.' This seemed at once daring and somehow shabby but hard to refuse. That's how she came to be wearing drainpipe black trousers and a black polo-neck sweater. It certainly felt like the latest thing. She hoped Enid would like it.

'Trousers aren't right for a celebration, I'd have thought ... and black! But then, no one asks me.' Beattie pulled the dowdy coat she wore for daily comings and goings over her gorgeous party attire and swept with what amounted to panache out of the house. She nursed in her arms a small package of bright red tissue paper. Martha, feeling twice wrong-footed, followed in her wake, while her father rushed to open the front gate for his transformed wife. There was suddenly a fizz in the air, a hint of their early life together. Martha felt his allegiance to her drain away.

The Johnsons' front door was ajar and the sound of Frank Sinatra reached out into the spring air, a small trickle of guests making its way inside. Beattie paused: 'I don't think we need to ring, do we?' A moment's uncertainty passed and she led her bemused family into the brightly lit house.

'Oh, here's Beattie – hello, Beattie, and Martha and Eddie.' Pauline Johnson waved happily even though she was standing virtually beside them. 'Dump your things and come on in.'

Beattie slid from her dowdy coat, looked round before placing the tissue-wrapped gift uneasily on the hall table, as though fearful it might be snatched by passing burglars. Then with a transformative little shrug, stepped into the party, smiling her broad beguiling smile. Martha and Eddie, her followers, shuffled in behind her and watched with both pleasure and trepidation as she fell into conversation with strangers.

Enid came jumping down the stairs, all smiles and eagerness, the wide skirt of her dress bouncing with her to reveal a bevy of flouncy petticoats, her hair in a pony-tail swinging from side to side with a life of its own. Martha's black ensemble suddenly seemed too severe. Enid rushed forward to greet her.

'Wow, you look like Juliette Greco – or someone from a French film.' Enid took both her hands and swung her round, giving her pride of place in people's attention, even though the flouncing skirts and swinging ponytail were what really caught their eye. Martha, surprised by this sudden attention, struggled to keep her balance. She was delighted by the reference to French film but wondered about Juliette Greco.

'Oh thanks, Enid. And you look great ...'

What am I saying, she wondered, and did it matter? The talk round her seemed to be a mindless babble, and across the room her mother was part of it. Her father, at her mother's elbow, was smiling with pleasure and relief.

'Come on upstairs, we've got some records from America.'

Upstairs in Enid's room a tan-coloured record player held pride of place. Three gangling boys and a girl in a too-tight skirt and pointed shoes were passing records between them.

'Is that your own?' Martha indicated the player.

'Yes, but I've only a few records so far. Others bring theirs round. I should have asked you to bring yours.'

Martha played along. 'Yes, I should have, shouldn't I?' Then, emboldened by the company: 'Perhaps next time.'

The three boys and the girl had been milling around, inspecting the posters on Enid's wall, posters of singers, legs splayed apart and guitars hung across their crotch.

Suddenly they slumped on to the bed and the floor and began inspecting the pile of records.

'Let's hear something good: we've had enough of this!' The tallest, all greased quiff with a thin tie, nudged his neighbour.

'Oh ... OK, Dan, if you say!'

'Oh, I quite like him.' A boy with acne offered the mild protest but was not so much overruled as completely ignored. The quiff thrust a record in a torn brown sleeve at Enid. 'Here, Nid, we've had enough of your pash. Loverboy Cliff's going nowhere.' Martha, who had perched thankfully on a little stool and was inspecting an exotic array of cosmetics on the pink dressing table, turned to watch the exchange. She felt something magical in their company that choked her with excitement. Calling Enid by her nickname meant they knew each other well. Could she do that, she wondered. The boy who had agreed with Dan, Steve they called him, had reached for the disc, read the label and whooped.

'Ohhh, yessss! Come on, Nid ... let it go!' Enid, whose skirts rustled as she moved, laughed, lifted the needle from the playing disc in mid-song, and replaced it. There was a hush of expectation and exchanged looks. Steve glanced at Martha and winked. 'Wait till you hear this.' Martha didn't have to wait long and there was no question of not hearing it. The noise blasted into the room and engulfed her. Martha found herself being grabbed by the boy who had winked: 'Come on, loosen up!' His limbs writhed and snaked as if they had no joints.

There was little space in Enid's dense little room, so they were soon out on the landing, thumping and yelling to the beat. Martha's heart was pumping, her cheeks burning. It felt good. Dangerous. Someone would disapprove of all this, and she knew who that would be. She even relished that disapproval. There still wasn't enough room so they invaded the bathroom. In the lead, the tallest, whom they called Dan, was setting the pace, his thin tie flying. He flung himself into the front bedroom. The boys followed. The girls hesitated. This was the hallowed sanctum, the parents' bedroom, a place where women left flimsy clothes and stockings lying around. Whenever she entered her own parents' room it was with a certain reserve and discretion; it always had a stale sweet smell to it. She looked to Enid for example. Enid, who had been spinning and turning at full speed, recognised the danger, ducked back towards the record player and lifted the needle. The music died.

'Sorry, sorry. But parents, you know, parents!' As they shuffled back muttering into her room they saw upturned faces at the foot of the stairs, among them Beattie's appalled stare. Martha stared back. This would be their battleground then. Martha transgressing and Beattie's silent disapproval. Well, so be it.

Chapter 6

The main feature was a musical: *Carmen Jones*. The Grande's Cinemascope screen came into its own. The film was a modern and daring version of the opera *Carmen* that had been released years ago, but the big circuits had kept it to themselves until recently. Now it was here it would run for seven days rather than the usual three and even then could expect to fill the Grande's one thousand two hundred seats. The excitement of it infected everyone. Bert loved musicals; he'd seen this one already, of course, but here it was under his own hands. He was rubbing them together, those little dainty hands, as they took the reels from the aluminium cans.

'I hear you've been living it up, Eddie. Word gets around.' Bert's ballroom excursions, when he and Mildred chummed up with other couples for an occasional Babycham or Tia Maria, had introduced him to a habit of gossip, as Eddie was well aware. 'Yes. The word is out. You can't keep anything secret any more!'

'Oh, there's nothing secret in my life, Bert. I only wish there was.' Eddie's chatter was familiar male talk and virtually without meaning. 'Yes, give me a juicy secret. Then you lot could really get going.'

Eddie knew the tight little cinema family watched the goings on of each other with a curiosity brought on by too many thrillers and fantasy adventures.

'So what have I been up to, eh?'

'I hear Beattie was the belle of the ball – it was quite a "do", at the Johnsons. So I hear. High ... high ... high society ...'

Bert did a little swooping dance across the narrow projection box, humming the easy tune.

'Oh, yes, she looked a treat.' Eddie had been moved to a sudden pride in his wife's appearance at the party. He had shepherded her round the admiring crowd with a glow of possession he hadn't known for years. She was still a good-looker and no mistake. When she tried, that was. Her looks – blonde hair, bright sparkling eyes – were what he'd spotted all those years ago. The factory girls had been chattering around the bar like a flock of parakeets. Beattie somehow carried herself apart but her open smile had winged its way across to him and snatched at his needful heart. Even now it could captivate him at the oddest moments. Ever since the party at the Johnsons he had been puzzling over her behaviour. He wondered what trick of events had triggered such a flowering. He realised he had lost the knack to do so himself.

'Who's your spy, then? Who's infiltrated my private life, I'd like to know: is this the House Un-American Activities Committee?'

'Oh, one of the lads there.' Eddie brightened.

'Yes, Martha, too, she had a great time, meeting boys . . . that's good for her, I think. Growing up. Daughters, you know, risky times!'

'Well, it was one of them as told Mildred what Pauline had said.'

'Oh . . . and what was that?'

'Don't get so edgy, mate. She'd just said that she thought you were the ideal family. Beattie so smart and friendly with everyone. You the doting husband and young Martha the new beauty.'

'Too much Hollywood, there, I reckon.' Eddie laughed off the exaggerated compliment. Still the incongruity hit him hard.

Bert began loading the newsreel.

'Looks as though the Soviets are beating us again: they've got a man in space. D'you know that?'

With the first showing under way, Eddie left Bert to it and went round to the Red Lion for his usual sandwich and pint of bitter. He found Josie sneaking a break from the box office, alone at the bar hunched over a port and lemon. The pub was a home-from-home to all the Grande staff; how else would a woman be in a pub on her own? He raised a quizzical eyebrow but Josie forestalled him. She was like that.

'It's OK, don't get huffy. I'm not neglecting my duty: the afternoon housewives are all in by now, and anyway, Daisy's keeping an eye open.' Daisy was always flattered to be asked to stand in for the glamorous Josie. She discarded her floral overall whenever the occasion arose. It was of course unthinkable she would ever ask Josie to return the favour.

The only problem was Gerald: his duties as commissionaire didn't begin until the evening performances and he always arrived brimming with suspicion that things could not have been running smoothly without him.

'Six o'clock and here I am,' he would declare swaggering into the foyer, for all the world like some ancient nightwatchman: 'Ten o' the clock and all's well.' Once into his maroon uniform with the braided shoulders he would exchange dutiful pleasantries with Josie. She would provide a teasing assortment of flattery, which he had come to regard as his due.

'She's a fine figure of a woman,' he told his mates.

She would need to be back in time to deliver her cheery greeting. But now she was far from cheerful.

Eddie climbed on the stool beside her. 'What's up, Josie? Not like you to be glum.'

She offered a weak smile and ignored his concern.

'I hear young Martha's doing well on the typing course. Sensible girl: she'll be sure of a job for life, won't she?'

'Yes, well, that's the idea: if she's lucky and gets to be a secretary she'll always be in work. But I'm not sure it'll be the sort of work she wants.'

'Tell her to count herself lucky; some of us could be out of work in no time.'

'Oh, I don't think there's much risk the Grande will go down. There'll always be people who want to go to the flicks.' He had taken upon himself to adopt Bert's optimism.

'The Westcliff over in Poynton closes next week; my friend Sal's got the push. She's nearly forty. What's she to do?'

'Well, she's married, isn't she? So there's a family wage coming in. She doesn't need to work.'

Josie turned a generous smile on Eddie as though humouring a misguided child.

'No, dear, but she wants to. Women do. You should realise that. It isn't all *Seven Brides for Seven Brothers* you know.'

For emphasis she patted his lapel with the flat of her hand, the ringed fingers and bright nails coming close to his cheek. For a second he was tempted to snatch hold of her hand and kiss her opened palm – like they did in the movies. But at two o'clock in the Red Lion it wouldn't be right.

'So you feel secure, do you?'

She was back to her concern for him and for a fleeting moment he felt she had seen into his heart and was stirring around in the shredded traces of his love for Beattie. Language was such a slippery business, with words – love, for example – meaning different things to different people. And now they hardly used them at all. 'Love' was just how you spoke to people when you couldn't remember their name. That's why people turned to the cinema; they talked in clear terms there. 'I'll love you for ever.' 'We are meant to be together.' Though of course things went wrong there too. But people spoke out about their feelings. That was the point of films. That's what people sat there to see – how love and beauty and truth got knocked around

51

and sometimes noble things happened as a result. But only sometimes.

And now here was Josie asking whether he felt secure: did she mean his job or his marriage, or the threats from Russia? Or all three?

'I guess they'll always be showing films somewhere. And there's loads of new techniques coming along. Not just Cinemascope, but others. Things television will never do.'

Eddie found himself on the receiving end of a long appraising stare. He knew what he must look like, lank and bony, sitting there in a dishevelled trench coat.

'You love it, don't you, your job?'

With some surprise he found himself agreeing. 'Yes, I do, Josie. I suppose I do.'

The fact of his surprise made him smile and that cheered them both up. And after a thoughtful moment: 'The thing is, I'm lucky. It's OK for me. But what about Martha? Will she find a job she enjoys, where she can settle down and be happy?'

'Oh young people! They're doing their own thing.' That was a new phrase he was hearing more and more often. 'Doing your own thing.' What did it mean exactly and what was Martha's thing? Perhaps she would go off and discover it for herself and leave him shut out.

The party had shaken the routines of Eddie's personal life. Beattie had raised his hopes and then abruptly returned to her self-absorption. He thought of her as he went about his work; her image in the red dress pleased him and hovered at the back of his mind, even as he was lacing up the latest films in the projection box. He was bemused by those at the Grande who had heard what an impression Beattie had made at the Johnsons.

He sipped thoughtfully at his pint.

'You know, life's funny, isn't it?' He found himself launched on an account he suddenly didn't want to unfold. Was he going to breach the unspoken code of his family, to spill out intimacies of unhappiness that were sealed within his home? Wasn't a certain loyalty still owed? Somewhere in his heart he was trying to retrieve the old affection. He and Beattie had begun so well. At the start, he had counted himself luckier than most. When he'd been wounded in the raids on the *Turpitz* and shipped back to a military hospital, he'd thought it was all over: no woman would choose a man with a limp. But he came home to a hero's welcome and a medal for bravery. The Air Force found him an office job and he'd kept the uniform. His good spirits revived. He'd caught up with Beattie again with a host of friends at some pub where the lads had invited along girls from the local aircraft factory. She had a long blonde bob and a red dress. He looked at Josie. 'You know what they were saying about us as an ideal family ...?'

'Well, it was a passing remark, Eddie. People admire you, even envy you.'

He smiled at that and stroked his fingers through his thinning black hair.

'But – an ideal family – I ask you! We're not like that, Josie. Really not at all.'

'Not what, Eddie? You're a family – sometimes you're happy and others notice. Sometimes you're not ... it certainly makes you typical. And think what would fill your life without it.'

This was an alarming thought: perhaps he was making a meal of ordinary disappointments to give his life a dramatic point. Had the tensions of the drama in the films he watched infected the way he saw his own life? How did any of us learn what to expect of life, how to behave, how to make a go of things? Had his love of films led him to over-dramatise?

'I think Beattie might be ill, Josie. I'm worried about her.' He veered from his intended confession and took refuge in fable. Ill-health was something Josie could deal with; she was generous with family details: her mother had arthritis, her auntie suffered from varicose veins.

'Oh, my lord ... what's wrong? Poor lamb.'

The commonality of women's suffering was a conversation familiar among them all, prompting suggestions of proposed visits and offerings of beef tea.

'Is it infectious?' Josie's flight of concern took active shape: arms and scarves were fluttering like trapped birds.

'No, no, Josie. It's not flu or anything.' Eddie's vigorous shake of the head made her even more alarmed, turning her voice dark and worried, her arms reaching out.

'Not ... you know ... women's trouble?' And then in a confiding whisper: 'You can tell me, you know.'

Eddie took a deep breath. He would try again, try to reach the warm-hearted woman he knew Josie to be.

'Sometimes Beattie seems ... well, depressed. She won't talk about why.'

Josie reached out her fleshy hand and laid it consolingly on his.

'Eddie, you're a fine man: I am very fond of you. I'm sorry you feel sad. But I hope it will pass. You deserve someone who admires you and feels proud of you. I do that, Eddie. I really do. But so does Martha. You've got her, haven't you? She's a wonderful girl. You're very lucky there.'

Eddie recalled a confidence of Josie's long ago that she would never be able to have children. Ah well, we all had our burdens. They returned together for the second showing.

Josie had never lived inside a marriage and, without being jealous, had brought an intelligent curiosity to observing other people's. You could only get so far, she had decided; only tell when some were tetchy and impatient, others smiling and complicit. Superficial stuff, all that, she was sure. The reality of things went much deeper, beyond any outsiders to disentangle. Eddie was feeling low, that much was clear.

That night's newsreels showed the Aldermaston marchers arriving in Trafalgar Square. Protests against the bomb were growing nationwide. Two thousand sat down outside the American embassy: police arrested many of them. People were beginning to fear for the future.

Chapter 7

Martha had been brought to the brink of tears by her mother's behaviour at the party. As they had walked home through the April air Martha held herself aside from her parents, hugging the privet hedges along the neighbouring gardens and refusing to join their talk. She had a lump rising in her throat in a sense of rage and hurt and kicked out with her black pumps at the low brick walls.

Beattie, too, felt a strange shift from her party performance. She had pulled it off throughout the evening. Everyone could see that. But even as she left the Johnsons' porch the veil of silence descended, trapping her inside. She felt helpless to resist it, some part of her wishing she could throw it off for ever and liberate herself to laugh and talk in ways that came spontaneously. It seemed all she could manage was the performance, her way of showing the world that theirs was a happy family. It was what her life was for, surely, to nourish and provide for Eddie and Martha in just the way the magazines said. She did her best, but the effort made her weary. And here she was between worlds ... the party over and her retreat home pulling her back into the old ways.

'I hope you aren't in a sulk, young lady.'

'Nice catering, wasn't it? Pauline had taken so much trouble. I loved those little pastry whatsits.' Eddie was making an effort to prolong the chatter with his wife. Perhaps this was a breakthrough, what with the glamorous dress and her smiling so easily at strangers. 'I could see you were enjoying yourself.'

'I was. Yes, I was ...' She was thoughtful. 'But I was just thinking what a pity we can't be a family like any other.'

Martha kicked again at the wall, damaging the shoe, hurting her toes. Once they were in the house, she stomped upstairs and into her bedroom.

Martha slammed her bedroom door behind her, feeling left out, jealous of whatever reviving family intimacy was under way. Eddie helped Beattie shrug off the dowdy daily coat to reveal the full glory of the red dress. She smoothed the line of its skirt down over her hips, admiring herself. She had always liked clothes.

'Hmm, wonder what's got into madam ...'

'Do you fancy a sip of Advocaat as a nightcap?'

Eddie ushered her into the front lounge, and when Beattie reached for a cigarette he rushed to light it with the table lighter he had given her last Christmas. He made no other move: in recent years he had known her body only as a curve in the bed beside him. At a stirring from him, a quiver from her shoulder had told him she was moving away. Now she sat back, picking a strand of tobacco from her lip, and waited. It had been so long, neither knew what to say. So they said nothing. She reached to tap the ash into the glass ashtray and stroked her hair, then the silk dress as it reached taut across her thighs. The sense of its texture pleased her, a pleasure she couldn't share. The cigarette burned low, and they each waited.

'Well, yes, the catering was good.'

'We'll need to watch Martha and those boys, you know.'

A little while later they had gone to bed in disappointed silence.

The phone rang two weeks later at six in the evening. Beattie put down the stack of newly ironed laundry she was carrying and moved to pick up the receiver. It was the only demand the outside world made on her and it was her prerogative to answer.

'Hello?' It was a tentative response. Eddie never rang and she had lost touch with her relations. One of the tradesmen she dealt with, perhaps, though it was late for them. Pauline might even want to be in touch. She handled the black receiver as if it brought menace into her life.

'Hello? Yes?' There was a pause until, with her hand over the mouthpiece, she called up the stairs: 'It's for you.' Martha had readied herself for the summons, standing by the door of her room ready to leap towards

58

the call. As she clattered down the stairs Beattie mouthed silently to her: 'It's male ... it's not Clive.'

Martha wanted to shout down the phone: 'Hello, not Clive! I'm here, not Clive, I've been waiting for you!' Her answer was as tentative as her mother's but carried a charge of expectation.

'Hellooo ... this is Martha!'

'Yes, hello. This is Alex. We met at the Johnsons' party. Remember me, do you?' This was awkward. She certainly remembered the party; she had been remembering it ever since. But as is the way with memories they had slid around in the telling. And there had been much telling. Returning the drainpipe trousers and black sweater to the girl in the typing class had brought out the full fantasy. 'So, yes, there was I pirouetting at the top of the stairs while everyone stood around clapping to the music. And this boy, tall, watching ... well!' She rolled her eyes. The scene had featured in a number of films and she felt a certain guilt at adopting it wholesale but it earned her instant recognition and approval among her dowdy colleagues. 'Gosh, Marty, wow!' Their responses too had been adopted from familiar fictions. The whole added up to their own reality: an imagined life that lit up the drab little classroom.

But Alex? Which one was he ... she wasn't sure. Was he the tall one with the quiff and tie? Or had that been Steve? Then there was the one who winked and danced with her ... had he ever had a name? Certainly this was 'not Clive', and therefore welcome.

'Yes, I do. Of course I do ... it was a good party, wasn't it?'

'I wonder if you'd like to come to the flicks, Monday?'

'Er ... well ... what's showing?'

Dumb question. That's not why boys asked girls to the cinema. Also they could fetch up at the Grande and run straight into Josie, Gerald and all her dad's cronies. Alex obviously sensed a delaying tactic and moved to deal with it.

' ... or we could go to the coffee bar, if you like. The one in the High Street. I'm a regular there.' It was where she had hovered in the rain gazing at the exotic creatures within.

'Oh, yes, I'd love that!' Not only 'not Clive', but someone at ease with espresso and French pastries. It really didn't matter which of them it was.

'Shall I call and collect you?' This was another hurdle. 'Call and collect' amounted to a serious date rather than a casual encounter. It also meant scrutiny from her mother which would certainly require a 'not Clive' explanation.

'Well, I'm doing a secretarial course at the Tech, and I finish there about five. We could meet on the steps of the college, if you like?' Best of all, they might run into the others and fuel the story of her emerging glamour.

'Fine by me. I know some of the lecturers there: get on with them a treat. So, yes, by the steps.'

Alex turned out to be the one with acne who'd not said very much and been largely ignored by the others. He had a high intelligent forehead and a great shock of dark hair, brown eyes set wide apart and a small girlish nose that made him look soft, even pretty. The acne spoiled all that, but was distinctly masculine. It was his mouth that was most expressive: wide and thick-lipped, always on the move flashing strong white teeth in smiles that came and went with a nervous energy. The reason he'd not made his mark at the party was because of his height. Martha was relieved he was taller than her, but only just.

Chapter 8

The coffee bar opened on to another world. Martha stepped through the red door and was now within its steamed windows and mingling with the exotic creatures she had so recently held in awe.

No one here was over thirty. Even the proprietor sweating beside his steaming Gaggia coffee machine looked like a handsome Italian film star.

'Hi there, Aldo,' cried Alex pushing his way clumsily towards a central table. 'How's things?' Aldo turned at the sound of his name, but didn't recognise who it was who had offered the greeting. Alex shrugged. 'He really knows me well, but when it's so crazily busy he can't spare the time.' Martha couldn't help noticing the place was only modestly full, but she was none the less impressed by Alex's easy familiarity. She wanted to be like that, spontaneous, with friends everywhere. She gave it a try, offering casual smiles in a multitude of directions, but felt a self-conscious inanity about the move and gave up almost at once.

'Due espressi, signorina!' Alex nudged a waitress who seemed to be dressed as a gypsy, in layers of coloured skirts and jingling earrings. Belatedly he turned to Martha.

'Oh, is that what you'd like? I just assumed ... ' He remembered suddenly that it was polite to consult her.

'What's dooey expressi?'

They were settled at cane chairs round a low pine table where she bumped her knees and struggled to look comfortable.

'It's the real thing: Italian coffee. Very strong. You've never tasted anything like it, and once you do, you'll never want any other!' The coffee came in small glass cups, little more than a thimbleful.

'Is this it?' She didn't want to seem greedy or ignorant but the quantity struck her as an outrage. 'Really?'

'Mmmm. But just you taste it.' Alex smiled benignly at her lack of sophistication.

'Well, it's little more than a mouthful. How much do they charge for this?' Oh God, a major mistake. Speaking of money was bad form, she knew that, and besides it wasn't resolved that he would definitely be paying. If he was, all the more unfortunate that she had mentioned the cost. Whenever the family ate out at a restaurant – which was rarely – she had learned always to choose the cheapest dish on offer, otherwise her mother would glare and go silent. Alex was breezily unaware of such constraints. 'Ninepence I think ... who cares when you're having fun? It is the Café Bocca after all.' Yes, he certainly had a point there. It was worth it to be at the hub of such a buzzing place. She winced at the black liquid but knew it was something she would learn to enjoy.

'Well then, tell me about the college: is it a great place to be? Loads of student meetings and things?' Alex was known as something of a swot by his fellow grammar sixth-formers, but it wasn't the image he was after. 'I bet you don't get much work done.'

Martha had never thought of doing anything but arrive on time, attend the typing class and leave when it was over. She scarcely noticed other students at all: they were noisy and always in a hurry, pushing past her on the stairs. Everyone had the air of knowing everyone else. Only Martha kept herself apart, cherishing her private hour, the time before catching the bus home. She tried describing it to Alex by way of showing she could defy the herd. He hailed it as though she were plotting a student revolt.

'Oh that's great: defy the norms, eh? Refusing to toe the line! That's the way things are happening. You weren't at the Marty Wilde concert by any chance, were you?'

Martha hadn't been to any concerts at all. She read about them, of course, and knew that girls her own age had mobbed stars like Johnnie Ray and Adam Faith.

She broke into a little hum. 'What do you want if you don't want money?'

Alex was ecstatic: it had been a hit song only a year or two ago. Not bad for someone who was really no more than a schoolgirl. 'Great, yes, I met him once. Adam Faith ... he was battling with fans who wanted autographs. I helped him out. He was really grateful. I might look him up next time he's on tour. You could come along too if you want. What else do you like?'

Martha was pleased with the effect she was making. Alex seemed really to approve. And he was so enthusiastic. She actually found herself smiling with him even when there was no reason. Now he was asking more of her. She searched her mind for more music she thought he might approve of.

'Do you know Peggy Lee, Duke Ellington? What about Chris Barber?' She was dragging up all the names that had featured on Clive's jazz records. Alex became suddenly solemn.

'Oh, yes, you're a real intellectual I can see that … good, that's good.' It was a qualified enthusiasm. He looked almost downcast and she didn't want that. With the mention of jazz she seemed to have taken a wrong turn. Jazz was Clive's obsession and he had convinced her that it was what all young people loved. Perhaps that wasn't the case. She must get back on track, keep Alex's spirits up at any cost.

'Yes, and Lonnie Donegan, too. I love "Rock Island Line".'

Alex brightened. He was back in his stride. 'Hmm, yes, well he was very popular, I'll say that for him. More my mum's taste than mine. The mums all loved him, didn't they?'

There was nothing Martha could imagine Beattie loving less.

'Really? That's nice. When your mum likes the same as you. Mine prefers Mantovani and his strings but she doesn't have any of his records. Just listens on the radio.' And they laughed together at the absurdity of liking Mantovani.

Martha began to feel she had found a fellow spirit. Alex unfolded many things about himself that appealed to her. He liked Ernest Hemingway and breakfast fry-ups with black pudding, woollen mittens with no fingers, long college scarves, even though he was still at school. And as he shared his tastes and preferences he began to inform her about things she didn't yet know. He'd read books she'd never heard of: he promised to lend her one called *On the Beach* and one called *On the Road*. They sounded like tourist guides, but she was happy to accept the offer.

There was just one awkwardness. His father worked at Granada television and when she told him her father worked in the cinema, Alex had looked dismissively snooty. Even the Grande didn't impress him.

'Well, poor old cinema's had it these days. They're closing all over the place. Maybe your dad should get a job directing for television instead. Many of the same aesthetics apply, and it's a booming business.'

She kept to herself the fact that Eddie was a projectionist. But she couldn't let the insult to film pass unremarked. Alex might live in a grander world but perhaps he wasn't always right.

'You're wrong there. Films are great – you can't do grand things on television. Just imagine *The Magnificent Seven* on television ... black and white and a tiny screen. What'd be the point?'

'OK, OK. Well I had asked you to the flicks, remember! Still want to go, with someone who prefers telly?'

Her eager 'Oh, yes please' had a little more ardour than she intended. They settled on *North by Northwest*:

the Hitchcock film she would be able to discuss with her father. Ideal, because it had moved from the Grande so there was no risk of running into people she knew. They saw it at a small cinema on the outskirts of town. Alex bought tickets for the back row. At the point where the crop spraying began Martha knew something threatening was coming and got tense with excitement so he seized the moment to put his arm round her shoulders and gave her a squeeze. She gave him a quick complicit smile but was really too caught up in the film for more.

The newsreel reported the Americans had got their own man into space: that'd show the Russians! The commentator was triumphant.

Chapter 9

The final performance of the cinema organ was to be a grand occasion. Derek was easily persuaded to go out in style. It would be a Sunday matinee, and a shower of leaflets had been scattered among evening audiences. Derek hoped for a loyal turnout. Most people regarded the organ as an out-of-date survival, but there was among the older cinemagoers a sense that they would come to regret its passing.

Beattie was pleased to come. She had been friendly with Derek during the war when Eddie had been away. He was one of several boyfriends but had carried a torch for her, stronger than most. His appearance had always been dapper and precise and she had liked that. A thatch of red hair had brought him catcalls at school and called for active remedy. Daily attention with copious quantities of unguent plastered the culprit hair to his skull. A small ginger moustache hinted at defiance. Forced to remedy his appearance, he took care to make his clothes distinctive. He took to sporting colourful bow ties with a pearl grey double-breasted suit. The dapper style had grown in emphasis through the years. For audiences at the Grande he embodied the phrase 'matinee idol', waving his farewells as the organ descended with a larger-than-life red silk kerchief.

Eddie and Martha were unsure how Beattie might respond to the invitation. Memories of the Johnsons' party made them apprehensive. But then she was suddenly taking charge of arrangements.

'I thought Clive would like to come.'

Martha replied warily, 'Well, I'm not sure organ music is quite his taste.'

Beattie did not react.

'I'll ask him, of course, but I don't expect he'll say yes.'

'I would have thought he'd appreciate being seen as one of the family, Martha. Let everyone know how things stand.' Things of course didn't stand like that at all any more but making that plain to her mother was something that could wait.

A day later, she made her move.

'I phoned Clive and he's sorry not to come but he's going to be away seeing his gran.'

'Couldn't he cancel? I'd have thought it a matter of politeness to us; we could be his future in-laws after all.'

'Well, no, it's not. Or he's not ... er ... I mean you're not.' Martha marvelled at how readily such exchanges were conducted between her friends and their parents. It seemed only she felt unable to speak directly to her mother: what was she fearful of? Further moodiness was predictable so why not speak out.

'I have another boyfriend, now, Ma. I hope you'll like him. He's called Alex.'

There was a long pause. Martha, trapped by her mother's stare, became fidgety and unsettled. 'We met at the Johnsons'.'

'Not one of those rocking types, I hope!' She spoke the words as though they had a bad smell and didn't wait for an answer.

By the Sunday afternoon Eddie had smoothed things over. The ritual of Sunday lunch had been forsaken to allow the hours Beattie insisted it would take to be ready. Here was another chance to face the world as she wanted to be seen. Another dressmaking pattern, chosen because it was harder than the last, had been laid out on the table, this time across the rich textures of dark blue wool. She had even made secret forays into town for ribbed trimmings and tiny mother-of-pearl buttons. It was a secret life of vanity and pleasure. Defiance, too. Surprising Eddie and Martha was a sort of triumph.

When the time came for their departure, Beattie bore herself down the shabby stair-carpet of their home with the hauteur that this time reminded Eddie of Ava Gardner. It seemed to him Beattie was consciously playing a part, acting out the self she wanted to be. It was distinctly eccentric. Here was another public appearance to impress not just those who saw her, but to define Beattie for herself. He frowned at the conundrum of why and how she was doing such a thing.

By the time they arrived at the Grande he was escorting her as though she were a royal visitor. 'What a lovely family,' Ethel confided to Florrie and even Josie couldn't help but be impressed. Eddie must have been low when he'd confessed his misery to her. Now look at them ... glowing, smiling. If theirs wasn't an ideal family it was certainly one she'd have settled for.

The Sunday recital was recognised by them all as an occasion for the cinema's employees to turn out in style. Ethel was there with her three teenage children: neat and tidy in their navy school blazers; it was the pride of the family that they had all passed the eleven-plus. Florrie had urged her ageing mother from her corner armchair with promise of a bit of a sing-song. The prospect brought a withered smile as she pinned a brooch on her faded Sunday dress. Gerald, who boasted to his bird-like wife of the authority he carried at the Grande, looked round eagerly for people to greet. He hoped to catch the eye of young Mr Colin but had to make do with joshing remarks exchanged with Sid and Daisy, whom he usually ignored.

'What's got into him, d'you reckon?' asked the startled and even flattered Daisy.

'Just wants his missis to think we all kow-tow to him, that's all.' Sid raised a hand and gave a mock salute to the former sergeant major.

'That'll chuff his bollocks, you see.'

Gerald bowed a response and muttered something proud to the tiny creature at his side.

Josie's arrival was the most joyous, ushering in a throng of friends, each of them as noisy and colourful as she was. At the centre of the group Josie herself was sporting extra scarves and heavier blue eyelids. She was the very spirit of gaiety, reaching out with little taps of affection for all she knew. She swept forward, overtaking the more sedate arrival of Eddie, Beattie and Martha, and patted them each with her plump ringed hand.

'Do we know her? I don't like being touched like that!' asked Beattie.

'We do now!' Martha could hardly suppress her giggles.

The whole event struck her as a bore, and she had been bottling her resentment. Josie's gesture triggered a choking sequence of laughter, until she had to bite into a handkerchief to stop the giggles.

Despite all efforts to gather in friends and relations, the cinema's vast auditorium was nowhere near full. At the front where they all clustered together there was a good-humoured murmuring of support and solidarity. But it was the echoing spaces behind that caused Derek pain. In a bid to save his job he had continued to urge upon young Mr Colin that there was still a loyal following for his recitals. And indeed it was a mighty instrument, a Compton, one of the first, installed back in the early 1930s. Its untarnished glamour survived in the mirrored glass panels etched with sun and clouds that enfolded the keyboard and even supported the organist's seat. Lights from within changed colour at Derek's whim and would be picked up and reflected in the surrounding mirrors, glinting and mixing as the mood of the music dictated. It was a glorious creature whose 140 stop tabs

72

and 15 toe pistons could mimic a modern dance band or transmute into the sonorous tones of a cathedral organ. Two organ chambers high over the proscenium arch threw out the sounds of drums, cymbals, castanets and tambourine, glockenspiel and xylophone. Yet over the years audiences had come to take its glories for granted, its standing debased perhaps by the habits of the sing-song, which bounced a ball along the words displayed on the screen. Only Derek still loved it.

Even with the offer of free admission, the public attendance was still fewer than a hundred, and several of those were seeking shelter from the rain. Derek peeped from behind the faded curtains in the wings, saw the truth of his situation and took a swig of whisky from the bottle in his pocket. Mr Vernon senior stepped forward and paid extravagant tribute to the man he was sacking, harping on the organ's glory days when the wartime sing-song roused everyone's spirits. The word itself prompted Derek to take another swig. He bit at the wrecked stubs of his fingernails, adjusted his red bow tie and the pearl grey suit and stepped forward to acknowledge the ripple of applause. Then he was at the console of the instrument he loved, his chubby fingers suddenly alive to its gorgeous sound, his feet nimbly feeling for the pedals, his whole body where it belonged in the comfort and reassurance of what he did best.

A medley of Noel Coward songs went down well; he could hear those in the crowded front seats humming along with the lilting tunes. In the pause, he took another swig, warming to the comfort of the company. This was his family and they appreciated his skills. After a selection from *Oklahoma*, and *South Pacific*, the mood of well-being had taken hold. There was good deal of talking in the stalls; after all, this wasn't a film where you weren't supposed to gossip and spoil other people's pleasures. Here gossip was part of the event: Josie was calling to Florrie, and Bert was in conversation with Sid. Several of the children were ducking and hiding among the seats. It had the air of a carnival about it, with a dangerous whiff of mayhem in the air. Beattie and Eddie kept their own counsel, sitting in attentive silence among the boisterous celebrants. Fortified by another swig, Derek stumbled to his feet to announce the final sing-song. But before that he had a few scores to settle.

'Well, ladies and gentlemen, I'm not going to close without saying a few words – yes, I hadn't planned ... but anyway, here I am, standing before you. And I know you all, know all about you. It's been eighteen-odd years I've been playing here ... the glory years, I call them. You see' – here he shuffled a little and his hand patted his pocket where the almost empty bottle offered false courage. 'Yes, great years ... when we won the war ... that was the thing. Won it, God damn it, and came smiling through, as the song goes. There'll never be a time like it again.' A frown grabbed his brow and he shook himself free of it.

Behind the banter, Beattie sensed a deep melancholy in Derek, a melancholy she recognised, born of high hopes and painful disappointment.

'Well, no, I hadn't been with the lads at the front, no, I wasn't medically fit. That's what they said, though what that Johnny who put me through my medical had against

74

me I'll never know. Anyway, here I was doing my bit, putting heart into the people . . . helping them sing along, singing our way to victory. Oh the sound of those voices! Real inspiration they were. Glory years and I spent them with you. We've grown old together, many of us. Josie, you've lost your bloom and put on a few rolls of fat since then but you're still the willing girl we used to squeeze on the back row.' There was an uneasy titter from among her friends and Derek gathered strength. 'I was a fine upstanding young man and you girls were easy fodder. Ethel and Flossie – d'you remember the day you arrived? Innocents straight out of school dead set on getting your boyfriends in free. Well, I've kept mum about it all these years but you've done Mr Vernon here out of a small fortune wheedling in all the boys you fancied.'

'Hey, put a sock in it, Derek!' It was the martial voice of the ex-sergeant, his face bright red. He knew all too well that Derek had been privy to some shady arrangements of his own.

'Let's get on and sing, Derek!'

'Yes, you're spoiling it.'

While the objectors were speaking Derek had swung round and, his neat back briefly towards his audience, taken a quick and frantic swig.

'Yes, they've been glory days. We'll not see their like again. All that singing. All those voices . . . Raising the roof, and bringing down the Luftwaffe.' He muffed the last word and, in a swoop of despair, sobered suddenly and became tearful.

'I have genuinely loved you all. You know that. Mr Vernon, Mr Colin, you've been family to me. Sid, Daisy, like my own kind. The war was worth it, wasn't it? We all agree, glory days. Now it's time to go, but I'll tell you this, I'm just the first. Cinema is on the skids: I'll tell you that for nothing. They're closing down all of the country … it's over, boys and girls. It's television's turn—'

'For God's sake, get on or get off!' His bluff was called.

'OK, OK, I've had my say. But one last word then. It's a lovely family you have, Eddie. Martha … and you there, Beattie.' He leant precipitously towards the stalls. There was a general intake of breath but he recovered his balance and addressed the entire audience. 'We love her, don't we? I certainly do; I always have. You're as much a part of the Grande family as the rest of us. So it's come to this, everyone … goodnight, but not goodbye.' And with a broad sweep of his arms he swung himself precariously back to the keyboard and slammed into the finale of 'We'll meet again …' The staff of the Grande, made nervous and then forgiving of the ramblings of a colleague, gathered voice and allowed him to go out in style. Swaying with the music and the drink, Derek raised his red silk handkerchief for the last time, pressed the pedal and, with a dramatic heave of his shoulders, disappeared from view as the mighty organ made its final descent.

There was a distinct chill in the air as people shuffled towards the sandwiches and cakes that had been laid out in the Grande's café. Eddie and Beattie decided independently to brave out the occasion. Beattie, who had once known the red-haired organist better than she cared to acknowledge, kept a private dignity that suggested that behind her Mona Lisa smile there was more to things than people knew. Josie took the uneasy silence and rent it asunder.

'Derek, God bless him, source of bad gossip and bad breath ... and I should know.' She rushed to greet him as he joined the party, planting a big red lipstick kiss on his now neatly restored head. 'What whoppers, Derek. You're the same old rascal. Just as well we none of us believe it, eh, otherwise you'd really be in the soup. Look at Eddie, there. He's ready to land one, I can see, defending his lady fair.'

Eddie forced a laugh. 'Oh, there's no offence taken. We all know Derek's a great romancer, don't we? Hey, Derek, come and have a Battenberg slice.'

Derek, who was sobering fast, had one final shaft.

'But I meant it about the war. I did mean what I said. Glory days, they were, when we were all at our best!' He fetched himself a cup of tea, nodding to Eddie in grateful relief. 'No hard feelings, mate! No hard feelings.'

Across the room Beattie was holding a dinky plate patterned with green leaves and watching. Derek took his time, as she knew he would, but eventually he reached her side.

'It was true, you know, Beatrice.' He was safely sober by now and anyway she knew how to handle him. 'I've always been devoted ...' He reached for her hand and raised it to his lips. She smiled with the glamour and the power of it all. 'Derek, you are always so flattering; you know how I like that. But it was really too much.' She gave a little Bette Davis laugh and took a tiny bite out of an iced cake. 'It's so silly, all these years later.' Derek bowed low and as Beattie turned to see whether Martha had noticed, he allowed himself to be swept away by more raucous friends.

Martha had spent the afternoon in horrified silence, frozen by what she was watching. Could Derek be typical of the proud wartime generation who had done so much? Her father had been injured, that much she knew, but how and where he never said. As to the rest, was this what was left of their effort and self-confidence? How could things get better with all this cheap chatter, this disparaging of women, even dragging her own mother into it? What the hell did he think that meant? She didn't want their tea, or their Battenberg slice. Somehow out of the victory days she had grown up with, they had salvaged only this bitter defeat of themselves. Wrecked, perhaps, by the scale of the effort they had made, they were left winded and ineffective in a world that was looking elsewhere.

She must get away. Not away home, or away to the Café Bocca. But away to America – full of people called Beats, away to Cuba where they'd had an interesting revolution, away to smoke and learn the guitar ... away, away and away. There was no time to lose.

Chapter 10

The family returned subdued to Galton Road and its familiarities. Beattie went upstairs to change out of the smart blue suit. When Josie complimented her on looking like Katharine Hepburn she had acknowledged the exaggeration with a quiet smile. But Eddie made no comment. If she wanted to confuse him she had succeeded. Perhaps, he speculated, that was her prime intent, adding to their domestic silences these baffling displays of public solidarity.

'Did she know Derek, then?' Martha was intrigued by the idea that her mother might once have inspired passion in a man, a man who wasn't her husband and with whom she was even now in touch. 'Was she his girl-friend or something?' Adding so her father wouldn't feel offended: 'It's hard to imagine.'

Eddie paused. He had tried confiding in his friend Josie at the cinema but had been met with only good-will and misunderstanding. Now he was tempted to confide in his daughter. But to talk with her of closer things felt to him like a trespass. He measured his response.

'Oh, well, there was an incident, years ago now.' He took a cigarette from his cigarette case, tapped the end against it to firm up the loose tobacco and lit it. Martha waited. 'They'd known each other during the war. And anyway, I was away at the front. Nothing serious, Beattie said. He was keen and she never was. His mother tried to push them together, and she'd gone along with it. He made a bid to be a bit of a ladies' man, in those days. The style is looking a bit moth-eaten nowadays. Anyway, about a couple of years ago Derek lost his wallet, it went missing somewhere in the stalls and Bert found it. Didn't know whose it was so of course he opened it up. Inside he found this photograph of Beattie, all brown and faded, but tucked away inside. He showed me. I didn't make much of it at the time and I still don't. I asked Beattie and she just laughed, said it didn't mean a thing, that he had always been keen on her and liked to harp on the fact. She wasn't cross or anything, rather chuffed I think. "It's nice to have an admirer," she said. "Nothing serious, but someone who notices." And we left it at that.'

After a pause, Martha said: 'I want to get away, Dad. I want to make plans. Once I've got my diploma, you know ... time to see the world!' She laughed a false little laugh and seeing the look on his face, reached out a hand. 'I've got to grow up some time, you know.'

'Yes, yes, you do. I know that. Of course I do. And I understand. I just hoped it wouldn't be so soon.' Tall men can look hangdog and Eddie did so now.

'Well, it's not yet. Not till after the course, and my shorthand's lousy.' Why did she always have to feel apologetic?

Eddie stayed up late that night. His only daughter, his only child. It was all happening so quickly. He had seen her growing into maturity with all the good sense he had hoped for, diligent, loving, confiding. At the same time she was gaining a gazelle-like grace, but with an animal shyness, too. She was leaving behind the lumpiness of adolescence, a process he had watched with anxious concern. She had become beautiful in his eyes – not as a child is beautiful to a parent but as a woman is pleasing to a man. The change extended to their relationship too. She had become more than his child: she had become his confidante. But there was a yearning in his heart that troubled him. Could he love her too much? What did that mean? He was moved by how precious she suddenly seemed to him. At any moment she would embark on a life that would go on changing her, taking her into other company with other influences, making other friends. He had a surge of panic at the risk she would be under, of the wrong encounters, the haphazard friendships that could damage the bond between them. It wasn't something he could share with Beattie. Beattie, who seemed to have something of revenge and jealousy about her.

'So what was it like? Did it go off in style?' Martha had told Alex of the approaching celebration but now it was over she didn't want to hear him mocking. It was one thing for her to sneer at the sad little occasion, but she didn't like him doing the same. She felt protective of her family, more especially her father's motley collection of colleagues at the cinema. She tapped her spoon on the froth of cappuccino. She still hadn't mastered how to deal with this smart new drink.

'Oh, it was great, really. Everyone made a fuss and Derek got drunk. He made some daft speech about how his cinema organ had won the war: sing-songs apparently.'

'Oh, the war, the bloody war. When will they get over it?' Alex called confidently over to Aldo for another espresso and was blithely ignored.

'Probably never: it was the high point of their lives.'

'Well, it's not a high point any more.'

'Yeah, but what is any more? You tell me. This place is a desert. Nothing happens.'

Alex, who seemed to take her comments as a slight on La Bocca itself, found it his turn to be defensive. 'Oh I don't know. This place is quite buzzy. And there's loads going on if you know where to look. Music and stuff.'

'But where can I go, Alex? Where is there?'

'I just said, concerts and things, all sorts of places, cellars, garages ... loads.'

'No, I mean to live ... I want to leave home. I'm not happy. I want to see the world.'

Alex concealed his shock. This was beyond choice as he knew it; and Martha only sixteen years old. How bold was that? He regarded boldness as his preroga- tive. He and his friends were rebellious in their hearts but in fact they all lived with their mums and dads. Yet here was meek little Martha making the running, stepping outside the conventions and exposing his own timidity.

'Well, yes, there are people that go on the road but they're, well ... you know ... they're in America usually. Kerouac and such. England's smaller. There's no need to go free-wheeling across the country.' Martha wasn't surprised by his response. She knew that for all his showy familiarity with new things, he was really as conventional and timid as herself. More so, it now appeared. But then he didn't have a seriously unhappy home to drive him away. They ordered more coffee and slices of apple strudel. He stepped across and put Eddie Cochrane's 'Summertime Blues' on the jukebox.

'OK, well, let's go somewhere, in England, at least. I've a friend over in Liverpool. We could look him up, go over at the weekend ... might even sleep on his floor.' It was as if he wanted to match her daring.

'Oh, yes. Yes, I'd like that.' Martha had in mind the chance to see a new city, hear some live music and meet exciting people. The practicalities of sharing a floor with Alex would sort themselves out.

'When? ... I'll need to get permission,' she added as an afterthought, and felt feeble for doing so.

That night she stood naked before the long mirror of her dressing table. She must be honest about herself. She liked what she saw: she tried considering herself as others might see her. Depending on who it was making the appraisal the view changed. Her girlfriends at the typing class would see someone much like themselves – middle

83

height, lanky with slightly drooping shoulders, her ribcage was small so her neat budding breasts spread across her torso, their flesh firm but widely spaced against her body. Other girls had narrow crowded little breasts, others limp and sad with scarcely any thrust, still others overblown and billowing ... how many different ways of being a girl.

Her mother would appraise her more critically: her daughter's body bearing the strap marks of the bra she had bought for her that didn't fit, her belly marked with the imprint of the elasticated roll-on that kept up her stockings, her child's body shaping up to be like her own. To her father of course, her body was now a secret, undisclosed even when she was changing into a swimsuit on holiday beaches, a curtain of towels required to cover what her mother called her 'modesty'. But what modesty was that, Martha wondered. It wasn't as if her body felt shy. Clearly she was meant to feel embarrassed by it. But she didn't feel that at all: she felt rather proud, flamboyant even, that her shape showed signs of being womanly, sexy. She turned and adjusted the lozenge-shaped side mirrors of the dress-ing table to see how she looked from behind. How she might look to others, skipping naked towards the sea on some liberated holiday. Her hips looked pleasingly rounded, her waist neatly indented, her back, though narrow, had the same smooth look you saw on women in magazines wearing backless evening gowns. So, boys ... how would they look at her? Clive she decided was virtually a write-off. She could dance naked in front of him and he would turn aside in alarm and

84

embarrassment. Alex she knew would be excited. And the prospect excited her. On looking in the mirror again, she perceived a glow to her skin, a slight tightening of her nipples ... or was it the draught from the bedroom door? Alex would like seeing her like this, and she would like his liking it.

The immediate question of growing up was who were you meant to please? She had an uneasy sense that she wanted to please herself; after all, her life was her own and its satisfactions were owed to her alone. Yet she knew this couldn't be true. Too many things already indicated this wasn't so. An anxious knowledge told her she must please her mother, at any cost she must satisfy her ill-defined expectations. Martha already suspected that her failure to do so had helped produce her mother's silences. Now, from day to day, she had to be vigilant against making things worse. Nothing had been explained, nothing had been made explicit, merely a deep sense of unhappiness had somehow contrived to transmit itself from her mother and lay the blame deep into Martha's soul. Her father – ah, her father – she basked in his approval. It was the pivotal point in her security, the linchpin of her confidence. It made her happy. His love of his work, his eagerness to share that with her, the good feeling that prevailed at the cinema when he was among his colleagues ... all these told her he was a good and sympathetic man. She ached when he was downcast; she hated to see him worried and bemused. And pleasing him seemed to come without effort: she felt she would always do that.

And the others? What about the others? The typing

class was amiable and unexacting but they could take her as she was, she was indifferent to their judgements. Alex, yes, Alex she wanted to please. To do more than please. She wanted to win his approval, to make him laugh, to share her growing up with him. The following morning she called him even before she'd had break-fast.

Chapter 11

'So, is this the address he gave you?' They were standing on cracked paving stones on a street of Victorian villas and looking at an imposing double-fronted house with bay windows, fancy ceramic tiling along the roof and funny little turrets at each corner. They reminded her of the dancing chimneys. 'Is this really it?' Martha was both impressed and concerned. She admired its grandeur but was disappointed that it seemed more shabby than the rest. Neighbouring villas had well-tended front gardens of laurel bushes and yew trees, but this one had run to seed and was now a mix of brambles and collapsing crates of empty bottles. Stranger still, the front door was boarded up with a single plank of wood nailed across the pretty period glass. 'Are you sure this is where he said?' They had arrived at Liverpool's Lime Street station with a small cardboard suitcase and a khaki rucksack left over from Martha's days as a Girl Guide and had taken the number 82 bus to Sefton Park.

'Here's the note: see for yourself.' He handed her a crumpled envelope with crabbed writing. He had claimed to have friends whom he knew well enough to ask for a bed for the night. But where were they? Venturing up the curving drive they saw flimsy curtains drawn across both bay windows. One had its wire dislodged and hanging loose. The address was correct enough but it seemed no one had cared for this place for a long time.

'Shall we look round the back? All we want are signs of life.' It was a month since Derek's calamitous organ recital and Martha's enthusiasm to get away hadn't dimmed. But in her eagerness for something new she hadn't reckoned with the totally unknown. Alex always boasted that he would take her to exciting places where people read poetry aloud and everyone had records of the new music. The reality could fall far short.

A few weeks earlier Alex had been in Liverpool and met an art student at the Rumbling Tum coffee bar, a tall ungainly creature with angular limbs and long limp hair. The two of them had moved on to a local pub hoping to hang out with the group that was playing there. Once the clutch of young fans had departed, Alex got talking to the drummer: he found they'd both had similar jobs on the railway during the school holidays. Alex was impressed by the glamour of his kit. He'd love to play drums himself but where could someone still at school get that kind of money? Monkey – that appeared to be his name – just raised an eyebrow, nodded to the student and turned away. The student grinned.

'No one has any money round here, you just cadge and borrow ... or nick from your family. By the way, they call me Topper.'

'Why's that? Topper.'

'Oh, it just is ...'

Alex hadn't much money either, so they shared a Tizer and a pie. The group had climbed into their van and driven off. Monkey left them with a broad grin and a thumbs-up. When they eventually stumbled out into the street with nowhere to go, Topper didn't seem to mind. Alex was impressed by his indifference: struggling to break free of family convention clearly meant having no bed for the night.

'I've got friends over in Sefton Park. Well, I think I have. I don't think it's far from here.' They caught a bus and got off near Princes Park. Topper appeared vague about directions. He leant against one of the hefty trees that lined the path and rolled another of his loose shaggy cigarettes. He seemed in no hurry.

'Well, come along then, let's go.'

'You know, I think I'll just wander for a bit ... I like the moonlight ... look ... behind that cloud.' Topper took a long tug of breath on the fraying rag of whatever he was smoking and turned his wan bony face towards the sky. The state of the stars wasn't something that had ever detained Alex. Certainly not now he was tired and in need of home comforts.

'But what about your friends, the ones you said could give us a bed? I'd really like to meet them.' There was an urgency to his plea that irritated Topper.

'You don't know them, though, do you?' He got

vaguer and less helpful. A long thin scarf was wound round his neck; he began playing with it, holding it from his body so he could see it.

'Jess gave me this: I think she's keen on me.' He hadn't moved from the tree and began to slide down its trunk, admiring the silk scarf as he went. 'I think I'll just have a little pause.' His limbs splayed easily at the bole at its base. He rummaged in the pockets of a torn canvas jacket. 'Look, here's their address – you have it. I never liked them much anyway now I think of it.'

Alex had taken the crumpled envelope, hesitated and stuck it in his pocket.

Then he caught the last train back to Staveley.

'I don't know them exactly, just through mutual friends.' Her own stamina was still high, the surge of excitement at having come here at all still sustained her. But Alex was wilting. She would have to take charge.

'I'll go round the back, you wait here.' Martha shouldered the khaki bag and made for the side of the house. The front garden with its tangled dark-leaved shrubbery reminded her of the spooky films she had seen from her father's projection box, X-rated films for adults only. They had left her with fears of shadowy gardens, creaking gates and wind in the branches. Works of the imagination . . . she shook herself free of their hold. After all, it was daylight, midday with a bright June sky in one of the plusher parts of Liverpool. As she thrashed her way through fallen branches and tangled undergrowth, imagination battled with common sense. She must look for clues. The narrow path was muddy, churned up. In the side wall of the house there was a small window, on the sill a vase of very dead flowers and a small golliwog wedged into the sash. Children, then, or playful adults. The path opened out to where she could see an expanse of lawn and some rickety deckchairs, faded and scruffy from having been left out all winter. There was a bicycle leaning against the wall, and a back door of wilted green paint daubed across with random splashes of colour. In the top right-hand corner someone had crayoned the familiar cartoon figure looking over the wall: 'Jasper was here!' Although all this seemed quite promising, Martha was still gripped by a fear of surprise: the criminal's hand on Pip's shoulder in *Great Expectations*.

She knocked on the door, a pale timid knock that asked not to be heard. At that moment Alex's voiced hissed at her from where he had stayed on the pavement. 'Any luck?' It wasn't a matter of luck. She knocked harder, and listened with her ear to the flaking paint. Was that a strange rustling sound and possibly the strains of music? Imagination or common sense?

She turned the knob of the back door and opened it slowly, leaning her face close to the crack to peer through as small a space as possible. She stepped into the dark interior. There was a small lobby with doors leading off. One of these was open a chink and opened further as she ventured inside. The only light was coming from the golliwog window to the left which she could now see stood over a wide stone sink, stained with grime and stacked with leaning heaps of dirty dishes. The evidence of domesticity, however wayward, made her feel more at home. The rustling proved to be the quiet flapping of a distant door catching on a curl of carpet. She pushed the door wider and stepped into a large mess of a room, strewn with the debris of strange and intriguing activities. A vast sofa dominated the centre, covered with a disordered heap of coloured fabrics, silks and velvets, a bolt of worsted cloth, gauzy swathes of gossamer stuff and one or two actual garments, a naval uniform of an antique style and a skirt of bunched ribbons hinting at maypoles and village greens. There were a couple of old-fashioned round hat boxes, their lids off and hats with veiling and long feathers within. On a small neat table beside a converted oil lamp was a spread of coloured masks, their eyes staring vacantly at the ceiling as though watching a display. Martha followed their gaze and saw nothing more than a single bulb hanging down from a lone wire.

She moved over and examined the masks. They were things of beauty – blue, mauve, velvety and shiny; there was a tumble of ribbons at each corner and an edging of lace trimming such as she had on her pyjama case at home. Things of beauty and colour were rare in her life. Rationing was still a glum memory and young men had until recently been called away to National Service. For Martha this was a glimpse into another world ... the theatre perhaps, or films. Yes, perhaps films. Something to tell her father about. But that would have to wait.

She reached for a mask of red satin and put it on. It made her feel secure. There, under cover of its prettiness, she could be whoever she wanted. She felt like a snake sloughing off its old skin, moving its new and glistening surface with the confidence of rebirth. She helped herself to one of the gaudy hats and set it above her chaotic black hair. She had trouble with the fine elastic that held it in place, and wasn't sure how to deploy the copious veiling that looped itself across her brow. She looked round for a mirror on the wall. There was nothing but faded brown wallpaper and a series of disconnected shabby cupboards, one with its door hanging off its hinge, a litter of paper, bottles strewn around. She was still seeking to find a reflective surface in which to measure her own appearance when a door into the interior of the house opened slowly. A man stood there. To Martha he looked old, not as old as her father, but older than the boys she knew. He came into the room and stood there without speaking. They weighed each other up. Then with a show of exaggerated gallantry he made a wide and sweeping bow. Martha surveyed him, squinting through the mask trying to make him out. Then, on impulse, and behind the camouflage of the mask, she responded with a deep curtsy.

'Is that prick of a lad out front something to do with you?' Martha had forgotten Alex. Growing bold herself she had become detached from him. They were no longer in this together. She was further in and he was nowhere.

Still, she felt a certain loyalty.

'He's my friend. He's called Alex.'

'Why'd he let you come in here by yourself? It could be a den of vice: white slave traffic, that sort of thing.'

'I rather hoped it might be ... ' She giggled. The mask was giving her false courage. Still the confidence it gave her was important. She wasn't going to discard it yet. Instead she cleared a space on the sofa, made herself at home there and waited. The man shuffled into the room. He was wearing large carpet slippers, the sort old women wore, with pompoms on the front. But otherwise his appearance expressed everything she imagined about poets and beats, strong men who spoke poetry, talked all night and drank whisky neat – black leather jacket, narrow black jeans and a loose and grubby T-shirt.

'Whisky? ... Or would you prefer a nice cup of tea?' He picked up a tin kettle and turned on a ring of a grubby gas stove. He was tall and substantially built without being fat. What her father would call 'a fine figure of a man'. His face was pale but he had very powerful black eyes which he focused with great deliberation. He had heavy eyebrows and a moustache that drooped down over his mouth concealing his lips as he spoke. 'I think it'll be tea. I had a heavy night.'

'Is this your home?'

'Tell me first why you're here. You must have had some reason to come snooping in in the first place? What's the idea?'

'Some friends of Alex gave him this address. We're from over Staveley way. We heard things were good in Liverpool. So we just came.'

His laugh was loud but generous. 'Yes, the address does get around. That's why we boarded up the front door ... to repel all comers. But not you, eh? Are you at school? Or looking for a job? What's your name? And please be so kind as to take off that daft get-up.'

Martha did as she was told; she felt happy to obey him. His demands were benign and in truth the mask had begun to itch and she didn't like the distance it put between her and the person she was addressing.

'I'm Martha; I'm doing a typing course. Who're you?'

'I'm Duncan and I'm all sorts of things. This is my parents' home but my father's been working abroad for over a year. They left me in charge.'

'What does your father do?' She felt a fool asking such a question, the kind of question parents ask.

'What does that matter? Anyway, he's a psychiatrist; he lectures all over America. He's pioneering some new radical approach to things. I'm not quite sure what.' He handed her a cup of tea in a surprisingly clean cup with roses round the lip and on the saucer. 'The place has run down a bit since they left. Cassie and I like it like this. We've sort of made it our own.'

'Is Cassie your wife?'

'No, no she's not. I don't go in for wives.' He chuckled to himself at the idea. 'We're close but not that close. Cassie's my sister. She has some sort of job in an experimental theatre club. This stuff's hers.'

'It's lovely! Really lovely!' Martha's eyes gleamed.

'Is it? Then take it ... help yourself. She's chucking it out. At least I think she is.' Martha ignored this qualifying remark and began rummaging among the costumes. She took the coat that looked like an antique admiral's uniform, discarded her gaberdine and put it on. Once again she wished there were a mirror. Instead she twirled round in front of Duncan.

'Small man must have had this ... it fits me perfectly.'

'They were all small then, undernourished, no National Health orange juice.'

'When d'you mean, small when?'

'Oh, just in history ... the past. England's glory. Nelson was a really little fellow, you know. Another cup. I notice you're not worried about your friend.'

'Oh my God. Alex. I'd quite forgotten. Can I fetch him in?'

'He's probably given up on you.' Duncan swayed towards a shabby leather armchair and dumped his considerable weight within it, his clumsy feet sticking out on the rug in their granny slippers. Somehow his great bulk had a confidence to it, the dishevelled clothes bunched with a louche glamour around his belly: he held himself with an easy pride, a self that conceded to no one, took no instruction from any world but his own. 'Yes, fetch him, fetch him. But he'll have to make his own tea.' Martha smiled with gratitude and even pleasure.

She found Alex sitting on the kerbside reading a paperback he'd had in his pocket.

'Well, a fat lot you care!'

'Where the hell have you been?'

Their voices jumbled together as they calculated who was the more to blame.

'I could have been shipped off in the white slave trade and no help from you.'

'I thought you were on a recce: I was keeping watch.'

'But it was your address ... you brought me here.'

'I'm not sure we should be breaking in. You've no respect for property, you haven't – and what's that fancy coat all about?'

'Don't be such a ... prick, a prick, that's what he said. He saw you from the window.' Alex glowered miserably. Martha had been so bold and got away with it. He was meant to be initiating her into ... well, he wasn't sure what. He had even paid her fare from Staveley.

'Anyway, he said to come in.'

'He ... will he give us a bed for the night?' Martha noted he spoke of a singular bed, and remembered the actual purpose of her coming away with him. Well, she'd best go through with it now, even though the shine had gone off Alex. He was no more than an ordinary mortal after all, and one with acne too. His attraction for her had died on the instant. One moment she was eager for his ideas, his talk, even his boasting. In the next he was no more than a lanky schoolboy bouncing around like a young puppy. It was alarming to find her feelings could change so fast.

Something of Alex's joviality returned as he joined Duncan in the echoing kitchen. He strode forward, extending his arms to embrace the unexpected scene.

'Hello there! I'm Alex. Hi! You know, I've heard so much about this house! Topper told me all about it. Its reputation's spreading, d'you know that? A place where things happen?'

Duncan's eyes took in the duffle coat over what looked like school trousers. His stare gave nothing away. He took his time, waiting for Alex to calm down.

'What? What happens here? Or rather what do they say happens here? And who the hell's Topper?'

Alex looked to Martha for help. She was sitting among

the cloud of soft fabrics in her antique coat drinking tea. She stared back, waiting to hear what he'd say. He'd spun her so many yarns about things happening, 'Really happening, man,' but she'd never bothered to establish quite what such things were.

'Oh, music, people, you know, poetry readings' – he was getting desperate – 'cups of tea!'

'You'll have to make your own then.' Over by the far wall a mahogany display cabinet held a sparkling array of cups, saucers and plates of many sizes: its glass-panelled doors protecting the contents from happenings of all kinds. Martha thought it conformed more to her mother's dreams of domesticity than to this chaotically bohemian place. Perhaps Duncan's parents were as conventional as her own. Alex made himself a cup of tea.

'Topper's a friend. We met at a concert: great gig: drummer called Monkey's a mate of mine. Topper's a tall bloke, scraggy, nice though, wears a long silk scarf. Makes a great fuss of it ... Says Jess gave it to him.'

'You seem to know a goodly rabble of friends in Liverpool already, if I may say so ...' Duncan's black eyes were piercing but not ungenerous.

'Well, you know how it is ...' He looked uneasily towards Martha, who was realising he knew exactly no one. 'It's a start.' Silence fell and they sat sipping tea from the flowered cups like ladies in a Victorian novel.

'Right then! You two! What are you wanting?' Duncan slammed broad hands on his knees, pulled his weight from the depths of the chair and made for the bottle of whisky that stood on the drainer beside the sink. 'Let's sort you out then. Are you looking for work, is that it? A proper job or just something to make a quid or two? No drugs sold on the premises, by the way, I promised Da that. Or is it a social call? Is partying what you have in mind, knocking around? Music? Well, there's loads of that going on . . . I can promise you that!'

'There's nothing in Staveley. That's the problem. It's dull and boring. Nothing happening . . . ever. Totally dull.' In the corner of her mind she felt a sense of disloyalty; a pang of guilt nudged its way forward. 'Well, there's the cinema of course. We've got a great one, the Grande; but that's just two measly programmes a week.' That was as far as she need go. Pride in your home town was natural around these parts. But she didn't feel any duty to exaggerate. 'No, Staveley's not got it. We wanted to be where – well – where there's almost anything really.' Martha knew this was feeble and it made her feel limp and useless. Then she remembered the dancing chimneys, the curling red chimneys she saw all week from her typist's desk. 'Do you have any dancing chimneys at all? You know, odd strange buildings . . . built fancy just for the sake of it. I like that kind of thing.'

Duncan turned, the whisky bottle in his hand, and looked at her. His eyes widened.

'You like buildings, do you?'

'Yes. How they look. Not any buildings, of course. Not most buildings, in fact.'

'Just dancing chimneys, eh?' Duncan smiled and Martha's face broke into a broad smile.

99

'They're what I see from my desk: sounds desperate, doesn't it? But you've got to make the most of what's around.' She laughed at the nonsense of it all, but also because it was exactly true about herself and the chimneys. Duncan's black eyes wrinkled and responded.

'Or leave home, is that it?'

'Oh, well, no. Not exactly. I can't do that. I still live at home: I have to.' How to unburden the story of Galton Road and its strange constraints? 'Alex and me, we've come away for the weekend. Alex is in the sixth form.' This was a disclosure too far: it was for Alex to speak up for himself; now he risked being labelled a grammar school swot. She turned towards him.

'Yes, I'm ... er ... I'm keen to get to university. I want to read English. I like it, I really do.' His tone was almost apologetic, but Duncan laughed, the loud generous laugh that greeted Martha when she had first arrived.

'Of course you bloody do. So you should. It's great. Who's your favourite? Who do you rate?' Alex's eyes bulged, his relief at not being designated a swot cancelled by being set a sort of exam.

'Well, Yeats for one. I like the poetry of Yeats. And Dylan Thomas ... ' Duncan and Martha were attentive. Did he need to go on? 'And, well, Shakespeare of course ... '

In a quiet dark voice, Duncan began: 'I have met them at close of day / Coming with vivid faces / From counter or desk among grey / Eighteenth-century houses ... '

He paused, looking at Alex, who softly, in a voice Martha had never heard before, took up the lines. 'I have passed with a nod of the head / Or polite meaningless

words / Or have lingered a while and said / Polite meaningless words ...'

Wrapped in the poem and each other's love of it, Alex
and Duncan went turn and turn about, their eyes locked,
all the way through the long poem until at the final
refrain they turned in gentle triumph towards Martha:
'... All changed, changed utterly: / A terrible beauty is
born.'

She sighed, and the room held their silence.

Chapter 12

'It looks very much as though Derek has decided to drink himself to death.' Josie and Eddie were sitting at the saloon bar in the Red Lion. It was early evening, with the summer sunlight struggling through the patterned Victorian windows.

'Oh don't be so dramatic, woman! Who says so anyway?' Eddie's irritation with Derek had taken a whole month to surface. He'd chosen not to question Beattie further about the strange outburst at the organ recital, but that didn't mean that old fears hadn't stirred. Every day he was searching for clues to his wife's behaviour. Derek's drunken meanderings with their long-gone memories of her, even as she sat there, decked up, as though for a starring role ... well, was that some sort of clue or not? He'd decided there and then not to let it get under his skin. Not to mention anything about it, to deliberately stop his own thoughts drifting that way. And he certainly didn't want to hear about Derek's problems.

Most of all he didn't want Josie switching her concern away from him: he liked the attention of such a woman. Derek was the past now, the mighty Compton organ had made its last descent. It wasn't appropriate that he should come round, stalking them all, walking in just as though he still had a right to the place.

'He keeps fetching up at the café. But it's not tea he's drinking.'

'Hasn't he anything better to do with his time? I'd have thought he needed to find another job pretty smartish ... though I'm not sure what he's any good for.'

'Eddie, that's just not like you, to be so unfriendly.' Unconsciously Josie drew her fringed silk scarf tighter around her breasts. Eddie sensed her unease and turned to face her.

'What are you up to, Josie, defending him like this? The man's a tosser – excuse my French. But he is, he really is ...'

'He thinks his mum's dying. That and losing his job ... and not just the job, but the organ itself.'

'His mum's dying! Is that true, Josie? Or is he playing for sympathy?'

Josie slapped his elbow. 'Stop it. Stop it. You're being too hard on the man. Anyway, search me. He's got some bee in his bonnet about nuclear radiation. Apparently she was holidaying in the Lake District when there was that escape at Windscale some years ago. He thinks she was contaminated, or something. She's losing her hair.'

The image brought Eddie up short: he recalled films of futuristic calamity.

'Well, it certainly was a strange business, that Windscale thing.'

Josie looked thoughtful. 'I don't like that nuclear. I don't trust it.'

'There's stuff on the newsreels about it – they keep testing. Then they keep having conferences about it. I hope they know what they're doing.'

They were both thoughtful, contemplating the unimaginable.

'Yes, and these protests are getting bigger all the time. What d'you reckon, Eddie, d'you think we're heading for world war three and being blown to kingdom come?'

'Looks possible, but it's out of our hands, isn't it?' His head sank lower. 'I thought we'd done with wars ...' This was the big one, the haunting worry behind all their lives.

'C'mon. Daisy's standing in but she's not up to coping with the second house.'

Eddie had already seen it through several times, but he was needed to back up Bert.

'It's a nice one, this one ... *The Nun's Story*. Audrey Hepburn being noble in the Congo. The women like it.'

Bert had got the second reel on and was sitting back having a smoke before going into the cubbyhole next door that housed the rewind machine. Eddie couldn't throw off Josie's worries.

'Seen anything of Derek, have you?'

Bert turned to look closely at Eddie. 'Yes, I have. Why're you asking?'

'I hear he's hitting the bottle. That true?'

'Something like that. He's round here more than's good for him. Doesn't seem to have anywhere else to go.'

'Mr Colin wouldn't like that if he heard about it.'

'Mr Colin – give me strength. Can't say boo to a goose. Derek'd wipe the floor with him, specially if he's wielding a bottle. Poor old Derek.' Bert laughed his curious high-pitched giggle, and Eddie pretended to find it amusing. And then Bert made a mistake.

'You'll have to get your Beattie to sort him out – she's probably the only one he'll listen to.' Eddie's brow shadowed briefly. Clearly the myths prompted by Derek's odd farewell speech were lingering in people's thoughts. Why was it he couldn't laugh it off as he was expected to do? Again he pondered the yawning gap between their fantasy of his idyllic happy family and the deep sad truths of his home life.

'Don't you be talking such rubbish, Bert. It's not like you!' he said dismissively, and that closed the matter.

On the newsreel Rudolf Nureyev, the star of Russia's Kirov ballet, was claiming political asylum at Le Bourget airport. He ran towards French police crying, 'Protect me, protect me.'

Presidents Kennedy and Khrushchev held a two-day meeting in Vienna: test-ban talks remain deadlocked.

Chapter 13

This is wonderful, thought Martha, sitting in the silence with the poem still filling their thoughts; I'm happy being here. Just being. She had an impulse to join in, to be part of the words and the feelings the words evoked. She plucked idly at a gauzy blue gown that lay next to her on the sofa.

'I don't suppose I could read something, could I?'

Duncan was lumbering out of the armchair and putting the kettle on again, for all the world as though speaking poetry like that was just what you did around the house, as though there were no difference in mood or behaviour between domestic chores and being literary... because that was what poetry was, wasn't it, literary and high-brow. 'La-di-da' Marjory would call it. Martha had always been unsure herself, but she'd gone along with the idea that being literary was meant to be high-flown and special. Even Alex had managed to convey that, lending her strange stuff from America, people with names like Ferling-hetti and Ginsberg she couldn't begin to understand.

'Yes, why not ... have a go at this ...' Duncan reached out to a loaded bookshelf of planks supported on bricks and pulled out a paperback. 'Stick with good old William Butler.' He leafed through well-thumbed pages and handed it to Martha at a chosen poem. She had spoken from an eagerness not to be left out, and had been scouring her memory for scraps of school poems, daffodils and larks and such. Faced with someone else's choice, she suddenly felt shy and her voice when it came was thin and wistful.

'Never shall a young man,
Thrown into despair
By those great honey-coloured
Ramparts at your ear,
Love you for yourself alone
And not your yellow hair.'

'But I can get a hair-dye
And set such colour there,
Brown, or black, or carrot,
That young men in despair
May love me for myself alone
And not my yellow hair.'

'I heard an old religious man
But yesternight declare
That he had found a text to prove
That only God, my dear,
Could love you for yourself alone
And not your yellow hair.'

The stillness returned to the room. Martha closed the book slowly and put it on the table. She bit her lip, and her eyes darkened.

'I don't think I want that to be true: it's beautifully put, of course, but I agree with her, what she says. I want to be loved for myself alone, the real me ... but—'

'No, no, no. That's the point.' Alex blustered in with the energy of a bounding spaniel. 'Being pretty matters ... you'd better believe it. All blokes know it's true.'

Duncan smiled. Was he a teacher, she wondered. He was taking his time to hear their reactions, holding back, waiting to judge what they had to say.

'It's a challenge for women, isn't it? If you're beautiful and sexy ... of course people will fall in love with you. How'll you even get noticed if you're an ugly little mouse?'

Martha sensed he was on to something; clearly the poem said so. Hadn't she felt a whole lot more real, more alive since trying on these fancy clothes and the glamorous masks? But he was wrong, too. What about the Clives of this world ... a mouse himself, surely he'd want to find another mouse to match. And anyway wasn't it deplorable to be swayed by the superficial, the surface of things. She wanted to be taken seriously, not treated as a bit of fluff, to be gawped at. She wasn't even sure Duncan believed what he said and wasn't simply teasing her.

'Then it's up to them to sort out whether it's genuine love or not ... watch out, young Martha. It'll not be easy being a woman.' Then his eyes twinkled. 'Fun, though!'

'I think I'll have to become a nun.' She was teasing him now.

'What a waste: don't even think of it.' Alex was left out of whatever was going on.

This time it was a different kind of tea, so unusual they thought it was a different kind of drink altogether. It lacked the round gold colour they were used to.

'Er, this tea, is it?' In the homes of Staveley there was only one kind. It came from former colonies, somewhere called Assam, and was dispensed from tea caddies with small chrome-plated spoons.

'Yes, like it? It's called Earl Grey. My parents like this sort of thing ... I think it's a bit poncey myself. But that's what we found in the cupboard.'

'No reason why there should be only one kind of tea, I suppose.' Alex was struck by the possibility there might be an expanding number of all the things they were used to. Bread? Brown or white, those were the existing options, coming straight from the baker's tin, though you could now buy loaves made in factories, already sliced and wrapped in greaseproof paper. Most sensible families disliked it. 'Too tired to cut it yourself, oh dear!'; his father had mocked their neighbours' picnic sandwiches. Butter? Well, it came in a yellow slab from the grocer's who cut it up and shaped it with wooden paddles, so there was not much messing with that. Jam? Well, everyone's mum used to make their own when the fruit first arrived in the shops, but now they saved time buying jars of it. It was always brighter in colour than home-made, and one kind had a little golliwog brooch in the lid. Coffee? Well, he knew all about coffee from the Café Bocca, not the instant Nescafé they had at home. But tea ... this Earl Grey was new to him. He made a point to remember. This was what was meant by broadening your horizons.

Martha hesitated. 'I need to go ... ' Duncan looked non-plussed. Lavatory? Or should it be 'toilet'? She remembered her mother saying it should properly be 'toilet', even though they'd said lavatory – or simply lav – at home for years. Of course it didn't matter, of course it didn't. It would simply help to know which was right.

'Oh, the loo ... yes, of course.' Duncan bounded to the room's inner door which opened into a large square hall and the front door. The staircase rose through its centre towards a balcony around the first floor. 'Up these stairs, turn right along the landing and the second door on the left. You'll see stuff of mine on the way. I'd like to know what you think.' And left her to it.

Martha had been given access to the whole house and she would make the most of it. From the hall other doors stood open and through one she could see a couple of rumpled beds, unmade, mattresses spread directly on the floor. Through another a circular library table with a huge globe on it, and small flags sticking to different places, a scholarly room with dark curtains and a mood of civilised thought. The staircase itself had something of the same curving lilt as the red-brick chimneys she saw from her desk, but it was painted white. The treads of the stair were white too. No stair carpet at all. Her shoes made a clumping sound as she went, so she took them off. Her gaze went everywhere, hungry for what was new and different. At the turn of the stair, where it divided left and right, stood a large misshapen figure. It seemed fashioned out of papier mâché, but left deliberately rough and then splashed with bright colours. Its face was bright red with bulging blue eyes, the naked torso was bright pink and it had an erect penis which was painted purple. Someone had hung a bowler hat on it. She knew the colour because she lifted the hat. Then put it back almost furtively as though someone might be watching. She took the stair that branched to the right. Further along were a series of strange abstracts on the wall. They were constructed of pieces of string, the strands pinned out on a background of hessian. Each one was in a blond-wood frame hung in exact alignment with the others. She found them serene, calming.

The bathroom was spacious and chill with a big iron bath fixed right in the middle. On the wall there was a long rack with hooks and a jumble of dressing gowns. The washbasin overlooked the garden where Martha could see more of those wrecked deckchairs and at the far end a long-disused children's sandpit. Beside it was a rickety shed just like the one at home. Did all gardens have them? The Galton Road shed held her father's bike and the one she'd had as a child and lots of rusty stuff, old but not thrown away.

Then she heard Duncan calling up to her from the bottom of the stairs in a voice he was seeking not to make too loud.

'Oh, I didn't say, don't go further up, will you? Grandma's room's up there and she hates it being disturbed. Well, disturbed by people she doesn't know, that is.'

'OK, I won't. I wouldn't have anyway!' She felt a fool shouting from the seat of the lavatory.

Grandma's room upstairs! That was unexpected: even weird. Hadn't Duncan said he and his sister had taken charge while their parents were away? Was Granny actually living there, like the mad woman in *Jane Eyre*, or had she simply left her possessions? Martha imagined old moth-eaten clothes and the smell of embrocation. She felt a shuddery excitement about what might be going on. After all, she didn't know Duncan: she only knew people who knew him, or rather Alex had an address from people she didn't know, who said they knew him. The link suddenly seemed rather tenuous. It appeared that getting out of a rut meant making all sorts of random connections along a chain of contacts you didn't know. Perhaps that was the way the world was going. She turned back, wanting urgently to feel the comfort of being with Alex, someone she had met at a neighbour's house, someone her father had nodded to and appeared to approve of. She scrambled down the stairs swinging her shoes in her hand.

'OK, then? What d'you think?' Duncan looked up from the open book in his hand. He clearly expected a considered opinion.

'Oh, yes, the art! I like the figure! The one with the purple . . . '

'Oh, the cock . . . you noticed! That's by an art school student of mine. I'll tell her: she'll be pleased.' Martha's head swam with the idea of girls studying art and making such bold figures. They would be having so much more fun, and she was stuck with boring old typing. Oh, there was so much wrong with her life, and so many chances she didn't want to miss. But she had got this far. Her confidence swarmed back. She might be in the house of a total stranger wearing his sister's theatrical cast-offs but this was the way to go. And things got better.

'I've explained to Alex here, Saturday night's when we sometimes have a sort of open house. People come round, and there's drink and talk and whatever. Alex has said you'd both like to stay. You can have a bed in the room across the way if you like.' Martha recalled the glimpsed room with rumpled beds on the floor.

'Fine, great. Yes.' She rewarded Alex with a swift uneasy smile. He was someone she trusted, and although he swanked a lot about the books he'd read, she liked the smell of his skin, despite the acne. Sleeping with him seemed suddenly safe and adventurous at the same time.

Around nine o'clock people began arriving with records and bottles – cheap wine, some beer, the occasional scotch and vodka. They trooped upstairs past the purple cock and the serene abstracts and into the huge room that extended the full depth of the house. Tall windows rose at either end, a beautiful gracious room, that demonstrated the confidence and taste of its owners. Bookshelves rising to the ceilings bore sets of books with identical bindings: red and blue leather with gold lettering. And a grand piano that had seen better days lurked away in the back. There was an abundance of cushions, grand ashtrays shaped out of pottery or coloured glass and magazine racks in bamboo loaded with imposing magazines, some frayed papers spilling out onto the antique but thread-bare carpet. Serious sofas and chairs had been pushed back against the walls. In the front corner, catching every-one's attention, stood an impressive record player – walnut veneer with a hinged lid – and beside it, stacked on shelves above, loads of records, each in its loose paper sleeve indicating the recording company – Decca, Capitol, HMV. Martha had never seen so much music. It seemed others hadn't either. They swarmed towards it, pulling out and exclaiming over the thick black discs.

'Wow, Chuck Berry! How'd you get that? ... '

'Ordered it from ... have you heard the new ... '

Martha and Alex moved like smoke among the know-ing crowd, looking for a break, a way in, trying to infiltrate a conversation here, an argument there. Then suddenly standing above the rest was the tall lank figure of Topper, his nickname explained by the misshapen and dusty hat he was wearing.

'That's my friend ... the one who gave me this address.' Alex waved and pushed through the crowds towards him. Martha followed him close.

'Does everyone round here go in for fancy dress?' Martha addressed the remark to Alex but Topper assumed it was to him.

'Well, you're a fine one to talk.' Yes, of course, the admiral's coat.

'Oh, I'd forgotten. I found it downstairs ... '

Topper was pulling on the same long silk scarf. Alex knew its story.

'Is Jessica here with you?'

'Not with me. Bitch – downstairs with one of those types from the art college. Scouse phoneys.'

Martha assessed the crowd: lots of tall young men, all with long necks and heads like stalks of corn, nodding and leaning together, talking earnestly, nodding and agreeing, sometimes waving a hand, shaking a head. Arguments seemed to be flowing to and fro across the room. A particularly intense group were huddled together in the corner by the grand piano. They wore cord trousers and tweed jackets; one had leather patches on his elbows, another wore a flowery bow tie; not fancy dress exactly but clearly an attempt to snatch some individuality from among the throng. One of them she remarked at once: he had a bright yellow waistcoat and a bold large head with a dense slew of pale brown hair that grew down and over his collar. His shoulders were hunched in concentrated attention as he listened to each of the others, almost a parody of a mad professor in a children's fairy tale, eccentric but benign, smiling but tense.

There was little laughter from that group. They were handing around what looked like leaflets and drinking beer from the bottle, putting the empties on the piano's fine wooden surface. Martha imagined the damage it might do. Then she let the idea go. She must stop responding like her mother, who would have silently fetched a cork mat and slipped it under the bottle. As if ... as if. Her mother was never going to be in such a company, at such a party ... It was a measure of how far Martha had come, and how much her mother would disapprove. But then she wouldn't tell her. She had spun a story of being on a walking weekend with a girl from the typing class. The deception had come easily, and given her a thrill.

'Oh, I like your coat.' A chubby girl, eyes weighed down with mascara, was fingering the gold braid on Martha's antique coat. Her hand, loaded with chunky rings slid down the heavy navy serge, coming to rest on Martha's hip. It was a gesture more strange than friendly, almost threatening. 'In fact, I liked it so much I had intended to keep it for myself ...' The mascara eyes brightened and winked.

'Oh no, oh dear. You must be Cassie. Am I right?'

'Right about me: not right about the coat!' This was looking tricky and Martha wasn't up to it.

'Oh I love it, you know, I really do. I tried it on and Duncan said it would be OK. But if it isn't OK, I'm sorry. I didn't mean anything, I wasn't stealing it.'

'Oh heavens, calm down, chicken! Just relax. Help yourself. As you can see everyone else does.'

'And you don't mind? All your friends piling in like this. With your parents away?' Damn. The shadow of her mother still haunting all she thought and said.

'I'd say not ... and hey, look who the wind's swept in ...'

Two individuals were bundling into the room with long loping strides, talking together, ignoring the rest. They wore narrow black drainpipe trousers; one had a bright pink shirt, the other a black leather jacket. Their hair was piled high in what Martha knew was called a Tony Curtis, and the one in pink kept running his hand over it, whether out of uneasiness or pride she couldn't quite tell. They stopped as they heard the music, began clicking their fingers and moving their limbs. Martha had somehow missed 'Jailhouse Rock' and 'Love Me Tender' but she could tell they were moving in the same sort of way Elvis did. They exuded glamour.

'Who are they? Tell me who they are.'

'Yes, all the girls are crazy for them. They play guitar in a group just nearby, Wavertree way: they're big right now. Get lots of bookings at church halls and things. Someone said they've even played the Broadway Conservative Club. Young Conservatives, of course, not the old fogeys.'

Not everyone was as transfixed as Martha: the corduroy gang paused in their conspiratorial chat to give the newcomers a condescending glance then went back to the serious business of leaflets and phone numbers.

'Can you introduce me, then, Cassie?'

'You soft? What good would that do, d'you think?'

'Well, I'd like it, what's wrong with that?'

'Fans? You don't want to be one of them, chuck. They'll have your knickers off in a dark alley as soon as say "shoot" ...'

Alex had listened to this exchange and felt suddenly possessive. Martha was his and was staying with him; he'd already bagged the bed downstairs, leaving the cardboard suitcase on the mattress on the floor. He drooped his arm across Martha's shoulder.

'Anyway, Cass, tell us about this theatre group you're part of ... is it at a real theatre?'

'Oh, it's just a few of us getting together. We're writing our own stuff, about things that really matter. Then we put them on anywhere who'll have us. We hope we'll be getting a booking at the Students' Union.'

Alex perked up. 'Who writes your stuff? Duncan? And what's it about?'

'He does sometimes. In fact, he started us going. But Duncan's like that ... a real start-up merchant. Gets stuff going then leaves you on your own.'

'Is that what you want? Can you manage on your own?' Alex was edging closer.

'Oh, it's a bit hairy sometimes. We had to ditch it for a while 'cos we ran out of cash. That's why there's a heap of costumes downstairs. The Playhouse gave us a bunch of their old gear when they were clearing out. Not always appropriate. In fact, we wrote a play around Nelson just 'cos we had the costume.'

'What did you have to say about Nelson, then?' Alex was quietly attentive.

'That he was a victim of the system: a naval regime where cruelty and brutality were endemic.'

'Scarcely a victim: he was the admiral.'

'Right ... and with all that power, he did nothing to stop it. So he's complicit, isn't he? He's been brainwashed to be complicit. Most of what we do is shaped around people who're victims of the system.'

'What system is that exactly?' Bells had begun to ring in Martha's head.

'Oh, any system at all ... that's how the world's organised. After all, what do you do with your life?'

'Er, typing course ... and Alex is in the sixth form.'

'Yes, well, you can both work that out for yourselves ... it's pretty obvious, I'd have thought.'

Martha felt challenged. She bit her bottom lip. Alex offered to replenish their glasses, empty so long they had a sort of greasy sheen.

'I suppose you think the family is part of the system ... of a system, at any rate?' Martha was tentative but hopeful.

'God yes. Our pa taught us that ... for a grown-up he's pretty enlightened.' Cassie tipped her ringlets and looked directly into Martha's eyes.

'You having trouble there, then?'

'Oh, yes, you could say that—'

Suddenly Martha was distracted: the pink shirt turned and smiled, a big luscious smile beamed towards her across the room. Her brows wrinkled into an inquisitive little frown. But, no, something was happening: her imagination took off. Their eyes locked and the room went hazy around them: here he came directly towards her, the crowds parting to let him through; now he was upon her, his arms in their billowing pink sleeves spread wide and enfolding the admiral's coat; he snuggled close into Martha's neck, murmuring, licking and sucking her skin. There was a sweet spicy smell about him, as he nuzzled and hugged. His black curly hair tangled with hers. She knew this was the special moment: going on like this he might leave a bruise, a bruise to be proud of. A love bite.

'Martha!' Alex was back with the filled glasses and tugging her navy sleeve. She was standing like a pillar of stone, unblinking, expressionless, staring towards the pink-shirted one across the room. 'It's rude to stare. Stop it.' Her eyes were the last part of her body to swivel back towards Alex. They lingered on the vision she had just had. Was it just her imagination or had it been one of those impulsive party moments, when people grab and then go, a quick encounter for an instant's fun.

'Sorry, Alex, what were you saying?'

'You, you were saying about trouble ... Cassie was talking about the system.'

'Er ... what did you say his name was?'

'Which one d'you mean?'

Wasn't it obvious, him standing so close and their passionate embrace ... or perhaps not.

'The one in pink. I need to know.'

'I thought you said you didn't want trouble.' Cassie shrugged with a smile towards Alex. 'I think she needs some comfort.'

The party grew noisier, happier, full of bodies sweating and talking louder. Pretty girls made the boys livelier, their limbs twitching with excitement and anticipation. For their part the solemn crowd by the piano grew more intense. The 'professor' was spinning a magical tale and they were listening enthralled. Duncan arrived in the room with two buckets brimming to the top with baked potatoes, their skins glistening with salt and lard. He went round dispensing squares of newspaper in which to hold the steaming lumps. There were hums of satisfaction, squeals as teeth bit into the hot pulp; someone turned the music up.

'Come over here, there's a crowd I want you to meet.'

Duncan had dumped the empty buckets and was steering Alex and Martha towards the piano. Martha managed a deliberate bump to the back of the pink shirt as she passed. He turned and with a gentle smile and gentle voice nodded at her. 'Oh, sorry there.' Alex grabbed her shoulders and pushed her hard after Duncan who was already introducing them to the piano crowd. 'Felix, Martin, Pete and John ... they're going to save the world for us.'

Pete was the name of the benign professor. He turned towards her and disclosed the bright yellow waistcoat she had glimpsed across the room. He was young after all, much younger than she had at first supposed. No more than a schoolboy. Perhaps he had a wise head on young shoulders – it was a phrase people used which Martha had never understood until now. He looked sad and fragile and somehow in need of protection. But he was lively and assertive too, an odd mix – welcoming them into their conversation and giving Duncan the sort of grin that carried both disapproval and amiability. 'What Duncan means is that we're CND, you know, the Campaign for Nuclear Disarmament ... d'you know about it?' He looked at her and kept on looking.

Alex pressed forward, reaching out a hand to shake theirs. 'Yes, yes. You're doing a great job. It really matters ... yes, I'm with you all the way.' He turned as if to explain things to Martha, who had not once heard him refer to CND. She ignored him and spoke to Pete directly. He seemed quiet by nature but fighting back a natural reticence in order to make his point. She felt he needed protection.

'Yes, I've seen the marches on the newsreels; they look great fun ... all those guitars and singing.'

It was the wrong thing to say, but Pete was used to it. He flashed a smile and said with a grin, 'Here, have a badge.'

She felt she was joining something but she wasn't sure what.

Chapter 14

'Hey, hey, come and look!' Josie had waylaid Eddie as he was dumping his bicycle at the side of the Grande. With Martha away on her weekend walking tour his thoughts had drifted, wondering whether the weather had held for her. Josie had beckoned him over, with a dramatised tiptoe and whisper had led him through the panelled swing doors every bit as though it wasn't their usual routine to be in the building and getting ready for the first showing.

'What's going on, Josie? What's happening now?' He was keen to get upstairs and begin loading the reels.

'A bright spark has arrived; Mr Vernon is showing him round. Take a look.' They stood together on the spot at the back of the stalls sanctified by the usherettes. If they were intruding, as Josie seemed to feel they were, best take up positions that made them part of the furniture. The young Mr Vernon – Mr Colin – was down by the organ at the front of the stalls, talking with a young man of striking demeanour.

'He looks a toff to me. Just look at his shoes.'

Eddie craned to see but couldn't.

'They're black lace-ups, very polished. Who round here dresses like that?'

'Perhaps he's just a mummy's boy.' Eddie wasn't really interested.

'Could be both, but what's he want, d'you think?' From where they were standing at the usherettes' post, it was hard to hear what was being said or to lip-read the conversation. So they simply watched: the 'bright spark' was completely at ease, his hand in the trouser pocket of a fine dark navy suit. Mr Colin was bouncing and bobbing round him, wiping his hand from time to time across his thin flaxen hair. The move suggested thought more than anxiety, but anxiety too. The bright spark gestured to the fabulous interior of the Grande: its gilded stucco figures, the Egyptian-style frieze around the ceiling … did it speak of appreciation?

'It's not the bingo lot back, is it?'

'But trade's been good since we boosted the matinees and took space in the *Weekly Advertiser*. Tonight's full … but then it is Bardot. Anyway, he doesn't look like a bingo type.'

'What type is he then? He seems pretty intense, the way he's talking.'

'A one-off if you ask me.' They tiptoed out like wicked children who'd overheard something naughty from the grown-ups. But they had heard nothing. Eddie felt the foolishness of it.

'There's no need to be excited, Josie – you see a conspiracy in everything. It's just a bloke, quite a slick bloke

124

but he's too young to do any harm.' And he left her for the shabbier domain aloft.

Mr Colin was unsure how to assess his guest. He was prepared to be impressed. The man, so unnervingly at ease in his silk and mohair suit, was laying claim to quite a lot of influence. He represented, he said, a number of musical groups from across the north-west. He had good contacts with record companies – the names dropped smoothly from his slightly wet lips – and was planning to extend his business in new directions. He was always on the lookout for new venues and had heard that the Grande was struggling to survive and hoping to extend its appeal. His referring to the struggle to survive made Mr Colin even jumpier, and his hand swept his balding head a little more urgently.

'Oh, we've picked up quite well recently. There was an article in the *Weekly Advertiser* about the café's afternoon cream teas.' The stranger smiled benignly and was clearly not about to wangle an invitation.

'I suppose you don't have a licence, then?'

'Oh, no, no, no. But the staff use the Red Lion next door. It's a friendly place, welcoming – even to strangers.'

'What time does it close?'

'Well, eleven weekdays, and of course it's not open at all on Sunday.' He must know the laws of the land: was he asking merely to humiliate him?

'If I booked one of my musical groups here, they'd want to set up their instruments from about three o'clock, have a rehearsal after that, then a bite to eat, possibly at the Red Lion, and begin the concert about nine o'clock.' It sounded alarmingly late to Mr Vernon.

'And what sort of musical evening would it be, exactly, that your groups present?'

The stranger gave the first trace of tension, wiping the saliva that hovered on his lower lip. 'They're young people; talented, of course. I wouldn't have taken them on unless they were. Usually three or four of them.' He hovered between losing the pitch and directly deluding Mr Colin. 'It's the sort of music the young people go for a lot. It's very popular. You'll get a good house, you'll see.' For the first time the lips coiled into a smile.

'Rock and roll!! At the Grande?' The news sped immediately round the building. Ethel taking up her place just inside the auditorium was letting rip at Florrie. A voluptuous Bardot was pouting and bouncing around in *A Woman Like Satan* – shocking enough, but then she was French. In Florrie's book that was no more than was to be expected. But live music, live rock and roll, was altogether different. Ethel had three girls in their teens.

'They're nothing better than Teds, their long jackets and greasy hair . . . I'm doing my best to keep Hazel and Doreen immune. And Mr Colin's bringing them here?'

There were hushing sounds from the back row of the stalls where couples had paused in their own gropings to watch the screen and see how the French did it. 'I can't believe Mr Vernon would allow it.'

Florrie was bewildered rather than outraged. 'I think it was Mr Colin who made the arrangement. I don't think he quite understands . . . '

126

Latecomers arrived and Ethel tore their tickets before leading them down the aisle, her torch low and powerful like the landing light on an aircraft. She flashed them towards two empty seats. They, stumbling as they watched the graphic undulations of Miss Bardot, fell over other transfixed couples and began to piece together the bewildering elements of a plot joined halfway through.

'I don't know why they bother.' Florrie tutted once Ethel returned. She was never pleased by the behaviour of their audiences. 'Coming in whenever they like, in the middle of the story. It's not as though it's raining.'

'They're going to put a stop to it, I hear. That Alfred Hitchcock wants us to stop it for him. He's made a film so frightening he says no one is allowed to go in after it's started.' Ethel's voice had lost its outrage and they now spoke in the strong whispers of their regular exchanges.

'Oh, so how's that going to work then? Are you and me expected to bar the door?'

'Josie can do it: there's more of her, after all. She can fill the space.' They giggled noiselessly. Bardot strutted her stuff.

'. . . but who's he to decide? He's away in Hollywood making films . . . we're the ones who matter in the flicks.'

Chapter 15

Duncan's party was still in full swing. It was two in the morning, and Martha was privately thrilled at the thought.

The piano group – a bit more sober than the others – were still going at it. Martha realised she knew some of what they were talking about.

'Isn't there some fuss about the test-ban not happening?' She was marshalling some dim recollection from the back of her mind and at the same time it occurred to her she was trying to impress Pete.

Alex was surprised by Martha. The remark sounded grown up, like something from the papers. He moved his weight from one foot to the other in nervous resentment. She noticed his discomfort.

'You mean, you don't expect a girl to care about such things?' Martha remembered the poem she had read for Duncan and was pleased that no yellow hair featured in their interest. 'It's been in the newsreels, hasn't it?

I've been noticing for quite a while. And when Mrs Charlesworth down the road had a baby she was worried there was strontium in the milk. That was the tests, wasn't it?'

She could see that Pete was thrilled by the degree of her interest and by her seeming to defer to him.

'Right, that's right,' he said. 'Fallout, every test conducted in the atmosphere adds to the radioactive fallout.'

'I saw it on the newsreels. My dad works at a cinema, so I get in free.' She didn't mention that being sixteen it was sometimes illegal.

'But the newsreels don't tell what matters – you should know that.' Pete's pleasing dark voice was rising again, a bit frantic. There was almost something unstable about it, thought Martha. 'What matters is the risk to the world, risk of a war with Russia escalating and getting out of hand. Someone could press the button ... some mad general or ... ' Pete paused.

Alex rushed in, trying to be part of things. 'What was it like, Aldermaston? Did you walk all the way? Bet it was cold, wasn't it?'

Pete took his eyes off Martha. 'Easter is always cold; we've learned to reckon on that. But loads more people than last year. Lots of people lining the roads to watch us go by. Some of them cheering, yes, cheering us on ... ' As Pete paused for breath the others jostled to join in.

'We stayed overnight in schoolrooms and church halls – so the cold didn't matter. Local people brought us food: home-made pies, cakes. We had plenty to eat. There was jazz, too, the bands joined us for the day, and a couple of students had guitars.'

Martha stole a glance back towards the party, eager to keep her pink-shirted lover in her sights. He was still there in the middle of the room. Should she try and ... She turned her attention back briefly to the story.

'The only thing is, your feet get blistered. I saw one bloke whose plimsolls had shredded by the time we got to Trafalgar Square.'

'Yes, you needed the right clobber: heavy macs and windcheaters, and boots are best with heavy socks. Trouble was people joined who hadn't been told what to expect: they found it hard.'

'But you didn't notice the pain, did you, once you saw the crowds waiting for us.' Leather Patches was alarmed they were making it sound such an ordeal. 'Thousands of them. They had banners too, then Michael Foot spoke from the platform at the base of Nelson's Column, and Donald Soper too – he's a churchman of some kind. They were serious people, important people.'

'And more are joining all the time: think of the strontium ninety in the milk you drink. Everyone has a reason to stop the bomb.'

It was hard to take it all in – and was it true anyway? Martha's mind wandered and she glanced again into the heart of the party: her pink-shirted idol was looking as debonair as ever. And he had spoken to her, directly to her. Their eyes had met. 'Sorry,' he'd said. Well, romance had to start somewhere.

'Do you want to join?'

Pete, noticing her distraction, was trying to draw her back. How lovely she looked, and how her passion lit up her face, making her cheeks pink and her lips gleam. She was the sort he imagined campaigning at his side, a fellow spirit, sharing his thoughts and ideals. Her head of unruly black hair tossed and bobbed as she talked.

While looking for a piece of paper to write down her address for him, Martha realised with a shock she hadn't phoned home. When she had left she had promised her mother to call and say where she and her rambler friend had found to stay the night. She had shown her mother her old Youth Hostel Association membership card as assurance. Now here she was over twelve hours later and no call had been made, no phone box sought out and no explanation given.

It was already far too late to call now, beyond the time anyone at number 26 would think it conceivable to stay up. Besides, the background noise, the thudding music, the laughter and shouts would go spinning down the phone line. Her mother always worried about sinks of iniquity. Perhaps this really is a sink of iniquity; the thought cheered Martha up and she wrote out her address with an eagerness that convinced Pete he had a recruit. He touched her shoulder in gratitude and something more.

The party was changing. More people were sitting than standing. Some were even sprawled full length. A number of girls had laced themselves around the men, felling them to the ground and coiling them into human cushions. The drink had been exhausted, a point at which Martha expected them to drift off home. Many did. But others stayed and a few lay around smoking soft shapeless cigarettes. She turned down the one that was offered, shaking her head. 'I just don't smoke, thank you.' She wondered briefly if she'd have accepted it from her pink-shirt hero, but he had disappeared.

Alex was censorious. 'Wise not to get into that, I think.'

'I'll decide, Alex. It's up to me to decide. Anyway I'm tired. I want to go to bed.'

It had been tacitly agreed when they contrived the weekend that they would sleep together and have sex. They would find somewhere with a bed to spare and people who didn't care too much who they were. Since then Martha's view of Alex had shifted uncomfortably. Back in Staveley he had seemed to offer glamour and the prospect of escape. After the clammy loyalty of Clive she was thrilled by his liveliness and charm, the range of friendships he spoke of, the books he urged her to read. He had ushered her into the coffee bar and had made a difference. But here he was diminished. He had been timid about coming into the house and only warmed to Duncan when he knew the same poem. He suddenly looked no more than a show-off, a know-all. She began to wonder whether he'd even read *On the Beach* and *On the Road*. Did she want to have her first sex with him after all?

But arrangements had been made. Alex had colonised the mattress in the ground-floor room. His cardboard suitcase lay across it, waiting. There was nothing to do but go through with it. Alex would pretend to know what he was doing, she supposed. She didn't know much about sex herself, but she had seen films of people in bed together. But even the X-rated films didn't go beneath the sheets and the hero of *Room at the Top* had kept his vest on. She had never seen a man naked. Her knowledge of male anatomy was gleaned from what naked sculpture was around: and there wasn't much of that. Mostly what stood aloft in Staveley's meagre civic buildings were Victorian efforts tastefully draped. She was, out of sheer curiosity alone, keen to see and touch what Alex had inside his trousers.

The ground-floor room turned out to be the place where everyone had dumped their coats. Clothes lay in heaps jumbled together – gaberdines and duffel coats; there were girlish coats of splashy checks and big black buttons, one or two tired furs, all laced and muddled together with long scarves and heavy leather gloves. Someone had left a pair of squirrel-fur-backed mittens on the end of the bed. Somewhere under it all was Alex's suitcase, and under that the promised mattress of seduction. Desire died on the spot.

'We can't sleep there, for God's sake. What can we do?' Alex was irritable and possibly, thought Martha, relieved.

'Well, let's see . . . ' Her chances of taking the sexual initiative now fading, she remained practical about what should happen next. 'We can wait for everyone to go home, or we can strip down and climb in under it all, or we can go back upstairs and rejoin the fun.' Alex was about to declare which option was to his liking when the whole mound heaved and shook like a tidal wave. The fur-backed mittens slid to the floor, the big-buttoned checked coat gave a dizzying lurch, the great pile swayed and began to pitch and toss. Martha retrieved the fur gloves and put them on; they looked incongruous with her admiral's coat. She liked that. She stood watching.

133

'Let's go ... come on.'

'Alex, you have no curiosity: watch, why don't you?'

'Because, well, you wouldn't like it if ... '

At that point the pounding intensified; slowly the mass of clothes slid from the mattress to the floor and a pair of white buttocks emerging from narrow black trousers came into view. A girl with a bright purple skirt pushed up around her waist, an expanse of suspenders and white flesh, was moaning about the interruption. But Martha only really saw the man: she saw that he had kept his shirt on; it was crumpled and billowing and pink. Her only thought was that she wished he had chosen her.

Chapter 16

Coming home would be different. Martha had been away only twenty-four hours but she felt like a stranger in her own place. Something had changed in her head, which put a distance between herself and her parents. It felt good still, just as it had felt good all the time she was in Liverpool. But there was something ... a melancholy, a strangeness. She wondered whether they would notice from looking at her, and whether her speech had changed, whether the way she walked and held herself had shifted from the little typist they knew to a nascent rebel against the system.

And yet she wanted to be back with them. She had a yearning for security. Even her mother's moodiness gave her a sense of who she was.

And yet her father – her lovely father – how she wished she could tell him of all the dizzying ideas, the new friends.

But she must remember the fiction that she had been walking the Vale of Edale with a typist friend, climbing stiles from field to field and eating sandwiches in the lea of dry-stone walls.

She got on the bus at the end of the station approach, then travelled on through the wet leafy evening to her home stop. As she came nearer there was much to consider. She had made sure the rucksack was jostled and bruised; she bunched back her chaotic hair behind her ears, chipped off the red enamel varnish Cassie had urged on her and dirtied beneath her nails. She resumed the presentable face of Galton Road's student typist ready to confront her mother.

It was Sunday evening and as usual Beattie was sitting before the television while Eddie busied himself around the house. But the tilt of a head, the lie of a hand on the arm of the chair could tell her much.

Martha breezed into the room with false high spirits, speaking before either could look her in the eye.

'Hello, there. I'm home.' Her mother's head was out of sight behind the high-backed chair but the hand on the arm flinched.

'We'd expected you before now – what kept you?'

Oh, speaking. That was good, even if the words were critical.

'It was the train times. We couldn't get one before five o'clock ... and then ... '

'Why was that, I wonder? We thought you'd be here for your tea. I laid a place.'

'I'm sorry, Mum. But I hadn't specified a time, had I?'

'No, you hadn't. Exactly. And why not?'

Martha took in the 'laid place'.

It was one of the activities a mother must carry out.

The place laid, the child cared for. The underpinning of generations depended on it. And yet it seemed to Martha that in Beattie's case, the intent and the fulfilment were out of kilter, the kind thoughts spoilt by the sour welcome.

Martha felt she was being blamed for something and didn't know what. Slowly and unobtrusively it had entered the family mythology that Beattie had made a mighty sacrifice and one that carried with it obligations. Beattie was owed. She had a claim on both husband and child that gave her power over them. Quite what the nature of the power was proved elusive, yet at the same time implacable.

'I'm sorry,' Martha said, looking fleetingly towards Eddie, who she felt was deliberately avoiding her gaze. 'Yes, I'm sorry, but I thought ... '

'Yes, it's always "sorry, but" isn't it? "Sorry, but", always an excuse.'

'More an explanation really.'

'Don't bandy words with me, young lady – we sent you to learn typing, not philosophy.'

'I only meant—'

'But I don't care what you meant. Don't you see that? Your food was almost ruined. As it is, it's on a low light in the oven: you'll be lucky if it isn't a shrivelled mess.'

Martha yielded to the situation. 'Thanks, Ma. Thank you.' She fetched a dish of macaroni cheese now crisped round the edge and set it on a tray. What if she'd lost the spat, after all? She was, she had to admit, greedy for the taste of home cooking.

*

'Dad, do you remember when they dropped the atom bomb?' Beattie had bundled off to bed at the closedown of the evening's television, happy in her own disgruntlement. Martha must now try deceiving her father without actually lying to him. Diversionary tactics were best. She was genuinely curious about the atomic bomb stuff, of course, but she surprised herself with how smoothly the trick of duplicity came. Emboldened, she began to elaborate. 'It's just that we met someone who talked about how dangerous it was.'

'Oh, and who was that then?'

It had been a mistake to go so far.

'Oh, a student we met; just in passing. Don't know his name.'

Eddie was startled and even a little impressed that Martha had picked up on the matter. There had been plenty in the papers and on the newsreels at the time of the Aldermaston marches, but they tended to show lots of students laughing and singing as they walked along, for every bit as though it were a holiday. He'd not given it much attention. But the meeting in Trafalgar Square had been different: serious talk of how at the next war we would have weapons that could destroy us all. He knew that was true.

He remembered the dropping of the atomic bomb all right. It was one of those moments, frozen in the memory. He had been watering geraniums in the back garden with a battered green watering can: he could see the spray sparkling in the sunlight, still warm in the early August evening. Beattie had come bustling out of the back door, her body – she was slender then – agitated and quivering, as though there'd been an accident in the house. But it was more than that.

'They've dropped some huge bomb on Japan: so big it's wiped them out. It's on the news. Looks like they'll surrender any moment. Oh, Eddie, it'll be over. The war'll be over!' She was shivering with excitement, laughing and coughing at the same time with the confusion of it all, and hugging her arms around herself for joy. Eddie put down the watering can and took hold of her shoulders. She needed steadying.

'Now don't get so excited. One bomb can't do that ... it just can't. Surely it can't.' Eddie's dismay waited on further confirmation, which came a moment later.

Bill from next door, who was allowed a couple of weeks' leave from the army now the war in Europe was over, called to them over the privet hedge.

'Heard the great news, Eddie? Looks like they've done for the Japs: really walloped them. Some amazing superbomb that blows everything sky high. Tojo's lot will have to surrender now.'

'Is that what they said? Is that what it said on the news?'

'Not about any surrender, no. But this bomb's different. Some great invention: no one can survive it ... that's what they say.'

Eddie remembered them standing, the three of them, in their summer gardens full of lupins and dahlias, looking from one to the other in surprise and bemusement.

Beattie had calmed down and was smiling wildly. 'And

isn't that wonderful? Just wonderful. It means peace. At last.'

'But this invention, whatever it is ... it'll make a big difference to things,' Eddie said.

'Yes, of course I remember. I was in the garden with your mother ... watering the lupins, as it happened. You were in your pram. She was thrilled to bits. She heard the news on the radio. Of course it didn't end the war. Not right away. They had to drop a second bomb to do that. Or that's what they said. There was lots of talk after about whether the second bomb had been necessary.'

'Or either of them – it was a terrible thing to do. You can see that now, Dad, can't you?'

Eddie felt his heart lurch. She'd grown up sharing his tastes, listening to his judgements. She admired the same stars and knew who the directors were. Even when she'd begun to prefer the sort of kitchen-sink cinema that wasn't to his taste, such differences weren't serious.

But now he could see a gulf opening up between them. How could anyone who'd not been old enough understand what the war had meant? But a bolder, cheekier generation of youngsters was coming along and questioning everything. Well, that was a good thing of course, as far as it went, but there were some things they mustn't touch. He reached out a hand to hold her arm, as much to steady his own rising irritation as to confirm the bond between them.

'Look, you can win a war by dropping lots of bombs for a longer time – or you can drop one big one and be over and done with it. It's likely the same numbers get killed either way. But we were desperate for the war to be over.'

'Driven by desperation, yes. I can see that. But the suffering! You can't have known about the suffering: this was something never seen before ... '

'Martha, Martha.' He held her arm more firmly. 'Look, you know Pete Sampson who lives over the fields ... lives alone, a pitiable lad ... '

'Oh, him. He's a bit of a recluse, isn't he?'

'What the Japs did to Pete doesn't bear telling – animals, they're no more than animals. So please –' he realised his grip was getting frantically tight so he let go and stroked her forearm – 'don't tell me about suffering. The Japs were terrible: they inflicted suffering with pleasure, they were merciless. Please, girl, don't lecture me about suffering ... ' His voice petered out, his eyes brittle with tears held her gaze; he patted her arm, seeking her understanding.

Martha tried not to flinch. How could she pull away from his hold on her? For the first time they were completely at odds. Who was this Pete Sampson anyway? Not a close friend of the family, just someone local they greeted warmly when passing before hurrying on ... She had always regarded him as a bit of an eccentric but not bothered to ask. Now it turned out he must be an ex-prisoner of war, one of those who'd come back years ago and never quite got back into the routines of life. He had some job minding the greens up at the golf course, and occasionally went on drunken benders where he'd shout and scream in the pub car park when they threw him out.

Eccentric, yes, but hardly a justification for dropping the atomic bomb. Martha winced at her father's pathetic logic. How could he leap from such a single tragic case to the whole nightmare of the atomic menace? She patted the arm that still held hers. But there was melancholy in her heart.

'I've got a friend who knows a lot about it, and he says it'll destroy the world for sure next time there's a war. He really is very, very worried.' She realised she cared about Pete's anxieties and wondered too whether he was exaggerating the risk.

'Well, he's right to worry, I give you that . . . but it'll be for your generation to see it doesn't happen.'

Chapter 17

Eddie steered his bicycle round the corner into the square and was amazed by what he saw. It was Wakes Week so he'd expected most people would be off on holiday in the resorts along the coast, Blackpool and Southport. The square was full of young folk. You could hardly call them a crowd because they were so disparate, loosely scattered across the square, enjoying the summer air. The bright colour splashes of their clothes – red, orange and an acid green – brought unexpected cheer to a place used to people wearing greys and browns. Some of them were walking in twos and threes around the perimeter, others were draped in the doorways of shops drinking Coca-Cola, watching and waiting. The more serious had posted themselves in a queue up against the locked doors of the Grande. The concert wasn't due for another two hours. Why had they come so early, and why were there so many young girls?

Eddie had been phoned by Mr Colin early that

morning. It seems the promoter, the smooth mohair-suited young man, was issuing orders about how what he called 'his' evening should be organised.

Mr Colin would have to marshal his staff without appearing to give way to Mr Smoothychops – he had picked up on Josie's nickname for him. He was nothing but a boy, after all, but Mr Colin had been told by the family who ran the Forum in Liverpool, that the promoter's father owned one of the largest radio and record emporiums in the city. They had expanded their corner shop and taken over the failing gents' outfitters next door and fitted it out with glamorous posters and boxes of records categorised by names: Elvis Presley, Buddy Holly, Bill Haley. Mr Colin began to feel that he was inheriting the wrong business.

Martha was planning to go to the concert. It was three weeks now since her weekend in Liverpool and she was eager to get back there, but she didn't know how to arrange it. Beattie had retreated again into her circle of misery, monitoring Martha's every outing. The secretarial course was over but even Alex was reluctant to help. The heady episode at Duncan's house had left him feeling the outsider. Anyway, he was preoccupied with his exam results and getting ready to apply for university in the autumn term. There was nothing wrong with Donne and George Eliot, after all. And Duncan had approved his love of Yeats. He had to admit his attempts at the beatnik life were laughable, were even laughed at by Martha herself, the one person they were tailored to impress. When she asked him to

144

come along and help her buy a white duffel coat, he declined.

The letter with handwriting she didn't recognise posed a problem for Beattie. Watching her turn it over and over, Martha almost relished the tension between her mother's sense of curiosity and her own wilful refusal to be forth-coming. Beattie handed the letter across the breakfast table with dead eyes and lips clamped tight.

'Oh, thanks.' Martha was cheery. It was a new tactic. She had tried for so long now to minister to her mother's distress and she was fed up with it. By what alchemy did her mother demand such attention? What trade-off in the normal relations between mother and daughter existed in their case? And why did she have to play along? Well, she didn't any more. Let the dutiful daughter die a death.

Martha had now walked and talked with people who were normal, easy to be with, undemanding. Well, Alex could be a bit pressing at times and she knew he was dis-appointed that they hadn't had sex, but so what. He'd recover. He'd turn up with her at the concert. To hell with it. She pocketed the letter and went upstairs.

My dear Chimneypots,
You see, I remember what you asked me: were there any interesting buildings in Liverpool. I never had the chance to answer though of course the answer is yes, plenty. I've been waiting each weekend for you to come back so I can show them to you.
Will you come back? Or have you given up on us? Cassie's staying here regularly now together with

one or two of her old acting pals. It's getting to be
quite a little commune: and we want to extend it.
Come and join us, why don't you? That typing
course will get you work: there are loads of jobs, and
not very long hours.

I hope you will: we can read poetry together.
Duncan.

He must have got her address from Peter. Not a word
about Alex, she noticed. That was embarrassing. But
otherwise, what an invitation, what a fantasy of the
future … living in Liverpool with all its music, and
freedom. It seemed almost too rapturous to con-
template: independence to come and go, unchallenged
by anyone, being unaccountable, above all not being
blamed for the misery of others. She was sixteen, after
all!

But of course she couldn't go, not just like that. There
was her father to care about, and, yes, even her difficult
mother: Martha couldn't just walk out on them. She was
needed, she was part of their pattern, she completed their
small presence in the world. So her mind closed the idea
down. But it was not forgotten.

The queue of girls was sprawling across the square by
the time she and Alex arrived, but a little wave from Josie
invited them to the back of her box office cubicle where
she slipped them two complimentary seats. 'Family favourites,' she explained. 'And I've put you in the dress circle.
All the shrieking girls will be at the front of the stalls; you
won't want to be with them, I know.' Martha wasn't sure

she agreed. There was something thrilling about this surging mass of girls her own age; she would have been happy to merge into such a crowd. But she was with Alex, his arm round her waist, and an old-fashioned kind of decorum set them apart.

There were three groups listed on the programme, and the stars of the evening – The Brigands – were last. A crescendo of noise rose from the stalls below when they finally came on stage: long, lanky, with greased quiffs of hair, they all wore the same sort of clothes: narrow black trousers and open-necked black shirts. Their skin looked pale even in the lush and changing lights of the Grande, lights awkwardly adapted from the defunct cinema organ. Martha stared. From the upper reaches of the dress circle he was unmistakable: there, with a guitar slung low across his hips, was the one she loved.

The cacophony of screams died away at the jolting impact of their first chords. From that point on their music drove forward, harsh and throbbing, the singer clutching the microphone and coiling round it as he jerked out the song in sharp thrilling stabs. Martha was on the edge of her seat, her eyes staring so hard they almost hurt: her mouth was dry, her hands catching at the folds of her skirt and clapping through the gaudy fabric. She scarcely noticed that Alex was sitting back in his seat beside her, frowning.

One song led on to another, with rising screams between. She ventured a scream of her own, then felt sheepish and fell silent. The noise from the crowd almost drowned out the music. But the music wasn't a matter of tunes and lyrics to listen to. The music just *was*. It was the enveloping place she wanted to be: it invaded her, made her pulse race, made her sweat; it excited her all over. She was considering again flinging herself into the sort of hysteria that was taking over in the stalls when Alex grabbed her elbow.

'Let's get out of here! Come on . . . let's get out of here! Please.'

What was he saying? Why was he interrupting? Martha shrugged and turned her attention back to the stage. There was her god: he was standing, very tall, his shoulders flexed, his body scarcely moving but gripped by the focus of his playing, his head nodding to the rhythm and throwing his black hair across his face.

Alex was not to be ignored. He grabbed her arm brusquely and tugged her from the row. Martha struggled to resist and break free but was held by what was happening on stage. Her full skirt was getting crushed.

'Let go, let go, will you, Alex!'

'It's not for us . . . that stuff. You're not one of them, Martha, you're not!'

He was dragging her with him and gradually she stopped resisting. But once in the empty foyer she was a tiger.

'Don't you ever – do you hear me – don't you ever treat me like that. I'm not some common tart to be dragged around by a bully and a lout. Do you hear me, Alex?'

'I only wanted to bring you to your senses. Martha, for God's sake, don't demean yourself.'

'*Demean?* What's that then, when it's at home?'

'Stop this. It's not worthy of you!'

148

'Worthy! Now is that it? Just let me get this clear – "worthy", you say, and "demean". It's not me you're talking about, Alex, it's some two-bit goody-two-shoes you want me to be.'

'No, no, Martha. I like you as you are.' He had opened the floodgates.

'Oho, my true self, is it? And just who is that, do you think? I'd like to hear because I don't even know myself. But I'm certainly not some pussy-footing little nobody who can't let rip if she wants, who's so bottled up she can't stand up for herself.'

'Well, that's great, isn't it?'

She could see something come over Alex. His cheeks blazed red and he spoke low and mockingly: 'You, Martha, Daddy's girl, such an obedient little daughter ... destined to a nine-to-five typing job somewhere that mother can keep an eye on you, and you on her. You can pretend that tapping your feet to some teenage would-be Elvis is freedom. But it's not!'

Martha burst into tears and rushed past Florrie and Ethel, out past Josie and into the now cloying summer night.

'She's not waiting for Eddie then,' observed Florrie.

'Well, she'd have found him in the Red Lion. He's only standing by 'cos Mr Colin's afraid there might be a riot.'

'Hoping, more like ... wants to make the place famous, does he? Like *Sunday Night at the London Palladium*?'

'It's this music, it gets them all overwrought. Still, it's not like her not to wait for her dad.'

*

The square was empty, lit up by the lights blazing from the Grande and the drift of music from its inner depths. Martha waited, trying to calm herself, for her face to lose its puffiness, then caught the bus home.

She clumped her way up the stairs to avoid bumping into anyone she might know. Noisy children were chattering and laughing in the seats ahead. The crispness had gone out of her skirt, the petticoats were a wilting mess. She gave them a flick, then scrunched up the fabric in a spasm of rage. Alex's stinging words nagged in her head. She was behaving exactly as he said, rushing home, seeking refuge, hiding away. She had let Alex bully her.

And she had left the music and her idol behind.

She raised the latch on the back door, grateful for once for a quiet house, thinking how she would have to explain being home early and without her father. Summer light still lingered over the garden, but indoors the dusk was seeping into corners and blurring the outline of things, familiar, shabby homely things, jaded, tiresome reminders that nothing was changing.

But all was not silent. There was a murmur of voices somewhere in the house. Aged routines left over from wartime habits meant that doors in number 26 were kept shut, ostensibly to retain heat from coal fires. And even though it was summer the doors along the hallway stood foursquare and solidly closed in her face. She stopped and listened.

The sound came from the front room, the room kept for 'best' – sterile and chill. It was meant for occasions of family jollity but Martha couldn't recall any. It was also meant for entertaining visitors but that habit had died.

Her mother's voice was speaking slowly and regularly, its cadences falling pleasingly although the words were muffled. Remarkably Beattie was speaking continuously, a murmur that came back from Martha's childhood, a kind of cooing reassurance that felt like kindness become sound. A yearning to be back within that reassurance warmed her for a moment, but just as abruptly shocked her into resentment. Who could it be, the person with Beattie, who deserved such confidences? For suddenly Martha decided they were confidences: this was the sound of intimacy, of familiarity, all those things for which she longed.

The other voice was male, dark and more insistent. Its urgency had a passion to it: it came in sudden gruff outbursts, falling away again before the balm of Beattie's tenderness. But it was becoming dominant, prevailing over what seemed to be Beattie's modest protestations. She shook herself and turned the doorknob. The talk fell silent.

'Eddie? Is that you?'

Martha opened the door and looked into the room: it was like looking into a story other than her own. It was like looking at a still from a film: a moment full of meaning but only if you'd seen the film from the start.

Beattie was wearing the elegant red silk dress she had worn at the Johnsons' party. She was standing tall in black high heels, her full height surprising Martha, who was used to a hunched and scuttling figure. She looked ... glamorous. A drift of fragrance as Beattie moved, which she did now. She reached out and placed her hand on the sleeve of the man who was standing beside her.

'Derek, I think you know Martha, don't you? You must have met at the Grande many times.' Derek smiled warmly and reached his two hands out to seize Martha's.

'Of course I do, of course. I am so pleased to see you again. I'd been hoping to for some time . . .'

Martha stood in the doorway, unable to speak.

There was a suavity about him that repelled her, like some oily salesman in a gentleman's outfitters. She almost preferred the swaying lunging figure who had delivered the drunken tirade at the Grande's farewell. This was like a rehearsal for some local amateur dramatics: Beattie and Derek speaking their lines with false and emphatic style. But they had the better of Martha, who stood blankly staring at them both.

'I've been watching you grow up over the years, and now I've time on my hands . . . since the organ was discontinued, you know.'

'Well, not that much time, Del. There is that job I mentioned seeing in the paper.'

Del? Del! What kind of familiarity was that? Martha withdrew her hand with some effort from Derek's grasp.

'Oh, well, perhaps, but, you know . . .' Martha found herself backing from the room while struggling not to offend. She had caught in her mother's eye a hint of that disapproval that led on to another of her silences. But this was amateur dramatics, wasn't it? And silence was not in the script. Her mother's fluency gushed on.

'I was just explaining to Derek how you've just finished with your typing course and will soon be applying for a job.'

'You're at a great moment in your life, Martha. Anyone

would be proud to have you in their family, or indeed their firm. I suppose you will be applying to one of the companies in the vicinity?'

This is a film, thought Martha. It could be one of those her father so admired by his favourite directors, Douglas Sirk or Carol Reed – one of those plots full of hints and innuendo, and bogus talk just like Derek was spouting now. But what would the intruder – the heroine – do next? That's what Martha needed to decide: she wouldn't hang around to be betrayed, that was for sure. OK, if this was a game, she would give the hypocrites who were deceiving her a knowing look and leave them to it.

'I just called in to say ... to tell you ... I'll be away for a while. I'm staying with friends. OK? Yes, of course it's OK. I'll let you know when I'll be back. Bye, Mother ... oh, and ... bye, Derek,' and then cheekily, 'Del.'

She closed the front room door quickly but precisely: she didn't want it to fly open, propelled by her mother's surprise. She went upstairs, sat on her bed and thought hard. And then she took her suitcase down from the top of her wardrobe.

The Grande was closed by the time she got back there, but the Red Lion still glowed with light. She was only sixteen, too young to enter, so she pushed the door open and peeped round quickly. She was spotted by Josie, who set down her port and lemon and came rushing across.

'For Pete's sake, Martha, what are you doing here? Your dad left about half an hour ago, and anyway –' She saw Martha's ashen face. 'What's up, chuck? What's going on?' She spotted the suitcase and frowned.

Martha looked at her evenly, showing no emotion. 'I don't know. I don't know, Josie, that's the honest truth.'

'Wait here a mo.'

Josie ducked back inside the pub, downed the rest of her drink in a gulp, called a cheery goodbye to the others from the Grande, and came out to take charge of whatever was upsetting Martha. She steered her along the street to where a flight of municipal steps took off to join the street above: they were dusty with summer detritus but warm and familiar. They sat under a street light.

'Sit here, love, mind your skirt.' Josie dusted a drift of concert tickets into the gutter and sat beside her. She waited.

Martha could feel tears pricking her eyes. She exhaled.

'Oh, Josie, I've got to get away: I really have, you know. In fact, I'm on my way –' She indicated the suitcase collapsed on the bottom step.

'You've not, you know, done anything silly? Not you and that Alex?'

'No, no, no, I haven't, it's nothing like that.' Martha managed a smile at the most obvious reason a girl of sixteen would suddenly need to leave home. 'It's not as obvious as that ... nothing obvious at all.'

Josie's head swam; was she wasting her time on some teenage sulk? 'Is it money? You haven't gone taking what's not yours, have you?'

'Heavens, no. Certainly not that.'

In the face of Josie's literalism it was becoming harder and harder to say what exactly was wrong. She brightened and turned a false smile in Josie's direction.

'How did the concert go? Sorry I missed the end ... everyone there and that.' And then, as if casually, pulling her skirt down around her knees: 'Oh, was Derek there at all?'

'No, Derek wasn't there. Is that it then?' Josie sat up smartly. 'Derek been after you? He's at a loose end these days.'

Martha paused, reluctant to tell too much, but wanting to know more.

'Do you like him, Josie? Do you think he's a nice man?' Adding a little awkwardly: 'I think my parents do.'

Josie frowned, looking away. 'He's all right, I suppose; no woman, that's his problem. Doted on your mother years ago, when they were all young. Till your dad came along and put the kibosh on things ... from his point of view, that is!' Then, suspicious: 'Why are you asking?'

Martha looked out across the square. The film was there again in her head: it was where she had come in, and the plot wasn't clear.

'He's seeing my mother, Josie, still seeing her.'

Josie started and then tried not to show it. 'Like ... how do you mean, Martha? Seeing her?'

'That's why I'm leaving.' Suddenly the prospect cheered her. 'I'm going to Liverpool. I have friends there and they want me to join them. I've decided to go now.' Then, crossing a frontier of behaviour she knew was treacherous: 'Josie –' turning a beseeching face to her – 'you couldn't lend me some money, could you?'

'Now look here.' Josie's voice was solemn. 'I can tell your father doesn't know about this and he wouldn't like it. And you can't rope me in as your collaborator. It wouldn't be right. Come on, Martha, you know it wouldn't. I don't know about your mother and Derek, but there's probably a sensible explanation.'

'I'm going, whether or not I can find some money, Josie. I've decided. I can always hitch.'

'But why? Look at you . . . a lovely girl like you, trained to be a secretary.'

'Typist, more like. That's not the point.'

'Happy home, doting parents . . . everything to live for.'

'Oh, Josie, that's the stuff you get from film trailers.' She put on a spooky voice. 'All seemed so happy in their lives . . . but what deadly secret lurks behind the façade . . . '

Josie laughed. '. . . come off it, Martha. You're living in a fantasy world.'

'No, no, I'm not. It's real, all too real . . . and I'm taking charge of my own life.' Martha gained courage from the sound of her own voice.

Josie shifted uneasily on the dusty steps, the summer night swirling gentle dust around them.

'Look, I'm getting stiff sitting here. Suppose you come to my place for the night and we can talk there?'

'You'll not dissuade me, I promise you that, Josie.' It sounded so ungrateful. Martha put her arms round Josie's chubby shoulders, comforting herself with this soft womanly feel. 'I could use one of your scarves.'

*

156

Josie made a large pot of tea and got out a packet of ginger nuts. She brought them to the small kitchen table where she'd sat Martha. She didn't know what to expect but felt sure they would be talking a good while. Where to begin.

'Now, I'm a friend of your father's, Martha. You know I'm very fond of him.'

'As if I didn't know that.'

Josie knew she'd hit straight to Martha's weakest point.

'I'm afraid he'll be very upset. Disappointed in you.'

Martha paused, a mix of emotions on her face. 'Dad won't, in the end, Josie. He won't. I know that, and I want you to know that. He'll know I'm doing what is right for me.'

Josie topped up their teacups. She was thoughtful. Perhaps she'd stormed in a bit there. 'How about we have a splash of rum with this ... '

'Thanks.' Martha smiled. And waited, as if for unpleasant but necessary medicine. The brown treacly liquid plopped into the teacups.

The conversation meandered – The Brigands, the crowd – then Martha said, her voice uncertain, 'Josie. I want to ask you something ... about sex ... I was wondering, you know, what's it like?'

'Phew, well, that's a bit of a tall order ... it's hard to know where to start. You've seen those seaside postcards, haven't you?' Josie pulled her scarf round her shoulders and cleared her throat. 'It's hard talking about it, your generation is different, speaking about such things.'

And so it was, on the night that The Brigands invaded

the Grande, and Josie heard perplexing news about her friend Eddie's wife, Josie found herself talking about sex to Eddie's girl.

'Well, I've not done it myself for a year or two now.' Ten years earlier Josie had been engaged to a merchant seaman who failed to come back from sea. She had taken off his engagement ring and put it among the scented linen of her handkerchief box. After that she had slept with two cats on her eiderdown. But young women needed help, there was no doubt about that. She had been ignorant herself when they first had sex down by the Pier Head. It was all his doing and he seemed to know about it, knew his way round, so to speak. In fact, he seemed to know more about her body than she did herself. So presumably that was what was expected.

'But you don't have to worry. It hurts the first time, but not after that. You can get to really like it ... well, I did. It's perfectly natural, Martha, even if you're not married. You'll need to keep a handkerchief handy.'

Martha squeezed her hand.

'Have you anyone in mind?'

'Not Alex, if that's what you're thinking. No. But it's bound to happen, I know that, and I don't want to get into trouble.'

'Oh, now that's a different matter ... that's chancy, that is. Sometimes the man takes care of it, but frankly, many can't be bothered. The best I can offer is it's safest either just before or just after you've had the curse. That's supposed to be safe; that's what the Roman Catholics say, anyway.'

'But, Josie, Roman Catholics have loads of children.'

'That's what I say, it's always chancy. But that's how it is, being a woman.'

They managed a weak grin of reassurance, woman to woman.

'Come on now, I'll put you in my spare room.' They went upstairs to a bleak box room with cretonne curtains and ill-matching sheets. But Martha looked content. Josie hovered on the threshold, wanting to give her a good-night kiss. Martha opened her arms and hugged her and they stood there, breathing in traces of each other's scent.

'You know something, Josie, I think I was wanting you to tell me about love.'

'Oh, love ... well that's another story altogether.'

Chapter 18

'I thought she was coming home with you.' Beattie was raising her voice and asserting her presence in a way she had not done for years.

'All I know is that she was at the concert: I know because I'd fixed it with Josie to let her have comps. It was a shouting, screaming business, so I'd no chance to find her.' And then, reluctantly: 'I took refuge with Gerald and the others in the Red Lion.' Information that might once have triggered some sort of disapproval.

'Well you better find out where she is. She is not in her room.' Then, suddenly aware of her own deception: 'In fact, she called in here briefly some time ago but I thought she'd gone to bed.'

'She called in here and then left? Is that what you're saying?'

Beattie decided to defend herself from any hint of accusation.

'Yes, she must have done, I recall now she did say something about going to stay with friends, but I didn't think she meant it ... at this hour.'

Eddie had wanted to talk over the evening's events with Martha, to offload on her the dislike he had for groups like The Brigands. But here was his wife, downstairs in her dressing gown, seemingly all set for a bout of boisterous disagreement. He shook his head. The thought of not knowing where Martha was troubled him, and who were these friends? She could be round at Marjory's or even at Alex's. She wasn't irresponsible, he knew that. Right now he was trying to make sense of Beattie's strangeness. 'It's been a funny old evening ... '

'Yes, and still is. It still is. Fancy a cup of cocoa?'

What had got into Beattie? She must have taken something, one of those exciting new drugs that pep you up. He'd heard Ethel talk of how their Doreen had got some. He felt the strangeness of Beattie's manner, a sort of defiant unease. Something about it hinted at the spirit of the girl she had once been: some shadow of her lost self caught his attention. There was energy in her defiance he hadn't seen for a long time. He found himself warming towards her. Perhaps he could reach out and catch the fleeting mood. He looked closely at her face. The porcelain skin was still fine, but tiny wrinkles beginning to spread out from below her eyes and around the mouth moved a certain tenderness in him; he even thought of reaching out and touching them with his fingertips. She was growing older.

'What is it? Something wrong?'

'Er, no, no, nothing. Yes, some cocoa'd be really nice,'

he said, adding dutifully: 'I'll set about finding Martha tomorrow. Don't you worry . . .'

He was less worried about his daughter than intrigued by his wife.

Beattie took two spoonfuls of cocoa out of the orange Bournville tin and placed them slowly into two large cups. She took two apostle spoons from the drawer and placed one in each saucer. Martha's abrupt arrival had shocked her. She had behaved awkwardly. She had seen alarm in Martha's eyes. And then her retreat. But Beattie wasn't to blame in any way. Derek's being there . . . well, he was a friend of this family. It mustn't become any kind of scandal. That would be dreadful. Yes, yes, this was how it goes, she was thinking, this is how life just happens. Making cocoa, sitting to talk.

But it had been the talking that warmed her. Derek, back from the past, voluble, insistent, the drink bringing the words tumbling out of him, making claims he might regret. His needfulness brought out something in her. And his compliments . . . And he needed help, that was clear.

She placed the two cups on the same Bakelite tray she had used earlier. She had offered Derek gin, which he declined; they had shared a sherry and she had washed up the two cut glasses and put them away in the mahogany cupboard the moment he left. She brought the tray slowly towards the door. Eddie jumped up to come to her aid.

'Oh, I could have carried that for you – you only had to ask.'

'I don't ask: surely you know me well enough to know I don't ask.' A weak smile took away the sting of the remark. They sat together on either side of the fireplace with its pattern of crossed kindling ready in waiting for a chill evening. There was a long silence, broken at last by Eddie.

'I know she was at the concert with Alex: he's a sensible boy. I'm sure things will work out.'

'But how sensible is she, d'you think?'

'Well, not too sensible, at her age, surely.' Eddie laughed into what stretched into ominous silence. He was laughing at the thought of Martha: her gaiety and the easy beauty of her long limbs. Her imagination, too, her hunger for the world. 'We want her to enjoy life, don't we? Like we did once. We weren't always sensible – you were quite a gay thing!'

Beattie turned a long look towards him. 'Was I? I must have been ... you forget these things, don't you?' She drank a gulp of the creamy brown liquid and it left a brown smudge along her lip. She wiped it away with the back of her hand and turned back to him. 'What happened, Eddie?'

She knew that if he could begin to tell her the answer, the talking would never end.

Eddie's heart failed him. 'Oh, you know ... nothing much.' It was the 'nothing much', he reflected, that was the truth and it had killed their spirit. Life had to have something more than 'nothing much' in it to keep the spirit alive.

His life had turned to the films he watched; the worlds he lived in at the Grande. But what had been her equivalent of his life in films? Did she have a lived imagination? Perhaps she had indeed and the burden of it had been too great, too explosive, driving her into the fearful silences he had had to cope with.

'We've done pretty well, haven't we? Much like all the others?'

He recalled the Johnsons' party and Derek's leaving concert and how they seemed to come across as the perfect family. 'Some of them think we've done rather well ...'

'And have we, do you think? Have we?'

This was too much: the hermit crab comes out of its shell and is briefly vulnerable to all manner of dangers. Here was Beattie taking risks that filled him with dread. He swallowed hard. He didn't know how to meet her.

'Oh, look, that's a big subject ... needs to be thought about a good bit. Perhaps now's not quite the moment, thinking about tonight and what's going to happen next.'

He saw the appalled look on Beattie's face. 'What I meant was, I'm sure she'll be OK: we've taught her – you've taught her – to be sensible. I'm sure she will be. Quite sure.'

He knew it was an excuse and so did Beattie.

A little later they went to bed. He came back from cleaning his teeth to find her lamp already switched off. He climbed slowly in beside her, and watched her hair as it fell on to her shoulders, a strand or two of her first grey hair straying across the pillow. She was silent, but her shoulders were shaking. He reached an arm out and hesitated. The sobs became convulsive. She made no move towards him.

164

Chapter 19

Martha humped her suitcase on to the rack. Josie had given her the fare and seen her off at the gate of the bungalow with the promise that she'd keep her secret. Now she was on her own. She had smiled at the porter on the platform, who had commented to other travellers, 'It's nice to see somebody's got something to smile about.' And a few people had looked upon her youth and her suitcase as though remembering their own earlier days. It would be an hour to Liverpool and she had nothing to occupy her. She examined the cheery railway posters commending Skegness and Eastbourne. Plenty of people were going farther than that nowadays, she knew, to beaches in Spain, saving up and taking a package that organised everything for them. They had passports with foreign stamps that they showed off at the office and the pub. The world was on the move simply for the pleasure of it. And now she was one of them.

She looked out of the window at the rows of terraced houses, red brick blackened by smoke, and every so often a clutch of factory chimneys and broad metal sheds where she knew people would be standing and moving between churning machines. With the late summer sun shining on them, she thought the factories had a certain gaunt resilience, as though they had been there for ever and would remain there, too. Well, they could be like that for all she cared, it was not where her friends wanted to be any more. Lots of girls at the typing class had come from homes where their dads worked in overalls and came home tired, if not wrecked by the work, by the chemicals, the toxins, the heat. The girls wanted to marry men with office jobs who wore ties and came home with clean hands.

The swinging banner of canvas had been tied between two trees in the front garden. It read 'Welcome!' in awkwardly painted red letters. Martha was intruding. She hesitated to arrive unannounced if there were important people around. So she loitered by the gate, put her suitcase on the pavement and sat down while she thought what to do. She had sent Duncan a postcard in response to his letter expressing only vague intent. 'I'll be coming some time soon: tell Cassie she must help me find a job. Martha.' There'd been no chance for him to react. The buoyancy that had propelled her so far began to flag. 'Yoohoo, yoohoo ... Martha!' Duncan and Cassie came bounding down the driveway of the house, waving and prancing around like kids in the back streets. 'You've come ... we got your card, and got the banner out ready. Great girl! Welcome, Welcome!' Duncan had reached her and given her one of his generous and indiscriminate bear hugs; Cassie's chalky make-up with its black panda eyes couldn't disguise the pleasure of her welcome. Martha, blinking with surprise, was paraded into the house to meet the others. There were three of them, two boys and a girl. One of them greeted her as an old friend. How easy they all were with instant friendships.

'We met before: you were with a bloke called Alex. We'd met up at the Rumbling Tum. I was Topper then; now I'm Jake.'

'Hello, Jake.'

Perhaps I can change my name too, she thought. Jake was very tall and angular, that hadn't changed. Nor had the fact that he wore a long silk scarf round his neck that hung loosely down. This one looked startlingly new against his drab old clothes.

'Yes, I'm not with Alex any more. If I was, I wouldn't have come.'

The two boys exchanged looks and she realised what she had said sounded awkward.

'He's expecting to go to university in October.'

Wrong again. Now it sounded as though he had given her up to serve his grand aspirations. She offered a weak smile.

Duncan introduced the other boy: 'This is Pete – he's big into nuclear disarmament.'

It was the dark withdrawn young man she'd talked to at the party; he still had that same haunted quality as before.

'Yes, yes, of course. We met here one night … Hello, Martha.'

His look was one of tenderness and for a moment it held her gaze. She returned it. She felt bold and new. Then he was suddenly urgent again.

'Yes, I'm still trying to convert this mob here ... it's the most serious issue of our lives, after all.'

He was too insistent for her. Martha nodded in acknowledgement rather than agreement. She was trying to be non-committal. She remembered the conversation with her father, who seemed to think the atomic bomb had won the war. She was touched by the enormity of the task Pete had set himself.

'Fine, good; you must tell me more ... '

'And this is Monica, she's one of Cassie's acting group. Mostly she wants to act in Shakespeare at Stratford, but is having to make do with us.'

An easy flirty laugh from the dark-haired girl. 'Oh, Duncan, that's not fair. I like what we're doing here well enough.'

'Yes, and she's really terrific. Helping write the scripts, too. You can't do that at Stratford.' Cassie leapt to defend her friend. Duncan gave Monica a little nudge that suggested other intimacies, then took Martha upstairs to see her room.

On the way he gave her a little speech – a lecture, thought Martha. 'We've asked you because we like you, that goes without saying. But we also want to bring together people who have things in common – like the same music, want to get involved with readings and things. We're not anarchists or anything – just people who don't want to toe the line. We're going to bring out a magazine of our own, publish people's poetry; I'm into organising evenings for people: booking halls and getting tickets out. And posters, too. There's so much going on – in cafés and clubs and places.'

Martha thought about the concert at the Grande – some far-flung wing of this same activity.

'We feel you'll fit in with us all, share our ideas.'

It wasn't quite a question. But it seemed to need an answer.

'I'll need to get a job. But I've just got my secretarial qualifications: that'll help.'

'Oh yes, none of us has any money, everyone has to earn. They just do it when they need to. Here, dump your suitcase here.'

The room was on the second floor at the top of the house, large, full of light and virtually bare. It had high ceilings and a broad sash-window that looked out on to the garden with its faded sandpit and the battered old shed. The room had the beauty of emptiness: bare walls, no carpets and a wooden floor that had been sanded. Why did people spoil rooms by clogging them with furniture? This looked like something in a French New Wave film.

'Come on down when you're ready. I'll take you to see some chimneypots you might like ... oh, and there's a shared bathroom next door.'

Chapter 20

Eddie wasn't cut out to be a detective. He might have had the trench coat and trilby of Philip Marlowe but his heart was wrecked and he simply couldn't get his mind to deal with what was happening. Taking his break from the projection box, he sat alone over a double whisky in the Red Lion, going over and over the events of the past week, trying to make sense of things.

Martha had left home.

After Josie rang to say that Martha had come by the Red Bull and asked her to give them a message, they were a bit lost. It wouldn't have dawned on them to ask Alex for more information, not knowing about the earlier trip, and Alex wasn't of a disposition to enlighten them anyway. They were sick with worry, wondering whether to call the police. Dithering, sweating, not knowing how to behave. Then two days later they got a postcard from Liverpool. It was of a painting called *Hope* from the Walker Arts Gallery. It was as minimal as Martha could make it: 'Am safe, don't worry.'

They choked with a sort of broken laughter when it arrived.

'Didn't I say she'd be sensible?'

'You said I'd brought her up to be sensible.'

Beattie relished a wisp of pride. Then a surge of anger at being caused such worry. The two of them were awash with emotions; it was like being swept in and out by the tides. Sometimes they talked, often they were locked in their own anxiety.

Grateful as Eddie was to know she was not in danger, he still puzzled over what had made her go. Beattie had said Martha had come back home after the concert: why would she do that and then leave so secretly, and suddenly? Leave home. Seriously leave home at her age, taking her old suitcase with her, packed with most of her clothes. And on the instant. Why had she not stayed to explain to him, as she had always explained, as he had come to expect her to do? That closeness between them . . . what had happened to that? He twisted open a little screw of blue paper and scattered salt over his crisps. And Beattie had been so strange, waiting up for him in her dressing gown. There had been a quivering excitement about her which she struggled to control, a feverish alertness. Could she have been in on Martha's midnight flit? If so, then the world wasn't as he knew it. But even women who seem not to like each other stayed close. He remembered his own mother and her sister, Maggie, who in their last years never spoke. Some quarrel about borrowed sheets, it had been. Then at his

171

mother's funeral, Maggie had been awash with tears, well nigh hysterical as the coffin was lowered. You could never tell with women: they were different. Something had happened in Galton Road that night after the concert. Something shifted the balances that held his life in place. He went back over it in his mind. The room, even the air, had felt different, it felt used, moved around. Something had shifted the staleness of the space and brought new feelings there. He had dropped his keys on to the sideboard and raised his head. The door of the front room stood open. He looked inside: nothing unusual. The soot fallen from the chimney on the crumpled newspaper in the grate lay there still. No footfalls on the carpets – they were too threadbare for that. Did the cushions seem a little newly plumped? It wasn't something he would notice. And all the while believing that Martha was safe in her room. Later when Beattie had cried in their bed he hadn't known how to respond. Their intimacy had its own rules. They could sleep next to each other, he could even enfold her, but it had slowly been stripped of emotion; the echoes of sex lingered as ghosts. He had felt a tenderness, but a tenderness born of their plight. What he recognised more clearly was his anger, a cold hard anger held back against his spine, held back lest it break out and crash and break things around his home. Where exactly was Martha? And what was she up to?

In the ensuing autumn weeks, as the weather grew chill but the sun was still golden, Duncan showed Martha the city.

'It's an old Liverpool joke: Hope Street with a cathedral at either end.'

They were having coffee together before embarking on another of their long walks. He had been touched by that first innocent question she had asked and referred fondly to her as 'Chimneypots' ever since. He took her to see the grandeur of St George's Hall, the decor of the Philharmonic Dining Rooms, and the three buildings – the so-called 'Three Graces' – grouped down by the Pier Head. She was his eager pupil and he her gentle tutor. His part-time job at the art college involved him with lively but often distracted young people. Martha was a captive audience, trusting and happy. And as they walked they talked. And always Martha was on the lookout for her hero, the one in the pink shirt. She couldn't find any mention of The Brigands in *Mersey Beat*, the newly launched magazine that told you all about groups and where they were playing. It might be that they had broken up, or changed their name. Their music had been very loud and that had been thrilling, but she couldn't remember any of the songs. Liverpool offered strong competition: every group lived in hopes of getting a record contract. A group called The Beatles had begun playing regular dates at the Cavern: she went along one lunchtime with Monica and they obviously had something special that put them ahead of the rest. They were so casually funny together, laughing at private jokes. They were good-looking, too, with a sort of vanity it was fun to share. Perhaps The Brigands had got lost in the crowd.

'The Anglican cathedral's not really finished yet, but

they have services. It's not got dancing chimneypots but it has huge expanses of red brick.' So they strolled to where the building stood isolated among the Georgian terraces of Liverpool's first great prosperity.

'Are you religious, Martha? You've got a religious name. Martha who did all the work looking after the house and the kitchen, keeping everything ordered. Is that you?'

Martha knew she was tidy: her sock drawer was orderly, her handkerchiefs kept in a neat pile. But about religion ...

'No. Nothing special. I was given the standard christening: my auntie May and Noreen are my godmothers and send presents each birthday but it doesn't have much to do with God. And you?' They were entering the vast arched space, the depth of it opening at their feet where the flight of steps went down into the well of the building.

'Oh, I'm typical of many round here: my mother came over from Ireland so I'm a Liverpool Catholic. My mother was devout without thinking about it, until she met my father, that is. Apparently she kept going on about sin so much he felt he should take her in hand.'

He laughed but the remark made Martha wonder. Was it drink, or women? Those were the only sins she knew anything about.

'He was a medical student at the time, later he specialised in psychiatry. Understanding people is what interested him. And interested him in her ... that's what he tells me. But she still insisted we go to a Catholic school. They seem happy enough, what we see of them.'

They were sitting side by side. Even empty the place felt hushed and awesome. His big warm laugh distracted several of the devout trying to concentrate on sins of their own. Martha wondered what was wrong with sin: as a child she'd believed it was just a fact of life. Clearly that wasn't so. At home things had been simple: things that offended Beattie were wrong; good was anything that pleased her. Much as she was glad to be away, Martha was missing such certainties. They were gazing at the great vaunting arch of the cathedral.

'I like religious things, though. And you were right to bring me here: I love it.'

She let the awe of the place, the emptiness that wasn't empty but filled with others' piety, reach into her. She didn't believe the stories they believed, but she liked the fact of their belief. It bound them together in a way she wasn't bound to anyone. None the less, something in her cared. She began to feel she was shrugging off the old boring sense of duty and finding something better.

She smiled at Duncan. 'How did you know I would like this?'

'Because *I* do.'

'You're like your father, aren't you? Interested in understanding people.'

'Oh, that's nice of you to say, but he's altogether something else ... quite a big cheese in the world out there.'

'Yes, but you collect people around you and watch how we all get on. I'm not sure why you do that – it's not as though we're your relations.'

'Oh, family ... don't pin your hopes on old-fashioned stuff like family. Mum, Dad and obedient children – too constricting.'

Martha recalled that Cassie had said something

175

similar. It seemed to Martha that, love it or hate it, we were stuck with it.

'If you've got nice parents, why do you and Cassie hate families so much?'

'Well, we happen to like our own parents, but, believe me, what Father tells us about how families behave, well, you'd surely rather choose your own family.' He paused and turned towards her. 'After all, you've chosen your family here with us. What's wrong with that?'

'Nothing, nothing at all. I like it here.'

Martha turned smiling into the broad expanse of the church. A lady passing across the great open space below the tower smiled back encouragingly.

Duncan was still talking. 'My parents sort of let me bring myself up: run wild. I was allowed to stay up all hours, dress how I wanted, cheek the grown-ups ... within reason, that is. Various busybodies said it amounted to neglect. I was generally a pretty obnoxious child. But here I am ... take me as I am.'

'You're not obnoxious now; it seems to me you're very kind.' Martha looped her hand round his elbow and gave it a squeeze. 'How old are you, Duncan?'

He regarded her with a long, close stare. 'I hope you ask because I seem old and wise – but I'm neither. I'm twenty-eight.'

Martha was thoughtful. 'Are you ever afraid, deeply afraid? Of what's to come?'

'I don't believe there's any life after death, if that's what you mean. I think my mother probably still has secret hopes. She'd like to meet up with those who've died: her mother especially, I think.'

'Ooh.' Martha's eyes widened. 'I can't imagine any-thing worse than an eternity spent with my mother; that's enough to put me off religion entirely.'

Duncan had the tact not to press for details.

'No,' she said, 'I meant fear of nuclear war. I wake thinking about it in the middle of the night. Then I realise it's not a nightmare and I get even more afraid.'

'You're right, you're right.' He stopped but he didn't have any answers. 'Most people just turn their minds away from it. It's there, after all, and can't be wished away. The thing is to enjoy the here and now.'

She could see that he wanted to move on, but she pressed: 'But that's not enough, is it? Turning your back on something evil. And yet it all seems so hopeless.'

'Pete doesn't think it's hopeless. It's taken over his whole life, haven't you noticed, trying to do something to stop it. It's all he thinks about. He's a sweet boy but it's making him neurotic. I fear for him sometimes ...' Duncan's voice trailed away as he spotted someone familiar.

'Look, there's Jen Sanderson. I need to speak to her.'

Martha felt the warmth leave her side as Duncan set off. It happened a good deal. He knew so many people and would stop and gossip on the streets for ages while she just hung around waiting. This time he bounded across the broad spaces to ambush a middle-aged woman in a floor-length coat who was picking at the leaflets at the cathedral door. After a moment's conversation he turned and beckoned Martha to them.

'This is Jen: she runs a second-hand bookshop along Hardman Street. There's a board in her doorway that takes cards advertising jobs. Jen, this is Martha – typist extraordinaire!'

Jen must be about Beattie's age but how different she was. Her camel-coloured coat fell untidily open. Beneath it she wore a bizarre miscellany of clothes – a calf-length skirt in crushed brown velvet, black riding boots, a green sweater that was clearly unravelling at neck and cuffs over which a cascade of huge amber beads hung to her waist. She seemed unaware of the incongruity of it all. Or perhaps, thought Martha, the incongruity is in my head. She remembered Cassie's theatrical costumes and how natural she had felt in the admiral's uniform.

'Yes, of course, I'll look out for you, Martha. Will you be coming to hear our next poetry reading … end of October?'

'Yes, please. I'd like to come. Is that all right, Duncan?'

His guffaw resounded in the arches above them. His presence was beginning to distress the worshippers.

'Don't ask me! I'm not in charge: you're a free agent. Do what you want!'

In the days that followed Martha went along to Jen Sanderson's second-hand bookshop, which wasn't the frowsty tired place she expected but an ordered treasure house where ranks upon ranks of shelves were labelled: philosophy, economics, world affairs, foreign books and, thankfully, foreign books in translation. Martha enjoyed the thrill of being impressed. Other customers, students pausing to examine individual tomes, must assume she was one of them. And then she realised the truth: of course she was one of them. There were plenty of jobs to be had on Jen's cork board. The Playhouse

Theatre needed a waitress for interval bar service; the library was advertising for a girl to check newly arrived books on to the shelves. Jen's bookshop was just the sort of place where such people might be found. A club needed a cloakroom girl, and a girl setting up her own dressmaking business was asking for general help. Martha noted the phone numbers of the last two. By the time she had got through to them, the cloakroom job had gone.

'Oh, sorry, we've hired someone already, but give us your number in case she lets us down.' Clearly commitments were verbal and casual.

The dressmaker asked her round at once. 'Dressmaking business' was something of a misnomer. Fee was a young woman in her early twenties, with shocking auburn hair, clothed in black with huge clanking bracelets on her arms. She was working in the bedroom of her home, on her mother's sewing machine, surrounded by confusion. But she had big ideas.

'I need to get some of this stuff out where people can see it; but I need to sort out bulk orders for clothes and buttons and such. Can you get me sorted, d'you think?'

Martha wasn't sure, but she'd answered the advertisement after all, so she expected herself to say yes. It was only polite. And Fee seemed easy-going enough. What an odd name that was, but then Fee seemed to be urging instant friendship and using slangy Christian names from the start. She certainly needed sorting out. Her sewing machine, a Singer treadle, over by the window was heaped with some sort of heavy black satin. Her bed was loaded with small boxes, some with their lids off tipping a cascade of twinkling buttons across the quilt. Martha thought again of Cassie's theatrical costumes and the chaotic heaps of fabric she had found at the house that first day. And Jen with her fraying jersey and amber beads. What was it about Liverpool's women?

'Well, yes, I think I could, yes.'

Martha's hesitancy stirred a sudden frown from Fee. 'Well, yes or no? Which is it? I can't mess around.'

Odd words from someone sitting at the centre of exactly such a mess.

Martha grew bold. 'It's like this: I'd like to. I think I could sort you out. But I only want to work three days a week ... will that do?'

Fee looked alarmed: then smiled a quick anxious smile. 'Well, yes, if you'll start now: today, I mean. I've a rush job for a group that wants something outrageous for their concert next weekend ... I'm up against it.'

Martha downed her bag, cleared a space and began. 'Oh, and what'll you be paying me?'

About what she needed. Five pounds sounded about right.

That evening Martha sat around the supper table with Pete and Duncan. Jake sat aside from them, rolling one of his odd cigarettes in a little machine. Pete was brooding and withdrawn, picking at his thumbnail. When he was in a mood like that they left him alone, Martha guessed. He would be off soon to join another big protest. Cassie and Monica were over by the stove cooking up something strange and vegetarian.

'The point is, it isn't a real job at all: it's just helping out a friend and getting some pocket money for it. I don't even have to turn up at a particular time.'

There was something not quite right about it. All the grown-ups went on about working hours, overtime and such.

Duncan couldn't see her problem. 'And how much better is that? The world of work is loaded against us, always has been. So the best thing is to find something you want to do, and do it.'

'But, I'm trained as a typist. I went to the Tech specially—'

Duncan interrupted: 'But that's the old way things are: offices and routine. Old stuff. Surely you want new ways of doing things? Like we do. Aren't I right?'

Martha wondered what Pete felt. He was usually watching, picking up on what she said and helping explain things. But he just smiled quietly and said nothing; his thoughts seemed elsewhere.

'I want a job I enjoy, I know that. But, you know, messing around with dressmaking is, well, just messing around.'

Duncan was roused. 'I hope you didn't tell Fee that. She wants to sell her designs to the shops one day.'

'So shops aren't part of old stuff then. Is that what you're saying?' She tipped her head to one side so that Duncan could see she was teasing.

Monica came across with platefuls of gooey food. 'Duncan likes to live by his own rules, not the world's. Right?' She addressed the remark to him with a pointed aggression, setting his plate down in front of him.

The food tasted of nothing much but nutrition.

*

181

A week or two later, Martha lay on her bed trying out her new habit – smoking – alongside her old one – reading. It was ten o'clock at night. Duncan had taken her that day to see more of Liverpool – the burnt-out church of St Luke's that had survived from the early nineteenth century only to be blitzed by the Luftwaffe in 1940. He had talked of Liverpool's pride at surviving the massive German bombing that had aimed to disable the docks. They returned with the pleasing exhaustion that goes with a day well spent and things learnt. Later with tired feet she had indulged herself in the big iron bath and gone to bed, all pink and rosy. She was reading *Franny and Zooey* by J. D. Salinger. Jake had earlier loaned her *Catcher in the Rye* and she had liked that. She was hoping for more of the same.

She heard feet clumping up the uncarpeted stair. Duncan came in without knocking and sat at the foot, and took up where his earlier talking had ended.

'Remember, the other day, I was telling you about Dante's *Divine Comedy* and how in the Third Circle of Hell he punishes lovers. What real torture they were given. Here, I've looked it up for you.'

She put aside her book and sat up. 'Oh, yes. You were saying how cruel it was, just for loving each other.' She moved to reach out and take the book, but had a better idea. 'Why don't you read it to me? Read it aloud.'

'Sure? Of course the original's in Italian. But it's just as moving in English.'

He left the room returning with two lit candles. He switched off the single bulb at the centre of the ceiling and placed a candle each side of the bed. Martha was prepared to enjoy the drama of what was to come. As

Duncan's melodious comfortable voice filled the room, Martha sank back on her pillows, her hands behind her head, watching him. Duncan read how Francesca had been unwillingly married to a deformed and ugly man and then fallen in love with his brother Paolo. One day they were reading together the story of Lancelot and Guinevere and as the story grew more romantic ... Paolo and Francesca themselves came closer, blushed, touched, and then Duncan read at the story's climax the famous line about what happened next, how –

'They read no more that day ... ' Duncan paused and spoke searchingly, quietly. 'Dante doesn't tell us any more than that, he leaves us to work it out. Should we should keep up the tradition, Martha? Why don't I set our book aside and see what happens.'

The next morning Martha lay alone in her rumpled bed and felt happy. She felt other things too: relief, gratitude, amusement and pleasure. Duncan had made her first experience a good one. That would never go away: he would always be the first. A huge wave of loyalty and affection bonded her to him.

He was buttering his toast and reading the paper at the scrubbed kitchen table. Monica was boiling eggs for them both.

'Hi, Martha ... want an egg, too?'

'Oooh, please!' Martha was ravenous.

Her eagerness caused Monica to pause and look up, then nod knowingly and glance towards Duncan, who kept his head down in the *Guardian*.

'Yes, well, it does give you an appetite.'

The eggs were served and the conversation meandered around.

Then Duncan exploded. 'Oh, my God, that's where Pete is. See this, see this.'

He flourished the paper towards them both.

'There's been a massive ban-the-bomb demonstration in London, hundreds arrested. John Osborne, George Melly ... I wonder if Pete's one of them; my God, that must have been why he was so clammed up in himself. He was always screwed up about breaking the law.'

Martha had hoped for a more tender morning, one that acknowledged the gentleness with which he'd treated her, but she could see that Pete's fate mattered.

'I'd better ring his parents and see if he needs bail.'

And Duncan swept out of the room without ever glancing towards her.

Monica shrugged, seeing Martha's face fall. 'Ah well. That's how it goes. Did he shoot you the Paolo and Francesca line, then? It's his favourite. I wouldn't mind but the book belongs to me.'

Chapter 21

Eddie called for another whisky. It was no time to get drunk. And yet ...

'How many've you had already?'

The second house was in and Josie was round at his elbow.

Bert with Tom was running *Sink the Bismarck.*

'Oh, don't worry ... I'm not another Derek. I just need a little comfort.'

They sat in companionable silence, Eddie vacant and lost.

Josie asked, 'Any more news of Martha then?'

It was now two months since she had gone and well into autumn. News had sped round the Grande that Eddie had broken down in the projection box when he and Bert were showing *Sons and Lovers.* The story's intensities had caught him unawares. He knew it was by someone they all thought of as a dirty writer, so paid little heed to the long lingering black and white shots of industrial landscape. But the dialogue's force had perked up his attention. The film was about a family caught up in awful conflicts, not the shoot 'em up conflicts he enjoyed so much in Westerns, but passions between husband and wife, and mother and son. He had lit his pipe and sat back on the stool to watch the second reel. The tears came slowly, and when Bert offered him tea he turned a face riven with pain towards his colleague.

'Hey, old man. What is it? Hold on there ... hold on.'

Bert reached in the cupboard for the half bottle of whisky that was always there, then placed an awkward hand on Eddie's unmoving arm.

'Here, this'll help, whatever the trouble.' He enquired no further.

'Martha's gone for good, Bert. She's not coming back.'

The words fell into the silence as the words of the film gushed over Eddie's grief.

'Well, she's a grown girl, Eddie: she's old enough, now, to make her own way. She's bound to know her own mind.'

This was poor consolation. Everyone knew that single daughters lived at home, and only left it for marriage and to create a home of their own.

Bert ventured a question. 'Where's she gone to? Are you in touch at all?'

Eddie shook his head. 'She sent a couple of postcards. That she was safe, then another one saying she was living with friends and had got a job. Both postmarked Liverpool. That was weeks ago.'

They were distracted at that point by the need to change reels. On the screen the Morel family were still breaking each other's hearts. For a moment Eddie felt he was part of a great sweeping mass of human misery.

'How's Beattie taking it?'

Eddie had turned staring eyes towards his friend. 'Oh, strangely. Strangely.' He hesitated as to whether to describe Beattie's behaviour. 'She's very upset, naturally. And coping ... in her own way.'

The curtain closed on further discussion.

'Let me know, won't you, if there's anything I can do. I've got cousins over in Liverpool ... Seaforth way. You never know, you never know.'

This last referred to nothing at all and was exactly what was needed. Eddie returned to the turmoil of Paul Morel with a chastened heart.

Bert would muse later to his wife that this was what came of letting a young girl see adult films: it gave them ideas, and that was the last thing you wanted. Look what happened!

Now Josie stirred herself on the bar stool. 'Still no proper news then?' Her guilt at helping Martha out on that strange panicky night had grown. The sadness of autumn, the nights darkening early, the steady rain, the leaves beginning to clog the drains all added to her gloom. But it was as nothing to what she saw in Eddie. His sadness persisted and she felt the blame. She watched out for him each day and cared more as the days went by. She had headaches and slept badly. She needed to act.

'Look, I don't know how much you and Beattie get out. It's none of my business, but I wonder if you'd like to come round for tea one night when you're not at the

Grande. I actually like cooking, believe it or not. I don't mean the usual – mutton stew, rice pudding and that. No, I try out these fancy foreign recipes they go on about in the posh women's magazines. I don't do it just for myself, of course. Only when I have friends round. Probably why I have so many friends ... they like to experiment.'

She'd got carried away and saw a look of alarm on Eddie's face.

'There's no point cooking fancy when you're on your own. It might cheer you up.'

Eddie looked amazed, nonplussed really.

'Or if you prefer I could make it a jolly get-together ... ask over Bert and his wife, even Florrie ... if you like, that is. I could try out something really adventurous.'

'Well, that would be very kind, but ... '

He explained that he'd rather it wasn't any kind of party. Just himself. Josie seemed content with that and they arranged for him to go round for high tea around six o'clock the following Wednesday. As he was coming alone, any later might have seemed inappropriate. Her neighbours in the tight little cul-de-sac would notice. Josie thought about the new paperback recipe book of Mediterranean food.

Since Martha's going, other things had begun to change. Beattie was out of the house more often. She seemed to be venturing forth on her own from time to time and returned seemingly satisfied but without explaining where she'd been. Something had changed in her for the better. Oddly, she never mentioned Martha's departure and continuing absence but she now regularly offered brief if not warm exchanges with Eddie, exchanges about mundane things like the gas bill, or the grocery order, and when something needed repairing. It would be wrong to describe her tone as friendly, nor was it hostile nor even cold. It was simply neutral. But at least the silences were ending. Eddie experienced this with puzzlement and relief. It was as though the conundrum at the heart of his marriage was being solved and, like the magician's box, turned out to be entirely empty. And to his surprise it had ceased to matter. Where he had once felt torment at his wife's behaviour, he no longer cared. He was preoccupied with what was a more shocking concern. Why had Martha come home after the concert and then left for good: what had happened in those moments?

At Josie's, she offered him what she called a quiche. To Eddie it looked like a pie with the lid off and tasted of egg custard with cheese in it. There were bits of bacon too. For some reason the French got the credit for it. It was the vogue thing now, he knew. All things French were in favour. People even asked why the Grande didn't show French films, which seemed to him daft as they mostly didn't speak French and he supposed they simply wanted to show off where they'd been for their holidays. Still there was nothing to be gained by making such comments to Josie. She was a strong woman with a mind and a life of her own. They ate the quiche with slices of bread and butter and cups of strong tea.

They talked of the fate of the Grande and cinema generally. Television was certainly gaining ground. People wouldn't move from their firesides when this new

Coronation Street was on. And with two channels to choose from there was always something to watch, something everyone was talking about at work the following day. Josie had a good-sized television of light brown wood that gave it a Scandinavian feel. The rest of her furniture was like that, too. When her mother had died ten years ago, she had sold all the dark brown furniture. The bulky armchairs had gone, replaced by starker seats with wooden arms and cushions bobbled in oatmeal tweed. The windows had curtains patterned in splashes of pale green and eau de nil spots that reached to the floor.

Eddie remarked how modern it all looked.

'Well, I have only myself to spend money on, so I like to have it nice.'

They settled into the armchairs with cups of Nescafé. Josie slid into the subject that had been on her mind for so long.

'I bet wherever she is, Eddie, Martha's making a good life for herself. I bet she will be: she's that kind of girl.'

Eddie looked straight at her. 'Do you think so, Josie? I'd like to believe you but do you really know her well enough?'

'Oh, Eddie.' She spoke with a new seriousness. 'I should have told you. I wished I'd mentioned it earlier. I should have, I know. But Martha came here that night when she couldn't find you.'

'Find me? Find me? What does that mean? I live at home – she can find me there, can't she?'

'The night of the concert. It all got confused. She left early and went home, then came back to try and find you. But by that time you'd left.'

'I was in the Red Lion all along. You know that.'

It was that same night, the night of Beattie's strangeness. Eddie stirred his coffee slowly and stared into the red bars of the fancy electric fire.

'Why did she do that, then?'

'She was upset about something. I thought it was that Alex. They'd had a row earlier. But she said it wasn't.'

'Alex? Are you saying it was all his doing?' He shook his head, confused. 'I'd come to trust him. I thought he was one of those nice grammar-school types.'

'Eddie, no, listen. Listen to what I'm saying. It was not him: it was something else. She said she had been asked over to Liverpool and she went the next morning.'

Eddie stood up abruptly, the coffee cup dumped swimmingly on to the little low-lying table.

'Are you telling me she stayed here?' He was clasping his hands and his lip was trembling. 'Here in this house, under your roof? I thought she'd given you that message for us at the Grande.'

Josie smiled grimly. 'I was looking after her for you, Eddie, as if she had been my own daughter. I was doing that for you. She said she wasn't going back home.'

She had risen and was standing face to face with him.

'I was acting for the best. You must know that.'

The moment was clumsy and awkward and stupid. Suddenly he lunged towards her, pulling her within his embrace and burying his face in her hair. A dangling earring caught at the collar of his jacket.

'Oh, Josie. It's terrible without her.'

*

191

Josie held him to her but was thinking fast. For all her motherliness, this embrace wasn't entirely motherly. It wasn't even sisterly. This tall lanky man was her friend and she had always kept it like that. Oh, she flattered and flirted with him; she did the same with Gerald the commissionaire and at desperate moments with young Mr Colin. But she kept in check a strong impulse that would have liked something more. And now here he was, angry one moment, needful the next. 'Men are like children, aren't they?' She'd heard it said often; it cropped up regularly on *Coronation Street*. But Eddie's neediness was pitiful and she was full of pity.

She raised a ringed hand towards his cheek. 'I'm sure it is, Eddie, I'm sure it is.'

He slumped back into the spindly chair. He looked wrong, somehow, against the pale colours of the room. His gaunt face was strong and assertive, his long legs sprawled across the speckled rug. His maleness had invaded her home. Josie fetched something more substantial than coffee. She would comfort him, but only so far. She wondered if she should have mentioned who Martha saw with her mother?

Chapter 22

Pete was in a bad way; he came back traumatised from what had happened at the protest. The sit-down in Trafalgar Square had been massive. The crowds came in response to their personal anxieties at the sudden escalation in the risk of war. In mid-August the East Germans had driven a huge impenetrable wall through the middle of Berlin. The four-power agreement on ruling the city had been torn up, cutting off all former contact, separating families, threatening with shooting those who tried to cross. Individuals had been making last-minute dashes to the West but the East Germans had destroyed any cover, trees, even woodlands uprooted. The place, shown everywhere in the newspapers of the West, looked desolate. Evidence, surely, of the increasing escalation towards war. Things had got worse: by the end of the month the Russians had resumed testing their nuclear bombs: almost instantly the Americans had declared they would do the same. There was only one direction the world was heading: another war and this time it would be nuclear. The crowds in Trafalgar Square and at Holy Loch were puny in the face of such insurmountable menace. Pete felt he could faint with the pressure of it all. But it was the thought of Martha that kept him going. He recalled her tousled head and laughing mouth and suddenly persuaded himself he was doing this for her. She stood for all that he wanted to save in the world: what was worthwhile in his life. He hoped thinking of her would give him courage.

He had put himself deep within the phalanx of people sitting down. There were hundreds of police around, backed up, he knew, by loads more in buses parked in Parliament Square and the side streets. It was the biggest confrontation the Campaign together with its militant wing the Committee of 100 had ever mounted. There was a high degree of excited talk in fear of what might happen, nervous laughter between those who had only just met, giving them courage and a sense of their own rightness. Then around seven in the evening, the sky still blue but darkening, the police reached to where Pete was sitting, his hands clasped round his knees, willing himself to hold fast and not be easy to move. He tried to think of Martha, but a couple of large and impatient policemen had made short work of his feeble effort, grabbing his feet and shoulders and swinging him like a child's skipping rope with little thought of how he would land on the floor of the van. The exhilaration had gone: those in the van with him were angry and muttering. Some had been hurt hard; Pete's ankle had twisted and his jacket had been torn at the shoulder seam. He was grinding his teeth with rage and defeat.

He was bailed by a friend who had money from his parents. They got there before Duncan. They knew what he was up to and as Quakers themselves were proud of his passive defiance. But they knew his frail nervous state would be hard hit by many nights in a police cell, so they had posted money to London. Pete felt deprived even of the satisfactions of suffering, and took the train north with his spirits low and his body throbbing with pain and injustice, thinking about the people in the house, feeling alone. Only the ticket collector at the gate, noticing his CND badge, had slapped him on the back:

'Good on yer . . . the country's with you, lad!'

That was some comfort, and after all only last year the Labour Party had voted to make Unilateral Disarmament their policy.

Martha had expected at first that she and Duncan would constitute some kind of couple together. It hadn't turned out like that. Whenever she turned to him in the hope of some sign, there was nothing there for her. He still made unpredictable visits to her bed, yet she was too timid to ask where he was spending the other nights. She deduced from Monica's impatience that she was no longer numbered among what seemed to be a sort of harem. She could hardly see Duncan greet another woman without wondering whether she too counted among his conquests. Was there anything wrong with this? Weren't they trying to live in new ways? Martha tried to embrace the notion in principle, yet when it came to acting it out she was having to steel herself against feeling too much pain.

But she only had to recall Clive and even Alex to know there was no going back. At least this was a new kind of pain, a positive exploratory pain, the pain of discovery and growing up, a pain that made her stronger every day. All she must do was remember Josie's practical advice.

The poetry reading was in a cellar of the Why Not Pub in Harrington Street. There were lots of cellars in Liverpool and many of them were being pressed into use for concerts. The Cavern was one of the most established with regular jazz and country and western: it was so deep underground that when it got overcrowded the walls ran in condensation, saturated with the general fug of people and dampness. You came out with the smoky clag clinging to your clothes. Still, it was worth it: the music was so good. This cellar was less celebrated and far less crowded, about fifty or so people. The first arrivals had occupied the faux-leather benches around the perimeter, their glasses of beer from the neat corner bar set on Formica-topped tables. Across the room a medley of chairs and stools provided for the rest. The poetry crowd was sparse but dedicated, seeming to know each other, exchanging complicit smiles as newcomers arrived. Martha went along with Cassie, Jake and Monica. Duncan said he had other things to do and Pete was too busy addressing envelopes. He said that settled routine work made him less frantic. He liked the sense of calmly doing something that mattered.

Jake was wearing his battered top hat, which drew attention to their little group when they pounded down the steps. Martha liked that: it gave them identity and gave their arrival some significance. She felt part of something, rather than just a hanger-on. The effect was dissipated as a gaggle of friends hailed Jake as their own and drew him away with them. Jake, pliant and amiable, simply responded to whoever called his name. Martha was wearing one of Fee's creations, a machined-together medley of strips wrapped into a jazzy skirt that daringly stopped well above Martha's knees. She had taken her cue from Cassie and embarked on an exploration of her face, painting her eyes and cheeks in colours she had only ever seen on Josie, who was judged at the Grande to be rather tarty. If dear Josie could see her now! She had teased her unruly hair into a tall beehive and secured its balance with a heavy dose of a glue-like spray. She wasn't sure about the hair, but you had to try new things, didn't you? Duncan hadn't noticed: he was preoccupied with whatever he had to do that night. Monica had nodded in acknowledgement rather than approval. But the skirt was a hit. Girls she didn't know came up and fingered it enviously. 'Where you get that, love?'

Fee's future looked good.

The poets, all men, were clustered at one end, conferring. For them there was a small table with jugs of lemonade and a pile of tired biscuits. Jen from the bookshop arrived with a tall stooping man with a substantial grey beard. The word went round that he was from the publishing world in London, but there was no evidence. If you looked different, people spun a fiction round you.

Martha was asked: 'Who are you here for, pet?'

It seemed the room had different clans of followers, but Martha was for them all. She was for the whole thing:

197

the cellar, the lemonade, Jen's unravelling sweater, her own swinging skirt, the unexplained delay in getting started . . . it was all still new and easy-going. There were four poets in all: as a group they looked lonely and drab. Their faces were devoid of expression; were they, Martha wondered, thinking of higher things all the time, living at some sublime level where poetry flowed like honey, or were they merely worried about how their poems would be received.

One poet, no more than a teenager, fidgeted with his frayed cuffs. The buttons had gone and he seemed unsure as to whether to let the sleeve hang loose around his wrist, or roll it up securely around his elbows. It preoccupied him while the others read. Martha knew this wasn't polite. You should concentrate on the reader in question. She concentrated like mad: her eyes scanned the poets' faces, their clothes, their fingernails and the papers in their hands, often scruffy scraps with lazy writing. One had neatly typed pages; one had a published poetry magazine, copies of which stood in an untouched pile by the tired biscuits. One read funny poems about dogs, and saucepans and catching the tram; another, mesmerised by a girl in the front row, read in a choking voice a series of explicitly erotic love odes. Martha twitched the strands of hair straying from her beehive: these weren't words she was used to hearing at all, let alone in a place of culture. The audience applauded him with extra gusto and turned towards the urn of tea thankfully brought in by two jovial women who'd been smoking next door.

Martha lit up a cigarette. This was the interval in the

proceedings. The erotic poet joined his girlfriend, who smiled wanly and gave him a restrained pat on the arm. The funny poet became serious and asked around as to whether his humour had gone too far. As it was mostly about domestic detail – socks and clogged hairbrushes and such – there didn't seem much occasion for offence. Perhaps it was an anxiety transferred from the shock impact of his fellow performer. There were two more readings. Before then Martha tried to make new friends. It seemed to lie at the secret of being Duncan, or Jake too, and she wanted to be like them, to take on their confidence and all-purpose amiability. Twice she asked total strangers for a light for her cigarettes. The first flame was provided by a tall loud-speaking man who reached in his pocket for a lighter, flicked it alight and held it towards her, all without pausing in his tirade or taking his eyes from the burly tweeded figure to whom it was addressed.

Her next was far more fruitful: a pale boyish creature, with big teeth and a waxy skin, who looked and smiled, noted the jazzy skirt and grinned some more.

'When did you arrive in Liverpool, then?'

Martha explained only a little.

He asked admiringly about the skirt. Was he at the art school perhaps? No time for more but she added his name – Nigel Quince – to her list of helpful contacts. Well, she hoped they would be helpful. Merely asking made her feel active in her own life, though for what and towards what she had yet to define.

The poet with the frayed cuffs went down well with some windy lines about fields and trees. Then the final one rose uneasily with a bunch of stained pages in his hands. His voice was faint and monotonous as though he were only unwillingly sharing his words. They spoke of strange feelings, love for a distant woman, guilt about a child seen in the street, the touch of an old person's skin. He was heard in respectful silence and given a ripple of gentle applause. Martha looked round searching to see whether others were as moved as she was. The jazzy skirt suddenly seemed a flimsy bit of tinsel, little protection against her unsettled feelings.

That night Martha lay alone in her high wide bed, the light from houses behind theirs casting shadows on the wood floor from the two shabby armchairs marooned in the middle of her big echoing room. The poetry had moved her. She remembered home. Her years there all seemed a long time ago. She wondered that she had lived so long in a place where thoughts and feelings were never spoken of, where there had been so little talk. Where no one had the words to express what they felt. Coming here had unlocked her tongue, and no one frowned or disapproved or thought she was dotty. In Duncan's household they never stopped talking, arguing, blaming, confessing, criticising and forgiving. And she grew to do the same. But there were threads that clung. Something echoing from what the listless young poet had said, not his exact words but the mood they gave rise to, had been unsettling. She stared at the light mottling the ceiling. It was almost two months now since she had left, Josie waving her off. Since then she had sent home a couple of terse little postcards of vaguely reassuring clichés. She had given no address and no clue as to the sort of life she was living. As communications they were very much in the style of the home she had left. In particular she offered no words of comfort or insight to her father. She sent him no love, none of the abundant love she felt for him, and which from time to time came lurching back with terrible force.

She lay on her back, her hands across her heart and slowly sad silent tears trickled down to the pillow. That night she dreamt about her mother. It was a violent and shocking dream. This mother was not the timid tyrant who had driven her away but a raging fury, huge and naked, savaging through the distorted rooms of what seemed like Galton Road, screaming after Martha. As Martha fled upstairs from room to empty room she was increasingly cornered and more and more desperate. Moving towards the open window she saw below her the figure of Derek, also naked, standing in moonlight in the middle of the lawn, his own arms spread wide and urging her, 'Jump, Martha, jump.' As her mother's figure closed behind her, she woke with a shock. Her body was soaking and the images still vivid. She shook herself awake, head and body quivering with fear and rage. She got out of bed, stamping her bare feet on the bare boards to establish reality and banish the ghosts. But they lingered.

Chapter 23

Martha's continuing absence released something in Beattie. She didn't quite know why but partly it was because the obligations that went with bringing up a child and running a house were diminishing. Meals, laundry, cleaning were all part of what mothers did, and did almost simultaneously in all the family homes across the country. She often thought you could have told the time of day by where she, and all the women on the street, had got to in their list of daily duties. She had tried to take her cue from magazine pictures of smiling housewives in skimpy aprons carrying casseroles of home-made nourishment triumphantly to family tables. She had acquired a sewing machine and learned quickly how to make clothes. She had cleaned the house. She had bought into the dream long ago and it had failed her, and now her own child had rejected this fastidious care. In truth she knew that Martha treated it with insulting disregard, preferring her father's easy-going ways and staying up late with him exchanging gossip about his films and his cronies. And now she was gone. Well, that was a burden off her shoulders, at any rate. It was growing to feel like that most of the time, a sense of relief, even a feeling that she could begin to please herself. But then she would be surprised by sudden alarms. And bouts of rage. Sometimes in the night she imagined cruel accidents befalling Martha and awoke in a panic, tempered, if she but knew it, with the tincture of revenge.

Out of the blue, a letter arrived for her with an American stamp. She sat down immediately to read it. It came from Muriel. Fancy her trying to catch up after all this time. That was friendship for you, at least as Muriel knew it. They'd exchanged the odd Christmas cards since she'd moved years ago to Florida, but it was unlike either of them to take the trouble to write a letter with proper news. Beattie allowed herself a sigh and a shake of the head. But a smile too as she read that: 'Gee, life is great. Gus has proved a great hubby and Natasha and Benedict are planning to go to college soon . . . ' Come the winter she and Gus were Europe-bound. 'What say' – wrote Muriel – 'we meet up, talk over old times. Gus doesn't know the half of it. Bet Eddie doesn't either. Toodle pip. Muriel.'

Beattie sat down to write a cautious reply using words like 'welcome' and 'gossip' and even reminiscently 'good times'. She felt strangely moved by the possibility of glimpsing back into her girlhood: what reminders might there be of how she had once laughed and joked, shared gossip and even clothes. What would Muriel think of her now, grown so silent.

*

Gus and Muriel were to dock in Liverpool in November and come over to Staveley to stay with Muriel's parents in one of the more prosperous suburbs, and soon after, the phone rang in 26 Galton Road. Beattie had grown used to flinching at the sound, being both nervous and hopeful that it would be Martha calling. Instead, she was startled by the crashing excitement of her wartime friend, now speaking with the American twang of her GI husband. Muriel decided that her invitation to 'come round and dish the dirt' would be an excuse to get out the red dress.

She dressed carefully and took the bus over. Gus and Muriel had an odd view of the England they had last seen some sixteen years before.

'My gosh, d'you know there are still bombsites in Liverpool ... and the war ended sixteen years ago. What's wrong with you people?'

It was well meant but put Beattie on the defensive. 'There are still shortages, you know. Things aren't easy.'

'And they say some of your young people are still doing National Service: is that true?'

Beattie wasn't sure; she knew Marjory's brother had had to go just a couple of years back.

'Still, at least you've got a gorgeous young Queen. It's the turn of young people, isn't it? That's what I tell Gus. We've got ourselves a young president and he's a honey ... even if' – she lowered her voice as if mouthing an obscenity – 'even if he is a Catholic.'

They seemed to believe England was under some sort of siege – 'What with the Russians putting up that terrible Berlin Wall and you getting all those negroes from the West Indies. You must be really scared. But then America'll take no nonsense from them Ruskies.'

It was not a political landscape Beattie recognised. Perhaps she should take notice; she could ask Eddie. He saw all the newsreels at the Grande. The news on the television never made much of such things. Macmillan seemed like something out of novel by Trollope she'd once read.

Gus was still a successful car salesman back in Tampa, Florida, and keen to get a look at British cars. He'd negotiated with a garage to take out one of their own for a rental payment. Beattie had never heard of such a thing. A Riley it was, and Gus proposed 'giving it a spin around your quaint little villages and leaving you gals to your talk'. He was off down the path, his casual swinging gait reminding Beattie of the glamorous figure who had once so charmed Muriel, except that now the tight high buttocks had softened into something more flabby. Ah, well, that was what age did.

'That's him out of the way. Now we can let our hair down.'

Muriel bounced into the depths of her mother's sofa, a dog-eared album of photographs on her lap. 'I knew you'd be just dying to know so I've brought along the family record.'

Beattie, who had stayed still and silent while these breezy Americans cavorted round her, settled gently beside her friend. They had once been so close, working alongside each other making aircraft components. Beattie had started at the factory the moment the war began. Muriel had come along a year or two later prompted by posters that proclaimed 'Women of Britain: Come into the Factories'. It seemed the patriotic thing to do. The whole thing seemed a great adventure at the start, but then the factory got targeted and they'd had to go down into the cellars. Muriel had taken down her wind-up gramophone and Beattie brought along her record of Gracie Fields. The girls had sung and danced; it was almost like a party. They laughed defiantly at how serious it really was.

Beattie had been promoted supervisor of section B, and soon all the girls looked to her for leadership. Taller than most, with her long blonde page-boy hair and bright little rayon blouses, she stood out from the rest: she had a knack for spotting the latest look and took the lead in whatever meagre style was possible, what with coupons and scarcities. She assumed her natural place among them, friendly but authoritative when the chatter got too loud to hear the all-clear. It seemed to her, huddling on the lavishly floral cushions next to her old friend, to be a world away, another life. Muriel was resolved to bring it all back.

'Oh my God, you were such a live wire. Remember that time when you . . . '

Beattie looked up with alarm at the resurrection of a self remembered by someone else. How true, she wondered, were people's impressions made long ago? They were subject, surely, to the waywardness of the person remembering. Here was Muriel, beaming goodwill and glowing with the glamour that attached itself to American women, claiming Beattie as her inspiration, her confidante, her buddy.

' . . . oh, but you were such a madcap, always off with

different boys. I think you went for sailors in a big way ...
until Eddie, that is.'

A breath of hesitation lingered over his name, then the
tidal wave of anecdote swept on.

'... yes, remember when the roof was leaking and it
was raining real bad. You fetched up in an ARP helmet
and worked in that till management noticed. Mr Hobson
could only laugh.'

'But they mended the leak, didn't they?' Beattie felt she
must defend an age-old prank she could hardly remember.

'Then you washed out your stockings in the water
bucket ... remember that? It was so cold they wouldn't
dry. So you went out on a date with bare legs. We
thought you were a right hussy!'

Beattie laughed at that. The warmth of Muriel's recol-
lections was compulsive. It wasn't so bad after all, sitting
with a friend who had known her glory days. She had
long dismissed them as reckless, days of misbehaviour
excused because there was a war on. But ... oh, they were
quite something. She leant across the sepia photographs
to conceal a smile.

'Come on now, you remember, don't leave all the reminiscing to me.'

Beattie looked up into her friend's eyes. 'Was I really
like that? I'm sure you exaggerate ...' She gave a feeble
little laugh, as though hoping for a denial.

'You were hot stuff, baby! Back in those days ... we
were free spirits, weren't we? After all, who knew when
we might get a direct hit?'

Beattie wriggled on the ample feathers of the cushions,
searching her friend for reassurance of some kind.

'They were our secrets, weren't they? Not to be shared, I hope?' A number of dangerous images were surfacing in her memory. 'They were so young, those boys, called up and going off together, so cheerfully. And coming back changed.'

'Those that came back, that is. You were lucky with your Eddie ... good to get wounded early on. Back home with a medal and still looking like Gary Cooper.'

Muriel raised excited eyebrows and Beattie grinned. 'I was so proud: we all were, weren't we?'

'Not so what's-his-name. Derek. He wasn't. He got his nose well and truly pushed out, poor dope.'

'Derek! Get on with you ... he was never in the running. Never, absolutely not.'

'OK, OK, keep your hair on. But he was smitten, all right. Poor lad, glasses and flat feet, and landed with that office job in the army recruitment centre ... no hero him!'

'No hero, that's true. Though he did write lovely letters ... sometimes poetry even. Like in a novel.'

'You led him an awful dance, you really did. His mother told mine she thought you'd get engaged. I knew you never meant it.'

'Well, he was at least at home; the others were all off to the front.'

'You were a real tease, you know. I always thought so.'

'Not like you, then, straight to the kill? One glance of those Yankee uniforms and you were checking your seams.'

Laughter broke through and Beattie's hand was patting her friend with something like happiness.

*

Beattie returned late to number 26 in a mood of bewilderment. There was lightness about her tread that wasn't visible to the eye, but the pavements noticed. She hadn't thought about the war for years. She felt she had survived it, as the boys in the forces had, as the cities had, in spite of the damage. She was like that herself, a damaged survivor. It had been wise to bury those memories deep. After all there had been the flurry around Derek and his hangdog devotion that she wanted to forget; it wasn't appropriate now she was offering him comfort. She was thankful for Muriel's breezy gloss on what had gone on.

She explained to Eddie about her returned friend.

'You mean the one who was always chasing Yanks? So she snared one after all, did she?'

'Yes, like I snared you, I suppose.'

He was pleased to see her wearing the red dress.

'I'm planning to see her quite a bit while she's here. All the others married and moved away, some to Scotland, some to the south. I'm all she's got of our lot.'

Eddie smiled; she was becoming quite loquacious, and he would do what he could to keep her like that. 'Remembering stuff, were you? Living the great days of your youth? And where did I come in, eh? I suppose I did come in?'

'You know very well, Eddie. Don't go fishing.'

'You were wearing red then, the day I first spotted you ... in the saloon bar of the Grapes Hotel. But I don't think you noticed.'

'I noticed everything ... that was my trouble.'

There was a certain strain in the remark that warned

Eddie to lay off. Beattie had once been piercingly exact about things – not just the time of meeting or where they should go but the affairs of others, their prospects, their outcome . . . and acerbic too. 'Too critical, by a long chalk' someone had remarked of her. He let the subject rest and they went about their different lives.

A couple of weeks later the two women decided to take afternoon tea in the Palm Court café at the Grande. They had been shopping together but Muriel was rude about the shoddiness of English goods compared to American so they had cut the excursion short. As they waited for their order to be taken, Beattie realised that she wanted to talk. Something had happened since their last meeting that unsettled Beattie and revived in her the old longing for confidences. It was Martha's birthday. It had come and gone without a word and Beattie had taken it hard. Martha was now seventeen and Beattie's grasp on her daughter's life was weakening further. She clutched at what strands remained. Shopping with Muriel she had made a point of buying a headscarf for Martha for Christmas. She didn't want to talk to Muriel of that, though, it was too embarrassing. But there was something else that she felt she could confide.

After their tea arrived, she smoothed the white tablecloth and slowly said, 'You know you mentioned Derek and the thing he had about me all those years ago.'

Muriel looked up from pouring milk. She sensed there was a revelation on the way.

'I certainly do: he was besotted.'

'Well ... oh, you know ...' It wasn't proving easy to put into words. After all, they were words she didn't like using – sex, French letter, pregnancy scare – but there was Muriel strong and shiny in her identity and waiting to trade sympathy for secrets.

Beattie picked up her cup and spoke quietly over the top of it. 'It was when I'd only just met Eddie, of course. Derek had asked me to the town hall dance and turned out to be a good dancer.'

'It's true, isn't it, how unappealing blokes can be fantastic dancers ... there's no knowing till they're on the floor, then wham, they're away. It makes them sexy in spite of everything.'

Muriel had come to her rescue. Somehow she had understood what had happened and was making it easier.

'Yes, yes, it was like that with Derek. He took it all for more than just the mood of the moment. In no time he started talking about having fallen in love. Just like the movies.' Beattie raised an ironic eyebrow towards the cinema next door. 'It was rubbish, of course, just one of those unwise moments, you know how they happen ... wartime and everything.' Beattie looked up and saw Josie barrelling over to their table.

'I was wondering whether there's any news of Martha; I wouldn't ask but I know Eddie worries. Have you heard anything?'

Josie's clumsy intervention hit.

'Oh, well, no, we haven't heard. We weren't expecting ...' Such revelations threatened the idyll of the happy family.

She leant confidingly towards Muriel. 'Martha's a grown girl now and making her way in the world.'

But Josie pressed on. 'I know she went off the day after the concert; I'm afraid I played a small part in her going . . . '

Beattie was flummoxed by the news but manners flew to her rescue. 'Josie, this is my friend from the war years, Muriel Goodman; she married a GI. She and I were reminiscing. She worked in the same factory I did. Muriel, this is Josie, the pillar of the box office staff.' Josie nodded briskly and went on with her confession.

'I'm afraid Martha stayed with me that night, Beattie . . . '

Beattie's family was being revealed as quite a bit less than perfect. She stepped in to save the illusion. 'Josie's a good friend of the family, you see,' and turning with a searchlight glare on the box office manageress: 'She did, did she? Oh yes. Well, Josie, that was kind of you, typically kind of you.' And she turned resolutely back to the collapsing meringue on her plate.

Their third reunion meeting was after Christmas. It had been a drab festival with Eddie and Beattie unable to pretend that it didn't really matter that Martha wasn't with them, the gift of the scarf wrapped but ungiven. Martha had sent nothing but yet another short message, this time a Christmas card from the Lady Lever Gallery of Holman Hunt's *May Morning*. Martha's interest in art was passing them by. What they puzzled over was the tone of her messages. Warm yet increasingly distant as from a friend on a sea voyage.

Gus had hired a Rolls Royce, 'like the Queen has', or so

he hoped, and headed off to see distant relatives in Scotland. 'The Goodmans are remote descendants of the Clan Macintyre.'

The myths had accumulated throughout their stay. Beattie distrusted such an unlikely connection. But then she hadn't been entirely forthcoming herself.

Once more the friends settled into the feathered comfort of the chintz sofa. Martha surveyed a sequence of identical pictures of growing children against the same picket fence, Gus growing fatter almost within each photograph. Muriel only figured in the records as the escort of her husband at official occasions when she stood frozen in tight satin next to her bulging companion in starched shirts. He had obviously made something of himself. She wondered what her and Muriel's lives would have been like if they'd not become simply wives and mothers.

Unthinkable.

Muriel harped on about the same old wartime memories. Beattie was growing irritated by their lack of reality.

'You know, after Eddie came back, he was such a star! And then he goes and sweeps you off your feet. A match made in heaven.'

'Yes, I suppose it was, for a while.' Beattie smile was tired.

'Oh go on, tell me the honest truth!'

'Is there any other kind of truth then?'

'Well, there's the truth you have to live with, isn't there?' Muriel had suddenly turned solemn. 'You know how it is ... for you too?'

Beattie took a deep breath. 'How is it for me? Well,

Muriel ...' What she would say would be disloyal to herself and her dream. She suddenly felt bold. Muriel would soon be leaving England.

'You remember while Eddie and I were courting I was made superintendent of the entire floor at Beesley's. I had to go to management meetings, things like that. There was even that time I challenged them about the pay. Remember that? The case for getting a bit more, more like what the men got.'

'Yes, game girl! It was terrific. Sad it didn't work.'

'No, it didn't work.' Beattie was not to be deprived of her triumph. 'But the girls were pleased that I tried. So they worked well for me. Our output broke records for the factory. Beesley's got a commendation.'

'Sure did – it was like you won the war for us, babe!'

Idiotic, wasn't it, she thought, two women on a sofa carried away by their own boasting. But it was what reunions were about. Rosy memories. Until Beattie wanted to tell the truth.

'The fact is, I'd never been happier. I loved working: I loved the girls, the jokes, even the work itself, getting the machinery doing precisely what it's meant to.'

She paused, finding herself becoming emotional, and blew her nose hard.

'I wanted to go on. They said they valued me. But then as the end of the war was in sight and the men expected back, they gave me my cards. Just turfed me out. It really hurt. They said my husband had a family wage, and the returning soldiers would want their jobs back. Well, I couldn't argue with that, could I? I felt my life was over.'

Muriel became knowingly tactful: 'But you did have Martha and everything turned out all right, eh?'

'Well, no, it didn't. It hasn't. You see, she's growing up in a different world, Muriel. It's all changed. She can train as a typist and expect a job that's hers by right. No man wants to be a typist. The fact is ... I think ... I reckon ... it's that ... I'm jealous of her, Muriel.'

Her voice rose and cracked: huge gulps of air threatened an outbreak of tears.

'Sometimes I can't bear her, and what her life is like. And it's even worse ... Eddie can see what's happened. He knows I'm unhappy but he does nothing. He prefers her to me. Well, who wouldn't? I'm a drag most of the time. But he loves her more; he lets her have a life of her own. Why didn't he let me have a life of my own? All I do is dust the bloody house, cook the sodding meals. I keep house, while he keeps me. It was a lousy bargain. I am jealous of my own daughter, Muriel. I can't bring myself to speak about it ... except' – the threat of tears was exhausting her – 'except to you. And that's probably only because you're going back to America.' Beattie managed a weak grin at this point, then stiffened again. 'But ... at least I've said it. Yes, I've said it.'

The effect left her winded and she sank back screwing a now tattered handkerchief into a ball.

'Whoa! Whoa! Take it easy, girl.'

Muriel had looked increasingly alarmed. This wasn't the sort of confidence she wanted to share. She had in mind to compare marriages and possibly to confide about the mistress Gus kept in a downtown rooming house. This outbreak was of an altogether different order. After all, she had managed Gus's infidelity very well. She had visited the startled woman unannounced and declared she could have Gus in her bed but she, Muriel, would be keeping him in her home. It proved a satisfactory arrangement; she was relieved of his cursory love-making, he knew nothing of the arrangement, she remained in control. But Beattie was a mess ... not in control at all. Poor feeble woman to have given up so easily and so long ago. She felt a pang of dislike for her. Why had the Brits become so soft?

Chapter 24

Gus seemed to be road-testing every car he could find on the winding lanes of the English countryside.

'It's such a pocket handkerchief of a country,' he'd declared. 'I can be across a county in little more than an hour ... and there's nowhere I can get a clear run of speed.'

Beattie let the comment lie: these Americans were full of criticisms. She felt it wasn't hospitable to remind them how long they took to come to our help during the war. And look what they were doing now with all this nuclear business. Besides, although Britain had opened its first motorway recently, Beattie didn't know exactly where it was and felt recommending it to someone from the wide-open spaces would be to invite further contempt. And whatever Gus thought of middle-aged women confiding with each other about their past lives, he put up with it.

And it was doing Beattie good.

'Muriel says you once reminded her of Gary Cooper.' Beattie and Eddie sat eating cheese and biscuits after *Coronation Street*.

'What d'you mean, "once"?'

Beattie actually giggled and this time just for him. It occurred to Eddie to make the most of the thaw.

'Look, Beattie, it's your birthday coming up. We'd missed out celebrating your fortieth last year—'

'I should hope so! Who'd want to celebrate being forty!'

He had not in fact forgotten but the gift of a small bowl had not been significant.

'Well, we could catch up a little late ... it wouldn't matter. Look, how would you like to make a weekend of it? Somewhere by the sea?'

Beattie didn't respond.

'I thought you might like the idea ...' His voice dwindled with disappointment. Better not to try. But a shred of hope spurred him on. 'I know I would ... I really would.'

Beattie moved to collect up the plates, brushing the crumbs together in the top one.

He wouldn't give up. 'I'd really like it: you could wear your red dress at the hotel!'

'Who mentioned a hotel?'

Llandudno in the early months of the new year was an empty and bleak place. The sea was grey and sullen, heavy clouds scudded across from Snowdonia dropping any rain left from its mountain downpours on the few who battled with straining umbrellas against the blustery winds. The hotel – a bow-windowed Victorian villa on the front – was home to a number of retired ladies, former teachers it appeared from their conversation. Beattie was respectful of their status, and nodded to them as they arrived for breakfast. It would be her birthday on the Saturday but she had little sense of anticipation. Memories of childhood birthdays with numbers on the cards and ribbons round coloured paper and a party dress with a big wide sash – all made her smile. Nothing matched up to it. But Eddie was making an effort, she'd give him that. He'd booked the hotel, without consulting her, and they'd come first class in the train. She was bemused by whatever he was up to. And she had gone along with it.

The red dress wrapped in tissue paper was taken from her suitcase and hung in the mothball-scented wardrobe. The present was in a long flat box. At six o'clock he disclosed that he'd booked a table for dinner at one of the resort's best hotels. She changed into the red dress. He held out the gift. She turned and he suddenly looked a bit like Gary Cooper. She caught a look that reminded her how they'd once teased him so much.

'It's like something in the films, this is . . . '

'Well, open it.'

Within was tissue paper. She folded it back, careful not to tear it: she'd like to keep the tissue and the box.

A pair of gloves.

'How d'you know the size?'

'Put them on and see . . . '

The gloves were black suede, and long. They would

reach to her elbow. How was she to wear such things?
'Oh, but they're . . . '

He was smiling and challenging her.

'They're very glamorous . . . but how . . . ' She fumbled
with the long sleeves of the red dress. 'How can I wear
them? They're film-star gloves. Meant for evenings. I
can't get them on with this dress.' This was a big mistake,
the colour, the style. She felt his effort was come to
nought.

'Then take it off.'

'What?'

'Take off the dress. Take it off and put the gloves on.'

Was he mad? 'Well, I'm not sure . . . '

'Come on, Beattie . . . you look lovely.'

He sat back on the bed waiting for her to move. She
waited.

'You'll have to help with the zip.'

The red dress slid from her shoulders. She was wearing a white satin slip, shaped to the contours of her
breasts and reaching to her knee. She put on the gloves.

'Well? . . . Will I do?'

She felt silly in a satin slip with long black gloves. But
she looked at Eddie, who clearly didn't feel she looked
silly at all. It is what men like, she thought. Who am I to
argue?

'That's exactly what I had in mind.'

He got up from the bed, reached his hand to her face and
stroked the fine lines round her mouth. 'Happy Birthday.'

*

The next morning they hovered on the promenade.
They ate fish and chips in a cheery café with blue-and-

white-checked tablecloths. The golden hunks of batter were so fresh from the boiling oil that Beattie burned her lip and couldn't drink the hot tea. But she didn't complain. It was even something of an adventure.

Chapter 25

'Last six months! Enjoy it while it lasts: summer closing ahead!'

Martha stood in astonishment and gazed at the make-shift banner hoisted over the cracked frontage of the Grande. Had it really come to this? The place looked tired and out-of-date ... just another of the buildings that planners felt had had their day. She knew there was a brittle new spirit in the air, of young men with slide rules and architectural plans who were keen to gut old jaded city centres and build new. They were getting busy in Liverpool. Surely the Grande wouldn't fall victim to them. It was too beautiful to lose, even though that beauty was old-fashioned. Besides it was a part of her life. Or had been.

There was no queue to see Melina Mercouri in *Never on Sunday*, so she could rush directly up to Josie presiding in her tight little cubicle.

'Martha ... oh dear girl! Oh, does Eddie know you're back?'

Josie left the kiosk and threw her arms around Martha, mewling with excitement and concern. 'Look at you! Your hair, and such a short skirt, Martha!'

Martha couldn't think of anything but the beloved Grande.

'Josie, what's happening? What does the banner mean?'

'Oh, I'll tell you, I'll tell you. But does your father know you're here?'

'No, no, I came back on a whim. I suddenly needed to.'

'Look, look here. You need to be careful. There's lots you need to know. Eddie's off for a few days; bit of a –' she wrinkled her nose – 'domestic crisis, I think. You can go up and see Bert, if you like.'

'But the Grande, Josie? What's happened? Is it really closing?'

Josie sighed and pulled her mouth taut into an expression of misery and disapproval.

'They've decided to sell. Takings didn't pick up enough – I know that for a fact – and apparently the bingo sharks offered more and more money. Eventually Mr Vernon couldn't resist. I've always thought that Mrs Vernon was a greedy so-and-so. To my mind she was behind it, but then no one's asking me. By July we'll all be looking for jobs.' Josie was falling into her routine huff of disgust and displeasure.

'Didn't the pop concerts help? I thought they were going to make a difference.'

'Oh, they did that all right. Daisy and Sid practically went on strike. Those young girls have no respect, you know. The state they left the place, you wouldn't believe. Young Mr Colin was very shocked. The staff weren't keen for any more. Ethel and Florrie said they'd rather not be on duty. So he gave up. Simply gave up. The fight went out of him ... not that there'd been much in the first place, sad little mummy's boy that he is.'

'How long have you known all this?'

'We were told a couple of weeks ago, just before the St Valentine's day programme. Your dad's distraught.'

Josie lowered her head and, looking up through her eyebrows with a frown of reproach that would do credit to a silent movie, added in slow and dramatic tones: 'As though he didn't have enough to upset him already.'

The display of melodrama irritated Martha. 'Yes, yes, all right. I know, I know. I'm going for a coffee to think things over.'

Aldo greeted her with a grin of recognition.

'Hi there, bellissima ... and where's Alexandro?'

Martha grinned briefly, shrugged and sat down without saying a word. Other coffee-bar regulars saw a slender girl of amiable but serious countenance, confident but subdued, seeking privacy to be with her own thoughts. She was clearly content to be alone, and that was unusual in a girl, they thought. Her gaze settled easily for long moments on nowhere in particular.

Martha noticed differences in the Café Bocca: it seemed more choked with chairs than she remembered, the little coffee tables seemed tawdry with use and the rubber plants had gathered dust on their big fleshy leaves. But the Gaggia machine still shone and hissed with a welcoming tone and the frost outside steamed up the windows as it always had. She smiled to herself and stirred thoughtfully at a cappuccino.

She'd had to come back. The nightmares had continued, not every night and not ever quite the same. But her mother was there, always screaming and coming after her. Sometimes her father was present, but she couldn't hold his image long enough to see what he was up to. She would wake sweating, then dash her head back on the pillow seeking to sleep again in the hope he might still be there and speak to her. He never did. It was impossible. The dreams left her bereft. She told Duncan about them, as much as she could. He stroked her face and listened. He could sense the turmoil she was going through.

But to Martha the nightmares were a strange contradiction to her days. For as months passed she more and more enjoyed waking to the prospect of talk and friendship and the zany crackpot times she had with Fee, making fantastical clothes and selling them to a growing band of enthusiasts. At Sibling Rivalry – the weird name Duncan and Cassie had now given their home – she felt secure. But one worry lurked always at the back of her mind. Pete spoke of it all the time, terrifying them with talk of nuclear destruction.

He and his friends spoke in terms of megatons of bombs, reporting to each other on the latest American tests, the French tests, and Russians too. Things were escalating at an alarming rate and Britain was going along with the frantic energy of the arms race. Could such momentum be thwarted? That was what they asked.

Martha listened to all they had to say, weighing up the unimaginable horror, seeking out pictures of what had happened in Hiroshima. A vast underground fear had become part of her life.

So the Grande was going to close. What must that mean to her father ... to all the workers at the Grande, losing not only the jobs but the comfort of their working family? Oh, they'd all known about bingo and the rise of television, but they expected, as all their friends and neighbours did, that once you'd found a good job, you had it for life. They would all be shaken by the news. She had planned to surprise her father and call on him in the projection box. Then she would decide whether or not to go home. But now? She would have to work things out for herself. Now that she was back, what was odd was how much she wanted to be at home, where all the misery had congealed around her. Being away in her light and airy room with its tall ceiling had made her forgiving of the early sadness. And yet she was still haunted by it.

She took the bus to 26 Galton Road. The house was dark. This was odd. Martha was still the child who expected someone would always be there waiting to make her welcome. In recent years, of course, her mother's presence hadn't had the qualities usually associated with welcome. But her presence itself did the job. Now the doors were locked; no light glimmered through the curtains already drawn against the night-time. And she had no keys with her. She thought of seeking refuge along the road with Marjory's family but that would require the explaining of matters that were none of their business. She strolled down the side alley and into the garden, still wintered over with a late frost and the frayed strands of last year's flowers.

A stray memory drifted up from the depths. When she was a child, her mother had explained there was a back-door key always lodged in a shelf above the door in the garden shed. Just a precaution, you understand, in case of emergencies. There had been no emergencies – until now. But would she find the key placed there so long ago? She put down her bag, opened the shed door and reached into the cobwebby dark. And there it was, rusted with time and neglect. She felt like a burglar.

The house was as ordered as ever. And silent. Even when her mother's affliction was at its worst, there had always been sounds: the rattle of pans, the squelch of cooking, the hiss of the iron, of needles knitting, the fall of coals in the fire, the tick of several clocks. Now only the clocks were still active. The place was like a museum, one of those places recreated to show how life had been in the past, but without life going on. Quite right, too. She surveyed the knick-knacks as though they were museum exhibits, a cut-glass vase set without flowers on the low windowsill, a coarse piece of pottery that Eddie had won at Blackpool fairground, a tray on the top of the sideboard with a wooden fruit bowl on it. But without fruit. She lit a cigarette and stood in the kitchen, smoking, looking in at her former life.

In the kitchen a surprise – a brand new fridge. They had never had one before. Inside a stack of butter, some rashers of bacon, some drooping vegetables and a row of tinned soups. Her mother clearly hadn't got the hang of it. She made a cup of tea and continued to poke around, looking for clues. Both her parents' heavy coats were missing from the hallstand. Her father's knitted scarf had gone, but his cycling clips and gauntlets were still there. Her mother left fewer traces. The shopping basket was in its place in the kitchen, but there was no fire lit in the living room hearth. The house was chill and had an air of incipient damp that suggested no fire had warmed its walls for some time.

On the wooden trolley that stood in its place behind the living room door, Martha noticed something not usually there. In a house where the correct placing of all objects was a serious undertaking, this was a surprise. A delight, too, for there lay a cache of dressmaking patterns: Butterick, Simplicity, McCall's ... names she knew from Fee, who affected to despise them. The outline sketches on the cover reminded Martha at once of the surprising red dress of the Johnsons' party, and the unexpected blue suit of Derek's leaving concert. Ah Derek! Where was he in all this? Was his mysterious presence on that strange night in some way connected with the house being so unexpectedly empty? Josie had hinted at something.

A snatch of professional interest surfaced for a moment as she examined the dress patterns more closely, for seams and tucks and details on cuff and collar, then tipped one of them into her bag to take back as a trophy for Fee.

She went upstairs. She looked into her own room first and was at once comforted by the sight of her old stuff: the pyjama case shaped like a rabbit with a zip down its back, a number of bottles of sticky pink fluid she once believed would make her beautiful. She stooped to look in the dressing table mirror: no, she was no beauty, but the high forehead, high cheekbones and full bright red mouth gave her plenty of style. She tweaked her hair as all women tweak in front of a mirror ... half pride, half correction. She gave a brief sashay, admiring something grown and confident she saw there.

At the threshold of her parents' room she hesitated. Was this too intimate? She remembered the Johnsons' party and how Enid had bridled at the idea of crashing their front bedroom. But then there were things Martha needed to know. The wardrobe doors released a sigh of stale scent. Her mother's few clothes were still in place. The sumptuous wool of the blue suit was there, beside it an empty satin-padded hanger, but no red dress. As far as she could see, her mother's routine tweed suit was also missing and a couple of drab silk blouses bought to match. She riffled through the drawers of the dressing table. A few peach-coloured knickers and satin bras lay folded and ordered. She swished them aside and in so doing found the parcel, what she suddenly knew had been the secret motive for her exploration. A small bundle of dog-eared envelopes held together by an elastic band. But the band had shrivelled and as she touched it, it snapped under her fingers. No, she hadn't meant to pry, or she thought she hadn't. It was enough to have found them at all. But here they lay in her hands, splayed and inviting. She could hear her heart beating at the intrusion, the transgression. But whose transgression, after all? Was her mother's concealment of letters worse than her own invasion of someone's private life? She bunched them hastily together and popped them in her bag next to the paper pattern.

She caught the next train to Liverpool, taking the shed key with her. The crude upholstery of the compartment seat scratched at her legs. She wriggled uneasily and thought of tucking her feet up on the seat beside her, but the daunting stare of a drab and serious woman opposite put her off. She fidgeted, plucking at her hair, moving her bag around, glimpsing rows of back yards through the grime-smeared window. With nothing to occupy her, she grew more restless.

She opened her bag and took out her mother's dress pattern. The outline drawing on the cover displayed an elegant older woman with tiny waist and long legs in glamorous shoes. Martha sneered at the datedness of it. Was this how her mother wanted to be seen? Perhaps this had been the point of her transformed appearances at the party and at the concert. Martha shrugged at the idea: such a puny ambition, and yet so successful. She was a wife and mother after all and supposed to be past such things. She rummaged around further into the bag. Ah, the letters. She certainly couldn't open them up in public, in the confines of the railway compartment and under the scrutiny of the woman opposite. She realised she didn't even want to very much. The act of taking them had been a sort of revenge, a way of hurting her mother. Whatever secrets they held would be mouldy and old, no longer of any significance. Like most letters in fact. And now she had them in her possession, her triumph in taking them was already accomplished. Maybe she would read them later, alone and in her tall room.

Chapter 26

Martha arrived back at Sibling Rivalry in a grey cloud of misery. Nothing had been sorted out and her spirits were low. Jake was readying himself to go with Monica to a club down in the Dingle. He was preening himself in some green velvet trousers devised by Fee. Monica, who was rehearsing a part in Osborne's latest play *The Entertainer*, was trying to identify with her character. So all day long she wore a drab tweed skirt and old-fashioned twinset and insisted on keeping it for their outing. Jake tweaked the long rope of pigtail that hung to her waist and they giggled together. To be silent and gloomy amid such exuberance was doubly painful.

In the days that followed, Duncan watched Martha with concern. She would move slowly into the collapsing armchair, avoiding eye contact with any of them. Once she unfolded the paper dress pattern and pretended to be preoccupied with it. She merely nodded when he set a cup of tea at her elbow, and raised only a faint voice as the others crashed out of the house towards their various playgrounds.

Duncan sat on the old sofa waiting for her to speak. He remained waiting and caring. Later he cooked and provided food which Martha scarcely touched; shreds of old manners told her she should not reject it, but her appetite had fled. She smiled weakly.

'I'm sorry about this.'

It was Duncan's next remark that struck home.

'You're behaving like your mother: that's if what you told me about her is true. You're living in silence, Martha!'

She took the remark without responding. But when the dishes were put away, she picked up her bag and went to her room. Its tall empty space cleared her head. There was nothing here to fret her spirit. She dumped herself on the bed and buried her head in her hands. She couldn't make sense of what was happening. She had gone home on a whim expecting all sorts of things – welcome, reconciliation, explanation – and found no trace of any. The welcomes – from Aldo and from Josie – were warming but superficial. With a pang of regret she wished she had left her address or even her phone number at number 26. Yet that carried risk. How could she know what strange story was unfolding there? What had Josie meant?

She stood to look at herself before the tall unframed shard of mirror propped against the bedroom wall. Different, yes, she was changing, but not different enough. Duncan had seen her mother in her behaviour. His remark had appalled her. She always hoped to root out all the miseries of her home life and yet she stood accused of perpetuating them by someone whom she had come to trust. It was worth thinking about.

That night in her high room, she pulled out the letters and opened them. She had anticipated some mystery, some challenge lying in wait. She felt a frisson of guilt and of justification in cheating on her mother. But the excitement fell to ashes as she read. Here were the stale worn sentiments of long-dead passions. She opened touching wartime letters from her father speaking haltingly of his love. Then she came to a whole set of urgent pleadings to Beattie in another hand. Derek. Their tone implied a desperate bid to have his love requited in the face of what must have been persistent refusal ... her own mother's refusal. He had wooed and he had pleaded. But he had lost. Was there a touch of bravado in her mother's keeping them? Evidence of having been loved. Of having been young. Her mother's lost life.

'Someone's been in.'

Beattie's existence was so finely tuned to her home that she sensed at once any falling away from the norm.

'I left the doors closed, and look now.'

There was nothing to see.

'Are you sure?'

'When do I not leave the doors closed?'

Even to her own ears it sounded a little obsessive. 'I always do. It keeps the heat in. You say so yourself.'

Eddie calculated it must be some ten years ago when they were first trying to afford their new home that he had casually remarked on the cost of coal. He knew better than to contradict.

'Who could have been here ... and why?'

They both knew the answer.

'Why didn't she leave any note ... not a single word? It wouldn't have taken much.'

'I guess she has her own reasons.'

Eddie was as bewildered as Beattie but the impulse to defend Martha was strong. They went on a tour of inspection looking for traces. They found an ashtray by the kitchen sink. The stub of a cigarette had a gash of bright red lipstick.

Beattie clicked her tongue. 'It would have been good to see her.'

Eddie's voice was low and disappointed. 'Wouldn't it?' Then, dangerously: 'Our little girl, huh?'

Beattie caught his eye and was suddenly close to tears. 'I'll look upstairs.'

Eddie slumped in an armchair imagining Martha coming back to a cold house, waiting around perhaps, smoking that glamorous cigarette ... a girl in a black and white film. Beattie returned with a slightly bemused frown.

'Nothing remarkable ... she's taken things from her own dressing table. I haven't noticed anything else ... Oh, and look!'

The frown resolved itself into a sort of relieved shrug.

'She's taken my dress pattern. Why would she want that, d'you think? It's useless without a sewing machine, and she hasn't one of those.'

'As far as we know,' said Eddie.

And both of them had realised they knew nothing.

Chapter 27

Dear Muriel,

Thank you for your letter. I am so pleased you enjoyed your visit and returned home to find Natasha and Benedict as well as could be expected. I think it is the case these days that young people left unsupervised will set about having a good time. It was lucky that your mother-in-law had moved in, otherwise the damage could have been much greater. I know from my own experience how difficult it is when young people get a mind of their own. All I can say is it wasn't that way in our day, was it? We did as we were told until we were old enough to earn our own money. Once we could do that, of course, we were considered grown-up.

I still miss not having any money of my own today. If I can be personal for a moment, you were very sympathetic, Muriel, when I got so upset that day in your mother's home. I really owe you an apology for making such a fool of myself. Having said that, of course, I don't regret the things I said about my life. I have been unhappy in recent years. It's almost as though a little part of those hopes have lived on, despite the evidence to the contrary. Sometimes I even have a sense of what that hope felt like and, needless to say, it just plunges me into ever deeper despair. But here's me getting all confessional again, when what you need is something to cheer you along.

I am sure it must be very lonely now that Gus is away for longer and longer on his sales trips. I hope this means the car sales franchise is proving profitable, and that he is winning customers from his competitors. It must get more difficult as you get older, and really, the way these young salesmen go about things, so pushy! Won't take no for an answer, will they? And that's not what customers want. Having met him, I am sure Gus remains a gentleman in all things. Eddie's a man without ambition and that seems odd when you remember what a live spark he was in the war years. I think the effort of winning took the wind out of all our sails.

You will see how I am rambling on, Muriel, just as if I was talking to you. I blame this new ballpoint pen!

Later:

Here I go again. This letter is becoming like a diary. We have had big developments here in Staveley: the rumours started before Christmas. The Grande is closing and it means that Eddie will have to find a new job. There's plenty of work to be had so he won't find it too difficult. But it matters so much to him. He loves his films and he once told me the Grande was like his real family. Not very flattering to me, but he is devoted to that place. He was plunged into gloom for quite a while. But he's had to buck his ideas up. The closing signs have gone up already: it will close in July. The fact is he's very lucky because Granada television is in the area. Eddie had applied for a job there as a film projectionist: it's almost the same as he was doing at the Grande but with different equipment. He goes along for an interview next week. He says it won't be anything like the Grande, but at least it's work. That's as much as many of us would like for ourselves, isn't it? There I go, my old gripe again. You must forgive me. This letter-writing has loosened my tongue and I feel just as though I am talking to you. Until the next time, then. Cheerio.

Beattie hesitated over how to end. Her writing had skidded so easily over the sheets of flimsy blue airmail paper, she was brought up short by the intimacy of signing off. She was embarrassed to have been writing so freely, and preferred not to read back what she had written. She steeled herself to extend the spontaneity still further. Then went ahead:

All my love,
Beattie.

*

She sat back from the frail heap of pages and felt good about what she had done. There were too many ways she might be misunderstood or be accused of being contradictory or even mean-spirited if she spoke like this. But Muriel was an ocean away and living in a world she thought of as perpetually sunlit and smiling. She recalled the style and wealth of the GIs when they were over here during the war. Admittedly Gus had run a bit to seed but he still exuded a spirit of breezy goodwill that she imagined bathed all Americans in an uncomplicated glow of achievement. 'Can-do' had been Muriel's phrase. Beattie had only ever once felt that applied to her.

The arrival of Muriel in her life began to feel like a lifting of the siege, the cavalry coming over the hill to clear out the old enemy and make the future different.

Eddie's key turned in the door and she lifted her head. Swiftly, with the old impulse, she hustled the pages under the blotter a moment too slowly to avoid his noticing. For Eddie it was no surprise. He accepted it as typical of her secrets.

'I'll get your tea ... I'm running late, I'm afraid.'

As she filled the clattering saucepans from the cold tap, she felt the warm feelings of her new friendship with Muriel drain away.

Chapter 28

The final days of the Grande came with few to mark its passing. It was Easter 1962 and the cinema-going crowds were thinner and indifferent. As for the staff, 'You're all demob happy,' Josie declared as sales slumped and nobody cared. Most of the staff were old enough to recall where the phrase 'demob happy' came from and how much those in the forces had looked forward to handing in their uniforms and getting back to civilian life as the different services disbanded – too slowly, it was thought, in the years after the war.

Of them all, Eddie was the most saddened. He stopped at the front and ran his hand over the cracked tiles he had noticed a year ago. At the time he wanted them repaired but no one had bothered and now it seemed no one would. The Grande had moved from being a precious temple of pleasure to becoming even in their eyes a shabby, run-down, out-of-date place that no one cared for. It would pass into the callous hands of money-making philistines who would savage its decor and transform it into the vulgar appeal of a silly game for lonely people. Bingo. What a terrible fate.

Only Ethel confessed to Florrie that she had once played and quite liked it. She was reprimanded, as though she had spoken slightingly of the royal family.

'I'd advise you not to let anyone else hear you say such a thing!'

Josie refused to be drawn into the general condemnation. No one noticed that the usually voluble box office manageress was saying nothing. Nor had anyone seen her slip into the Bingo Hall over Wythenshawe way and see for herself what fate lay in store. A week later she had written to ask whether she could train as a caller. Here was a job that offered scope for her sense of the dramatic. Josie had always embraced the new; this would be at one with her taste for quiche and Scandinavian furniture. None the less she felt furtive about her move. She knew the others would see it as a betrayal. They had worshipped at a glorious shrine and she was leaving it for an upstart cult. But there was the thrill of conversion, too; she felt daring and renewed. She smiled as she hugged her secret to herself.

As the company of employees fell apart, someone had to be to blame. Young Mr Colin was a ready victim. He cringed each time he toured the building, nodding in vague approval at everyone he passed. They seized on his distress to make it worse, ignoring him, never looking him in the eye, pushing past his stooping presence and greeting each other with loud cries of sympathy. He felt worse every day. Finally his wife found him in the garage crying as he sat in the Ford Zephyr afraid to go to work. 'Don't make me go!' he had pleaded. She phoned his father, who came round to sort him out. 'You're not the man I thought you were' – was her remark of surprised hurt that dealt the final blow. Mr Colin left home on the next train out of Staveley. He had an aunt who kept a boarding house in Rhyl.

Eddie struggled to deal with the change. He would no longer be close to the films he loved: there would be no greeting with delight the arrival of the latest cans from the distributor, the physical excitement of loading the reels and the emotional thrill of watching the stories unfold. He armed himself against the loss by involving himself ever closer in the films themselves. He would place himself on the tall stool beside the projector and give them his full eye-watering attention. He rode the roller-coaster of emotions, whether it was the exotic heat and sex of Monroe and Gable in *The Misfits* or the parochial entanglements of young British stars in *A Kind of Loving*. The latter woke in him fears of the kind of life Martha might be living and stirred up regrets he was trying to forget. He preferred the glossy conflicts of *West Side Story* or the tensions of *Cape Fear*, where he could live the exaggerated lives of others and feel emboldened by them. He would turn back from the screen seeing his own life as a tale of hopes and fears, ups and downs, especially the dramatic tensions around the two women in his life. And why not? If he was Gary Cooper, perhaps Martha could be conjured as Lee Remick and Beattie ... he had once fancied Beattie had the looks of Ingrid

Bergman. Imagining his life as some kind of film plot helped him like it more. He saw himself moving between scenes and crises: the disappearance of his daughter, his wife's fascination for another man, the sudden loss of his job.

But time was running out and as Eddie clung more earnestly than ever to his seat by the projector, Bert had begun to tidy up the accumulated bric-a-brac that had piled up over the years: old football pools, an unravelled pullover, empty tins of Fisherman's Friends, a glutinous lump of humbugs stuck in the corner of a white paper bag turned grey with age. Eddie kept his eye on the screen, even the advertising slides for the new Indian restaurant and the garage down the road. Even the Pathé newsreels. The Pathé style had changed little since the war and the famously triumphant voice that had hailed D day and VE night still boomed from the speakers. Audiences smiled indulgently at how dated it all seemed, especially compared to the brisk immediacy of television, which was so much quicker with the headlines. The younger audiences laughed out loud at the gung-ho tone and the threatening or jovial mood music.

It was while watching towards the end of April that Eddie was stunned by what he saw. It was over in seconds and gone before he could react. But it was certainly Martha.

Martha was on the pavement nearest to Pathé's cameraman: she was smiling towards him, and gave a friendly toss of the placard she was carrying. It said 'Ban the Bomb'. Then the moment had passed and she was gone. Eddie wished he could run the film back to see her again, but the story had moved on to some trouble with the police later. Pathé was doing a round-up of recent CND protests.

'Bert, it was her. My Martha. She's in London on the CND march. I've found her.'

'CND? What the hell she bothering with that for?'

Eddie hadn't considered. 'Well, obviously she wants to save us from a nuclear war ...' He made up his mind quickly and decided to back her. 'And I, for one, am with her. She's standing up for all of us, don't you see that, Bert? Doing something she believes in. But I'm proud of what she's doing. I'm staying to see it round in the second house.'

'Proud? More than many a parent would be. They mess with the police, these kids – some of them lie down in the street. I hope she's not planning to do that.'

Eddie was swung from euphoria to worry. Martha might push things too far ... she could end up being thrown into the back of a police van. He'd seen that on newsreels the previous year. Still, this nuclear stuff was getting urgent, he was dimly aware of that. Fear of another war like the last one made him blank out the prospect, but that was becoming harder. Meanwhile he had seen Martha, looking so bright and eager.

He was full of smiles, conveying the news to Josie.

'She's been down in London ... That's what she's doing with her life. She's gone all political, trying to stop World War Three!' His relief was investing Martha's appearance with the sense of a diplomatic mission.

'I wonder if that was what she came to tell us.'

Chapter 29

'I have seen her! I know what she's up to!' Eddie hadn't waited to get home but was phoning from the phone box outside the Grande.

'Oh, oh, that's wonderful! Or is it, Eddie?' There was caution in her voice. 'Where is she exactly? Is she all right?'

'She was on an Aldermaston march: I saw her on the newsreel.'

'But that was days ago. Where is she now?'

The voice had a certain spirit in it. Eddie warmed to the sound. But the warmth and this new Beattie weren't for him.

Beattie's moods were being dispelled by her correspondence with Muriel. Muriel's boisterous letters arriving in a steady stream from America somehow prompted Beattie to identify with the figure of herself Muriel painted. She cleared a regular space at the table where the dress pattern had gone missing. There she placed an old stationery case, a long-ago Christmas present never used and stowed away gathering dust. Now it was opened almost daily. Beattie drew back the zip on the three sides of the dark red leather and readied herself to encounter the new creature she was creating. As she took up her Bic pen and smoothed out the flimsy airmail sheets there was an excitement and expectation about what she was doing. It was as though a river had been blocked by silt and boulders and now the insistence of the water was forcing a way through. At first the trickle had been intermittent but as something in herself was released her fluency increased. After writing for half an hour, she sat back with a proper sense of achievement.

This sense she had of becoming a new person also owed something to her strange birthday evening with Eddie. That had been nice but it hadn't changed much. They were still awkward with each other. So much had gone wrong between them and over so many years. She thought of the cheery figure of Eddie conjured up by Muriel's letters. But Beattie doubted whether such an Eddie had ever existed. And besides, it was the awkward, ambiguous Eddie she had to deal with. Martha was gone and he was about to lose his job. She doubted whether much of their old love could be salvaged from the wreckage.

On the telephone she'd rung off being brisk.

'But, Eddie, that's over and done with. She'll be back to wherever she is living. In Liverpool according to the postcards.'

He felt suddenly deflated. Film on the screen of the Grande had a greater reality for him than the postcards that arrived intermittently at Galton Road.

'Well, I know. I know that!' He used his irritation to cover his error. 'But at least we know she's happy ... well, she seemed happy enough. And we know the kind of people she's with. They're trying to stop the next world war, aren't they?'

Beattie was blank. She wasn't aware that another world war was in prospect. 'We can talk about it when you get home.'

Eddie went back to the showing of *The Man Who Shot Liberty Valance* with a certain relief.

Beattie was thinking about Derek. There was something so straightforward and up front about him. No subtlety. His way had always been to engulf her with flattery, and needful as she was, that satisfied some superficial vanity in her. She liked to be thought well of, she liked to be adored. It had always been so. She was no good with disappointment. She mused that possibly she was as much in thrall to illusion as Eddie. Once her good opinion of herself was dashed she never quite recovered.

Mr Hobson had called her into the little office rigged up of prefabricated partitions that occupied a corner of the machine floor. He had indicated that she should sit in the upright wooden chair opposite him. She took care how she sat for the wood was splintered and she didn't want to snag her stockings. She settled comfortably, believing she was in for some sort of commendation, possibly even a rise, or in her highest hopes the prospect of actual promotion. She was buoyant with the good-will of the place. The blow fell like a hit across her head. Through a mist of shock she heard Mr Hobson mumbling on about the boys soon coming back, already arriving, jobs to come home to, war effort a triumph, brave little Beattie. She had stumbled to her feet and out through the door into the embracing noise from the throbbing machines. Leaning against the outside of the office wall, she gazed around without seeing. She hugged her arms around her for comfort, coming to a realisation of the many things she had not until then acknowledged.

She knew suddenly that the world did not share the picture she had of herself. Clearly they did not. She was able enough and they would be nice to her when it suited them. But that was a sleight of hand that had led her astray. She had believed she was more than that and making her way in the world. Her expectations were blown sky high. It made her wary, and watchful, cautious about putting her vulnerabilities on show. She took her wariness home with her but kept it in reserve for when it might be needed.

The birth of her daughter had come as another shock. No one had warned her how awful it would be, how raw and humiliating. Her body railed at the indignity, fought against the massive wrenching of her muscles, the implacable force that was generated from inside her and over which she had no control.

'Just give in to it, dearie, that'll be best!' The Irish midwife had urged. Then when Beattie gave out an animal cry of pain, she had turned in disbelief. 'Oh, I don't think there's any need for that, dearie: think what the saints went through and count yourself lucky.'

When eventually the scrap of life that was Martha was placed in her arms, already prettified, washed and cradled in shawls, she felt a deep resentment at the cause of so much agony. Their opening encounter would colour her days and those of her daughter.

After Derek was dismissed as organist, she had heard from Eddie that he'd been drinking heavily. She could sense, even at a distance, his all-consuming misery. His melancholy spirit reached out to her. It moved her to think they had something in common after all.

And then she ran into him outside the butcher's shop. He was buying bones for a new dog he'd got himself. A dachshund, he told her, and she imagined it as a mirror of his own lugubriousness.

'It's always good to see you, Beattie.'

Well, yes. We're old friends, after all ... She felt drawn to offer comfort. Emboldened, he invited her for a spin in the sidecar of his motorcycle. Well, perhaps another time, when the weather was warmer.

The warmer weather arrived, and with it a reminder from Derek. They agreed to meet outside the doctor's surgery. She climbed into the awkward space, feeling the thrill of some sort of risk, though the only risk was to her hairdo. The hedgerows were succulent with honeysuckle; she smelt it from the open top of the sidecar. As the cut hay lay in the fields she breathed in great gusts of it. She shook her hair in the wind. They went to a little pub down a country lane. 'Gin-and-It', as it was when she was young. She sipped at her drink and, feeling relaxed, leant forward and confessed she was thinking of getting a job. Derek was surprised.

'Why would you want to do that?'

She dropped the subject. It was an ambition she would keep to herself. Instead they began to talk of Martha and the possibilities of her life in Liverpool. Derek asked a lot of questions. Whether she had boyfriends, what money she had of her own. His curiosity made Beattie uneasy. This little meeting was supposed to be about Beattie.

He began to reminisce about the fling they'd had together. Did she remember the big bands, the dances, how close they had been?

She smiled wanly. 'No, not really. Not that close, Derek.' And she pulled her chair away from his in the inglenook.

They left that pub and drove on some more, then stopped and sat on the gnarled stone wall outside a hillside pub. He was fidgeting nervously, plucking at strands of weed and twining them around his fingers. He was looking around, jumpy, nervous.

'You know, all those years ago . . . and Martha now a grown girl. How old exactly? I used to know . . .'

Beattie clouded over. 'Seventeen, Derek, she was seventeen last November. Why? What's that to you?'

'Well, that's what I've often wondered, Beattie . . . what exactly she is to me.' He threw the strands of grass away abruptly and turned to her. 'I have wondered . . . you must have wondered too – whether I am in any way connected to her. And not in any old way.' Irritated with his own choice of words he grew suddenly emphatic. 'I have wondered, Beattie, we being so close, whether I might – possibly – be her father.'

Beattie frowned. Was he crazy? She shook her head emphatically. The idea was so wrong-headed, so fantastical. Was she dealing with a madman? She must be careful how she answered. But she couldn't find the words. The frown deepened. Derek, looking washed out and feeble, was seeking her eyes for some indication, some hope. This was obviously the momentous question he'd been nursing for years and at last had the courage to ask.

'Don't answer now if you don't want to. I can see it's hard for you. We need to think what it means.'

Beattie found her voice. 'No, no, no, we don't. We don't, Derek. Really we don't.'

She took a risk, resting her hand on his as it lay on the rough granite stone. Would he misinterpret this too?

He brightened at that. She felt she owed him something – a confession perhaps.

'It was over, you and I. It was just a single occasion . . . you remember that, don't you? The wallpaper in your mother's front room.'

Derek's head was bowed and his eyes were directed at the spread of clover at his feet.

'But, you realised, didn't you . . . that he was the one.'

Derek drew a deep sigh, lifted his head and gazed across the lane to where two cows were chewing the cud. He didn't speak.

'He had always been the one. He came back wounded and we married right away.'

Derek didn't know where to take his grief. 'My mother

always liked you … she always hoped … and when we went dancing, you were so lively and laughing. She said it must be love.' The word choked him. 'Well, that was the word she used.' He managed an awkward grin.

Beattie saw what a sad man he was.

'I fell pregnant almost at once, I'll grant you that. But … there couldn't be any doubt about it. You understand, don't you? Women know these things: it just wasn't possible.'

Derek shook his head hard as if to stop her talking any more. 'No, no, I believe you, Beattie. I know you wouldn't lie to me.'

They sat side by side on the wall, two middle-aged people unable to console each other, sharing shock and disappointment. Slowly he raised his head.

'You're a good woman, you know.'

He didn't need to say any more. But after a further moment he did.

'Thank you for being my friend.'

Chapter 30

Throughout the summer of 1962 Liverpool came more and more alive. Energy was seeping from its stones. It belonged to the young who, like gazelles, had raised their heads and sniffed the air appreciating something new. There had always been music: Liverpool was a port with all the folk songs that go with maritime life. But this was different. People said it came in on the liners from America, brought by brothers and cousins who worked the shipping lines. Every family knew someone at sea, someone they could badger to bring in Chuck Berry and Elvis records.

But Merseyside's own spirit was stirring, a mix of wit and defiance, joy and exultation, it was like an infection spreading out from the clubs and cellars, pubs and halls. Young people were discovering their own talent, making poetry and painting and above all music. The streets sang with it: the girls were dazzled by it, the boys inspired by it.

Martha, taking a bus into town, passed a group of lads, no more than twelve years old, messing around on a bombsite covered in rosebay willowherb. The tallest and scrawniest had a guitar and was moving and shaking as the others danced around on the old rubble. Youths of fifteen and sixteen were already forming and re-forming their own groups and giving them odd names: they played in cellars and above pubs, enlisting the support of sturdy scouse mothers to provide sandwiches and soft drinks for their friends. They in turn were inspired by others, regularly booked for formal Friday and Saturday night appearances in town halls, and at serious golf club evenings and Conservative balls. Those still at school skimped their homework; those with jobs snatched a lunch hour from their desks or got away when the whistle blew. Making music was what mattered. Everyone felt it and shared it.

The household at Sibling Rivalry was infected by it. Ever since their first meeting, Martha realised that Fee was wayward, disorganised in the way she worked and sharp-tongued to those she looked to for help. At the time Martha thought it was just how things were, and she must buckle under and set out to please. It was the lesson she had brought with her from number 26. But Fee was emotionally needful too, given to tantrums when Martha was late to deliver clothes, and ready to shout and plague her with nasty remarks: 'This looks all wrong, and you said you liked it.' 'How come I've run out of ribbon? I thought that was your job.'

Martha's job had never been defined. And nor had her pay. She had been happy to take the five pounds Fee had offered at the start. But as Fee's clothes were becoming popular and selling well in little shops springing up around town, she began to feel entitled to a larger share of the rising income flowing into Fee's bedroom workshop. Money suddenly seemed to matter, being a measure of how the world valued you. And after all, she made loads of bold suggestions, sought out fancy trimmings and bizarre ideas from around the city. She even wore Fee's creations with enough panache to have people enquire where they could buy them. She was of value in the business, and knowing as much buoyed her up.

Cassie's theatre group was planning a production of Sartre's *Huis Clos*, a strange dark play about people trapped in what they believed was the antechamber to hell, but was in fact hell itself – other people. Cassie wanted the cast of three to have simple striking costumes of a single colour and identical fabric. Fee's imagination let rip. She came round to Sibling Rivalry with some elaborate sketches and swathes of lavish materials.

'You tell her!' Cassie shouted to Martha. 'You work for her. She's just not listening ... Turning up here with costumes that dominate the play, distract from the ideas and probably steal the reviews. It's not my vision of the play at all.'

Cassie was being as dogmatic as Fee. Martha was trapped in the middle, calling on what her father referred to as her 'spirit of sweet reasonableness'. There was indeed something reconciling and affectionate about her;

she hated conflict and tried her best to say so before it arose. But Cassie and Fee were of a different mind. They seemed to relish their clash.

Martha still hadn't spoken to Duncan about where things stood between them, a situation that caused her silent misery but seemed not to be of concern to him at all. Other people were deciding for her how she would live her life. Mostly they were people she admired and even loved, and that being the case she could see that it shouldn't matter. On some occasions it even made her happy to go along with their expectations, seeking to please them. Then the house smiled and all was happy.

Being caught in the middle, like this, between two shrieking harridans must stop. She ducked out of the kitchen on an excuse – 'Just fetching my ciggies' – then stood behind the closed door tracking the sounds of their abuse and argument. It was seven in the evening. Outside it was raining steadily and the summer light scarcely penetrated the gloom. As she stood in the hallway away from the fight but still feeling part of it, Pete arrived back home, rucksack and duffel coat wet through. His spirits dampened too, as he trundled through the front door.

'Hi, there, little Martha, what's up? You look like a glamorous spy, hunched there.'

She felt guilty at once. She knew Pete as a beacon of moral probity. She abandoned the spying and put herself outside the quarrel.

'Oh, nothing, just some daft row about nothing very much ... and you? How's things with you?'

It was polite to ask, but she was fearful of the answer. Each time Pete was away on CND business he returned more anxious than ever. He had grown thinner and his skin beneath the helmet of brown hair was pale and drawn. She was fearful for his health. She knew that his commitment mattered to him but it made him at once exhilarating and exhausting.

Over dinner that night round the scrubbed table – spaghetti bolognaise was becoming the favourite dish – Pete updated them about how much longer they could expect to live. It seemed Britain and America had walked out of talks about banning atmospheric testing. Our own government, blatantly ignored the risks. Then America had slapped an embargo on Cuba, which was simply a brave little country struggling to get out of the clutches of exploiting capitalists and offer education and welfare to all its people. How could that be bad?

Pete would pause long enough to search out a direct eyeball-to-eyeball challenge to each of them, daring them to disagree. They all nodded vigorously; he was, after all, their appointed conscience. 'And now, imagine this for outright cruelty – they've imprisoned Lord Russell: a man of eighty-nine acting entirely for the good of humanity. It just shows how afraid they are of the voice of the common people.'

'Come off it, Pete. Lord Russell isn't the common people – he's a hereditary peer and one of the world's great philosophers!'

This was Duncan, who sat back tipping his chair on its two back legs as if to distance himself from Pete's fervour.

'That strengthens our argument, can't you see that?'

None of them could and the nodding had stopped.

'We must listen to the world's greatest philosophers ... they know more than we do or we can. Brainy people realise nuclear war will destroy the world. Loads of writers are protesting too: Doris Lessing, Robert Bolt, J. B Priestley, even plays on BBC television.'

They perked up at this. There had been discussion recently about whether to have a television set in the house. If they were serious about trying to forge a new way of living together and not fall in with conventional behaviour, then they should eschew television and all its ills. In the end they decided in favour of having one. As a concession to principle they bought one second-hand.

The affair between Cassie and Fee continued to rattle on over subsequent days. Each sought Martha's sympathetic ear. Cassie's production was working its way towards a first night at the art school: student bookings were strong. All things French were still the rage. France's tidal wave of new-style films was filling the small art-house cinemas. *Jules et Jim* had just opened in town and the free spirit of Catherine, its mysterious heroine, was impressing them all. Cassie's production was taking on some of its charm and defiance. Martha's loyalties were tipping towards her.

'I need to explain, Fee. I think it's time I changed jobs. We've had a good time, haven't we, and I want to do something different. I'll be finishing at the end of this week, if that's OK?'

'No, it's not bloody OK. What are you thinking of?' Then apparently anticipating with horror the chaos ahead: 'Oh, Martha, you can't leave me in the lurch. Not only Cassie's show depends on you, but there's an order you mentioned coming from ... '

Little of what Fee made was ordered in anything like an official way. There was no record of numbers, or prices, of orders and deliveries. It all lived in Martha's head.

'And just at the very moment when I was about to increase your wages ... '

Martha scarcely responded.

'Even double them.' She shrugged a grin. 'Even make you my partner.'

'No, Fee. I have decided. I am finishing ... I want something different. Please be reasonable.' They looked unblinking into each other's eyes, no expression giving away any thoughts. Then Fee caught up an armful of all her dressmaking stuff: bolts of cloth, boxes of buttons, even lace and pins, ribbons and scissors ... she grabbed them together frantically and flung them to where Martha was standing meekly making her explanation.

'OK, go, if you want. Go, yes, why not. Go now, bitch' – and Martha was outside the imperturbable suburban house, standing in the street while Fee, downstairs, raged in tears to her indifferent mother.

Martha felt the weight of conflict lift from her. Ever since she had left home she had avoided people who put on the pressure. She walked with a lighter step when she was running her own life. The sunlight glittered on the Mersey, where a brisk breeze tipped up little shafts of light from the edge of waves. The air was freshening from the sea, nosing its way through the cheap fabrics of the clothes Fee had made and Martha had taken. Her white duffel coat had the aged look of stale cream, smeared at elbow and cuffs as though dusted with the flakes of old charcoal. It looked like a working garment and that was fine with Martha. Everyone was starting to wear working clothes. There were clubs who kept to the old ways, turning away anyone in jeans. But that was because they hadn't yet caught up with the way things were going. Informality enraged the elders, who didn't dare do more than frown and offer sour glances at the queues outside clubs and bars waiting to hear the groups. Martha was often in those queues.

She took a part-time job in a milk bar on Church Street, and by taking on later shifts for her colleagues could get away at lunchtimes for whatever was going on in Mathew Street and Dale Street. Her life began to grow more buoyant. It seemed being assertive didn't lose you friends, as she had feared. Fee had made up their quarrel, becoming suddenly conciliatory when Martha left. She had come round for supper and apologised to Cassie for not heeding what she called her 'vision' for the play. They had all gone along to its opening night and retired to the Jacaranda to discuss the performance and Jean-Paul Sartre. Slowly as they drank the talk shaped itself into a game: what each would consider their personal idea of hell? Duncan nominated the absence of books and there were mutterings of agreement. Jake said 'the death of trees', and left them murmuring reservations and some kind of sympathetic sounds.

'But that couldn't happen, could it?'

'No, but this is in our imagination ... it's just a game.'

Cassie's fear: 'The loss of those I love.'

Pete had no hesitation. 'Nuclear war, of course ... and that's not a matter of the imagination. It's real right now.'

The others hesitated to agree. They'd heard it before and it held no originality for them. They were even getting used to the idea. Their indifference made Pete cross and almost spoiled the game. Martha retrieved it. 'Not knowing who you are,' she said finally. 'That's hell all right.'

They all frowned at that except Duncan.

Pete spoke up. 'But you do know who you are, don't you, Martha?'

He saw her as the strongest of all the girls. She had become to him like a bright and sure star in his sky. She smiled at his tribute.

'Oh, well perhaps I do, Pete.' She smiled her broad lipsticked smile at him. 'If you say so' – and began to believe it. 'I certainly know more than I once did.'

The enamel greens of springtime had long gone and mellowed into the tired dust of summer. The city seemed spilling over with new groups, and Martha had become a seasoned follower. She had seen them come and go: Ian and the Zodiacs, Kingsize Taylor and the Dominoes, Faron and the Flamingoes, Lee Curtis and the All-Stars. Always at the back of her mind she remembered that early momentary passion for the boy in the pink shirt and the roaring performance of The Brigands that night at the Grande. She asked around but no one knew anything about them. Occasionally someone admitted to a shadowy recollection, but she judged it was more to please her than to offer any established facts. Anyway, if they were playing at the Grande they were hardly at the hot heart of what was happening.

She came to see the Grande for what it was: a failing cinema in the dingy square at the heart of a minor town. And perhaps by now it was even closed. The thought came as a shock. What about her father? He would have found another job, but he would have lost his precious films. She had hardly been in touch and he would think she didn't care. She tussled with her conscience. What surprised her most was that at such moments images and thoughts of her mother surged into her mind too. So much unresolved unhappiness. Between them, between herself and them. Closing the door on all that distress was the best thing she had ever done. But it was no sort of resolution. It was a landmark, for sure. But it was not over.

Duncan cared for her but he cared for them all and for others beyond Sibling Rivalry. A dumpy girl called Charlotte with straggling blonde hair and torn jeans had begun to stay over for a night or two recently. Duncan had always insisted he belonged to no one. Ownership of people, he said, was the way to tyranny. Martha tried to believe him but still knew she wanted something more anchored in her life. She wanted to feel that her new family of friends was an appropriate substitute. But it wasn't.

She had turned out of the cobbled side street and was walking along a main thoroughfare. Buses passed close to her as she walked with sprightly steps clicking her stiletto heels along the pavement. The sun made her smile; the music made her smile. She swung her hips and her bag to the rhythm of her steps. Someone spoke to her: he was walking along too and had caught up with her and matched his stride to hers.

'Hey, there, I think I've seen you around, haven't I?'

'Probably.'

She looked him up and down. He was very thin, wiry, and gaunt of features with a strong bony face and wide shoulders where the collarbones stuck out. His shirt was unbuttoned down to his jeans and a soft flock of black hair filled the opening. He had a wide leather belt with a fancy brass buckle, the sort Fee would admire. He carried no guitar but he was undoubtedly of the fraternity. She looked up smiling as they walked together.

'What's your name?'

'Martha. And yours?'

'Jeff. And where are you off to, Martha?'

'I was heading over to Whitechapel to do some listening ... '

His limbs moved with a casual glamour. She was inclined to like him.

'And you?'

'Oh, I've an appointment at a recording studio. It's

quite a special day for me.' His eyes twinkled, boasting. 'It's on your way ... why don't you drop in? Have you ever seen a disc being cut?'

Martha took good measure of her man and decided to believe him.

'Sorry, but I've got to be back at work for the afternoon shift.' Not strictly true, but a delaying tactic.

'Can't life wait? It'll be fun, I promise you.'

It was a tempting offer and something to tell the others.

'What's the group?'

'Oh, we've only just come together: we're calling ourselves the Jumping Jesters.'

A new group cutting a disc. It might not be a serious recording studio. But there were loads of small spaces where hopefuls cut sample tracks of their work in the hope of impressing the likes of Bill Harry and Bob Wooler, even Brian Epstein. She looked at her watch. They had turned a corner and were heading downhill. In the distance the Mersey rippled in the sun.

'Look! We're here. This is the place. Come on, come on.' He laughed pleadingly and she gave in.

They were early because the studio was empty and the control room dark. There was a drum kit in the corner, a settee over by the wall and several microphones on stands scattered round.

'Hi, there, guys!' Jeff called out, circling as he did so as if they could appear from any direction. Martha hovered near the door.

'Come in, come on in. They're late, all of them.'

She moved into the room and with a neat little skip of

a movement he passed behind her and she heard the sound of a key turn in the lock of the door.

'What are you—? Please don't do that. I may want to go out.'

Martha moved towards him but he backed away, tossing the key teasingly in the palm of his hand. 'Not so fast, not so fast. We'll enjoy ourselves first. I get the impression you like enjoying yourself.'

'Well, it's the wrong impression. Now let me go.'

Jeff chuckled. It was a sound full of menace and Martha began to panic.

'It's a serious mistake. My mistake. I shouldn't have come. They're expecting me – and I'll be late.' She was babbling stupidly. 'Jeff, come along. What is this? You said you were going to a recording—'

'Woah, woah. We were getting along just fine . . . now why don't we keep it that way? I'm happy to.'

He had pocketed the key and held his arms splayed wide from his sides, his palms open in an apparent gesture of welcome. He moved towards her.

'Please, Jeff, I don't want to be here. I want you to let me go. Why won't you let me go?'

She backed away towards the wall. The studio walls were padded to make the place soundproof. No one would hear her call out. He had it all worked out. He moved closer towards her.

'Stay there. Stay away from me.'

Her voice was reedy and plaintive. She tried to recall whether there was anything useful in her handbag, a penknife, perhaps, or a hand mirror with a glass edge she could use in self-defence. But he was tall and agile.

It would be useless. As he moved suddenly to grab her, she swung her bag by its long handle and hit him across the face. It was the wrong thing to do. His response was instant. He hit her with the broad flat of his hand and sent her hurtling across the floor.

She was in pain but suddenly alert. Everything was very clear and somehow moving slowly so she had time to think. She didn't want to be hurt. She wanted to be back in the street, back in her normal life. She could feel it there just out of reach. She scrambled to her feet and confronted him.

'OK, what do you want? Tell me what you want? I want to be out of here.'

'I want you, little lady. You and your delicious little cunt. That's what.'

He had grabbed her by the wrist and was swinging her round.

'Don't, don't hurt me. Please. Don't hurt me.' She was squirming within his hold.

'Ooooh, that's nice, that feels good. You liking that?'

'Please, don't hurt me. Please stop.'

It was no good. She beat on him with her free fist but she had a sense of the strength of her resistance ebbing away. It was urgent he didn't realise that. Oh, he would win, but she would never collude: she turned her mouth to his arm and bit into it hard. He flung her away.

'Now look here, bitch. We can do this one of two ways. I can lay you out flat. Cold. Get it? Or you can make things easier for yourself. It's your decision? Right?'

'None of this is my decision. None of it. I want to go. I want to be out of here.'

'That's not an option, I'm afraid. I've set out the two options you have. Which is it to be?'

She stood there breathing hard, snorting with fury, her nose running with snot and the muscles of her arms quivering, so that she had to clasp her hands together to steady them. She faced him head on.

'Neither . . . '

She knew she could not avoid him. The thing was to play for time and think fast. He was big and strong. He was insistent. Half an hour ago she had found him attractive, relaxed and casual in the way they all were these days. He was one of them, the new musical crowd who talked and laughed, drank and played all over the city. In another setting he could be her hero, and she more than willing to give herself. So why not, then, just see it through. Was it such a big deal? It wasn't as though she was a still a virgin and living by those old-fashioned values of her parents' generation. Of course her mother would be shocked. Miss Saward at the typing class, dull Marjory, Josie at the Grande, even Enid and Fee and Cassie . . . in a split second they, all the women in her life, paraded before her. Each in her situation would have their own response, and make different choices. But would they blame and condemn her? And even if they did, what value did she place on their judgement? She looked around. She was on her own. And suddenly she was angry. Jeff had moved away and was leaning on the padded wall of the studio; he was fidgeting with a large shiny watch, admiring it, adjusting the strap as though it were new and not yet comfortable. All he had to do was wait. Her powerlessness appalled her.

'What instrument do you play?'

He looked up. 'Base guitar, since you ask.'

'What music do you like?'

'Well, plenty. Loads. Chuck Berry is tops. Elvis, obviously ...'

'No, but here, in Liverpool. Do you rate Gerry and the Pacemakers? The Beatles?'

'Look, kiddo, we're not here to chat about the music scene. I do that with my mates, with the blokes over at Hessy's, with that guy who's started up *Mersey Beat*. Girls aren't for talking music ... and I haven't all day.'

Idling towards him and keeping up the chat, Martha took measure of the room, the placing of the door, the distances to cover.

'And Rory Storm and the Hurricanes, how do you rate them? I saw him over at New Brighton Ballroom only last week.'

'I didn't know he was there ... go on, you're having me on.' He took the door key out of his pocket, shook it in her face and laughed. 'Yours – when you deliver.' He tossed it on a chair set far away against the wall. Then he reached out for her arm. 'Come on ...'

Martha was quick. She snatched off one of her shoes and aimed its sharp stiletto heel furiously at his eye but heard the crack as it hit his skull. She kept hitting. He moved to fend off the blows, crying out and writhing away from her reach. Again the heel beat on his face, his arms flailing to fend her off. He moaned in pain and fury, clutching at his cheeks where the blood ran. Martha turned and ran for the key. His vanity saved her.

'My face, damn you, my face . . . '

She tore off the other shoe the better to make a run for it. He simply gave up.

'You hell cat. Get out of here . . . get out!'

She was in the street without shoes.

'Oh, look, a gypsy . . . ' Two dowdy shoppers pointed towards her. She gave them an awkward little wave, gulping with relief.

Chapter 31

Martha returned from her ordeal in the recording studio with feelings of distress and triumph struggling to prevail. She offered a cursory greeting to the crowd at the scrubbed table, then headed for her room, tugged the flimsy curtains across and flung herself on the bed, huddling into a bunch, comforted by her own body. A sudden shaking came over her. She was shivering without being cold. She waited for the spasm to pass. Shock, this must be what shock was like. What shock was. She wished she had her old rabbit pyjama case for comfort. Her mind was racing. She couldn't stop it. Her mind filled with flashing images. The dark cave of the studio, the moment when she realised her visit was not going to be benign. She remembered the start of the encounter. Jeff had seemed nice. They had fallen into a shared stride together on the street. He was breezy, casual ... she had liked that. She could understand why she trusted him. He smiled easily and looked into her eyes. There was nothing shifty about him. He was like all the other people she was growing to trust. He dressed in a pleasing way, too: she recalled the shirt open down to his jeans, and the sprouting black hair. Duncan was hairy in the same sort of way. It was a reminder she felt comfortable with.

Then the leather belt with the gaudy brass buckle. It was not good remembering that. She had thought at the time of what might be Fee's approving response, but not any more. She could read menace into its swagger, recalling how Jeff had lunged his crotch towards her, the buckle an emblem of his virility. She shuddered. How much was she to blame for getting into such a mess? A twinge of conscience surfaced, but her mind hadn't done with its whirlwind of images. She rolled on the bed, groaning, beating the pillow with a feeble fist. She could hear the sound of Jeff's key turning in the studio door, a small doom-laden click. From that moment her life was no longer her own. The mistake she made had been to trust him. No, she could have trusted him and refused his invitation ... no harm done, meet up another time. She had fallen for the promise of glamour. She had wanted to see a disc being cut. Liverpool was awash with pop groups and his might be one of the latest. Imagine, being in the know, even a friend of one of the up-and-coming. Images of concerts, howling crowds of teenage fans, and the newest band of all acknowledging her as one of their gang, an insider, a girl who was in on their secrets. Songs dedicated to her, carrying her name ... making her famous. The fist that had punched the pillow softened in a movement of despairing self-knowledge. She covered her eyes with her hand, groaning and ashamed. Then she sat up suddenly. She brushed the black hair back from her face, anchoring it behind her ears. She had been a fool for succumbing to schoolgirl fantasies, but she had fought back. She had come to her senses. She was proud of that spate of sudden thinking that had seemed to be moving in slow motion. She had weighed up her options. She had made the calculations millions of women make when it came to handling men. And she had not been the loser.

There was a timid knock at the door. It was hours later. Sleep had come at last and her mind was rested. It must be late.

'I thought you'd like something to eat.'

Pete was at the door with a plate of sandwiches and a jug of coffee.

'You didn't come down so I thought something must be wrong.'

She knew at once he was the right one to come to comfort her. Duncan would have been huggy and full of strokes and caresses, but only finally for the sake of his own reassurance. He liked all his family to be happy: it was what made his life rewarding. Besides, Charlotte was here almost permanently now. Pete was the only one of them open to the brute hostility of life.

'Yes, I am suddenly hungry ... how odd!' She seized the plate and began gulping down slabs of the soft white bread. 'It must be late. I've been having such a good sleep.'

Pete looked at her, as though envious of her ability to sleep. She had become closer to Pete since she travelled to London at Easter to join up with him for the last miles of that year's Aldermaston March. This had been his fourth so he had been well prepared for its rigours. Fifty-two miles is hard unless you're in training. But this year the weather had been clement and he had enjoyed the company of those he'd got to know on previous marches. They all believed the impact of their movement was growing. Now they were pressing forward, going global with delegates visiting the USSR and stirring things up across America. Khrushchev and Kennedy must surely know the world was rising up against the prospect of a nuclear war. Martha saw that Pete wanted to console her for whatever misery had beset her, but was struggling to choke back his own concerns.

He tapped her hand fondly. 'Drink up ... then you can tell me what's happened.'

Martha dunked her face into the huge mug and drank in one great draught the milky coffee he had made. There was silence between them. A space to fill.

Pete filled it. 'Something bad has happened, Martha.' She looked up at him over the rim of her mug. 'The Americans have tested a hydrogen bomb so powerful that it lit up the sky all the way from Hawaii to New Zealand. Imagine that. Almost half the planet could see its effect. That's the sort of thing that will destroy the entire world. And they're already practising ... here, let me take that.'

Pete took the mug that lolled in Martha's hand. She stared at him.

'Well, that's terrible, terrible. But what can we do? What are we supposed to do, Pete? What are you asking me to do?' She could do without this. Pete, so gentle and so worried, asking her to rescue millions. 'It's not something we can change, Pete. It's out there, in politics and governments.'

He smiled wanly. 'We have to keep trying ... until the very last moment. We must not give up, Martha. Even when the planes have set off, even when it's reached the point of no return, we must still keep trying.'

She clambered across the bed to where he sat at the end and wrapped her arms round him. The impulse had been one of tenderness and concern. She stroked his head as if comforting a child. Then she held him away from her and looked into his eyes. And he looked back. She felt a sudden certainty about herself, an assurance in what she was doing. She was taking charge. She reached forward and for a moment held his face in both her hands, his mouth close to hers, she looking at the curve of his lips and the way he held them apart in a sort of anticipation as though not daring to be bold. It was Martha who would be bold. She reached his jacket from his shoulders and threw it on the floor.

'It's OK, it really is.'

And as if with her permission, he unloosed his tie and shirt.

There was a scramble of clothes and they were under the blankets and eiderdown. Martha surprised herself by her sexual confidence: she had learned enough from Duncan, but she had been his protégée, submissive and yielding. This was altogether different. Pete, if not exactly inexperienced, lacked the finesse of regular practice. And it didn't matter. Their bodies were eager and awkward,

273

and it didn't matter. Something else was happening ...
and that did matter.

'Pete, I'm –' she wrinkled her brow into a comic
frown – 'I think I'm happy. Is that allowed?'

'I don't know about allowed, but it's good, isn't it?'

For the first time in weeks he smiled a wide smile.

Later they lay beside each other, bemused by the strange
and sudden mood that had captured them. Everything
about the room seemed heightened – its pale walls, its
long windows, the small and only chair. It was the perfect
place to be. They turned to face each other.

'Good – yes, it is, and it's nice to hear you say so.'

Martha's eyes sparkled and her heart was caught.

Chapter 32

Martha slept again this time without the images troubling her, and with a new sweet confidence in herself. Pete had tucked her up like a child, reaching the eiderdown under her chin and kissing her cheek. He stroked the black curls back behind her ear. She wriggled and looked up smiling.

'Things will be all right,' she said, without quite knowing what she was referring to.

'Oh, I do hope so.'

Pete gave a disbelieving smile. Martha loved that smile. As she sank down into the bed a sense of deep well-being spread throughout her body. It had recovered from its shock and was more than restored to her. It seemed to be flowering with a sense of joy, of realisation.

'Sleep tight, dear Martha.' Pete tiptoed out of her room, taking care not to slam the door. There was something precious happening between them and he was careful not to make too great a noise. He was fearful the moment might pass or vanish at the slightest move to tie it down.

Back downstairs he joined a game everyone was playing, trying to weave a continuous story out of the titles of pop songs. Duncan had started them off with 'Are You Lonesome Tonight?', and the others followed: 'Only The Lonely.' Cassie grimaced and added hers: 'Tell Laura I Love Her.' It was Jake's turn; he thought for a while then came up with: 'Johnny Remember Me.'

Pete stayed quiet and smiling. 'What are you smiling at?' Cassie asked, nudging his elbow. 'Or do I know?' And she began humming the first release from The Beatles that was currently the rage of Liverpool. 'Love, love me do . . . You know I love you!'

Pete's friends called him brainy. But that wasn't quite right. It was true that he loved knowledge and was happy to immerse himself in his studies, but what characterised him more was an underlying unwillingness to engage with people. He enjoyed watching how others came together and made easy friendships. But he was aware it didn't come easily for him. He was neither critical nor shy of others. He simply kept himself apart. His tutors at the institute liked him; he was assiduous without being solemn and amiable without being familiar. He would turn up on time when they required it, with essays for his history course completed in a neat even hand, and took their comments about his work as offering an alternative view which was not his own. He was not to be deflected from his strongly held but mildly expressed opinions, whether it was about the legacy of Tom Paine, the importance of the Chartists or the strange friendship that seemed to have sprung up between President Kennedy and Prime Minister Harold Macmillan. He saw history as a struggle with the forces of evil gaining ground. His view of the future was that it wouldn't last long. He lived his life in the shadow of the bomb.

He had become more and more watchful of Martha as the months had gone by and found it giving him more and more pleasure. He had accepted her being drawn into Duncan's embrace because that's what happened. The absence of declared rules for living within Sibling Rivalry was what had brought him there in the first place, but he learned quickly that unspoken habits of behaviour take hold whether people meant them to or not.

Jake would never be found doing the washing-up. And the women automatically assumed the home-making duties, however much they protested that it should be otherwise. Theory simply never moved over into practice. In the same way no one had declared rules about fidelity or expected it. The newly arrived Charlotte had learned quickly enough not to lay exclusive claim to Duncan. Now Pete had a bond with Martha. An exclusive bond.

Pete's home had been straightforward. His mother was a rather untidy teacher at a local church school, his father assisted with a charity for African orphans. They attended the local Society of Friends where he met other Quakers, mild, quiet-spoken people who thought it their duty to do good in the world, an obligation they undertook without fuss or even any sense that they were unusual. For Pete this sense of obligation had grown to be a burden. He felt the weight of it from day to day; and though he felt no resentment, he somehow marvelled at how carefree and even reckless other people were. Their spontaneity delighted him, even as he withheld his own part in it. He made his way round the city smiling quietly at its innocent pleasures. He would call in to hear groups play, stand unnoticed with a glass of lemonade then leave without having spoken to anyone. Back at Sibling Rivalry he would tell them all what a great time he had had. But it was in the Campaign for Nuclear Disarmament that he found his calling. It was as though the apocalyptic nature of the threat called forth some latent messianic response in him. Even as a young boy he had sought out images and records of the explosions in Japan. He had read with a kind of macabre relish tales of people's flesh coming away in layers, of the only trace left of some individuals being their shadow imprinted on a wall. He was made almost delirious with panic by the way America, France, Britain and Russia went on exploding ever more huge devices of death into the atmosphere. When anyone showed similar passion to his own he marked them down as genuine friends. When Martha had come to share the protests with him, he felt bonded to her for ever.

But it was the afternoon when she had returned home in that febrile state, such a mixture of shock and exhila-ration, that his eyes had filled with a new devotion. She seemed to be quivering with some inner turmoil of her own. It seemed only natural that she should have reached out to him as she had done. From that moment on they had entered some magical and silent pact together. Their eyes sought each other's with a sense of finding their true home; they were reassured to be in the same room; they used every chance to touch, to pass close, to smile more broadly together at someone's half-amusing remark. The air itself was transformed.

It was within this new euphoria that Pete heard on the television news and read in the papers of the deepening crisis over Cuba. As far as he could follow the story, Russia had dispatched missiles there to counter the threat of an American invasion. There had been an abortive invasion back in April of the previous year at the Bay of Pigs. Ever since Castro's revolution America had been outraged at having an ally of the Soviet Union just ninety miles off shore. Suddenly the threat of actual invasion was growing stronger. There was an assumption that the Soviet missiles would be carrying nuclear warheads and could be deployed to destroy a vast area of America, taking out cities and reducing some millions of Americans to the skeletal figures of the old newsreels and many a shadow on many walls. Khrushchev was belligerent – a little ugly man who strutted about relishing his power. He was not to be trusted. Pete felt sick with anticipation.

The coincidence of his anxieties with his new passion for Martha produced in him a sort of delirium. He was stretched between the extremes of happiness and despair. Sometimes he could hardly tell the one from the other – his immediate love for the flesh and blood Martha, caught up in his paroxysms of fear at how they were all about to be incinerated. He was at first jumpy and nervous, quick to react and respond, though never taking offence. Slowly this mellowed into a bleak calm at the prospect of the inevitable. They would all die together in some Wagnerian climax of nuclear global destruction. He took to playing the final act of *Götterdämmerung* on the record player in the book-lined room upstairs.

In the days that followed Martha and Pete snatched whatever chance they could to go back to the big bed and explore each other some more. They regarded with delight the shape of bones, the paleness of skin. They laughed together as though continually surprised by pleasure. Back in the real world Martha tried to bring some of her lightness of spirit into Pete's life. He tried to convey to her the seriousness of his. He went along to the milk bar when she was on duty there and sat idling by the window watching her come and go. She looked across from time to time, smiling and happy, making the jostling young customers wonder. 'She's something, isn't she ... flashing around in that red skirt!' 'It's obvious, isn't it? You just need to look. She's sweet on him ... him over in the window.' 'The one with the long hair there? No match for her glamour, is he?' But Martha and Pete didn't care that the rest of the world thought they were an odd couple. They thought so themselves. It was a sense of being a couple at all that was new to them. When Martha's shift finished, they wandered holding hands down to the Pier Head to gaze at the autumn skies across the Mersey and out towards where the river met the sea. The seagulls screeched overhead. They talked fancifully of the future they might share.

'We could go away together, go somewhere safe. I

know someone who's doing that – to the west coast of Ireland. To make sure he and his family survive. I'd like to do that with you.'

'Pete, that's really weird. Who are they? They must be odd, thinking like that.'

'Not that odd. Really not that odd at all. After all, governments have built nuclear shelters – did you know that? So why shouldn't ordinary people protect themselves?'

He didn't wait for an answer.

'And you can't be safe within range of a target. Liverpool could certainly be a target. Think of the last war and how many places here were aimed at. I know of people, especially with children, who are planning to move where they can be safe. One family is even thinking of Argentina: they have Welsh in their blood so they could settle in Patagonia.'

'Oh, Pete, stop it, please.' She hugged at his arm and stroked his pale cheek where the lines of distress had reappeared. 'Please. Don't think like that. I can't, I just can't. This is my place, this country ... I just couldn't leave. And yet I want to be with you. Of course I do. I feel safe with you, wherever I am. I feel safe here.'

'Do you? Do you, little Martha? My adorable Martha ... don't you want us to have a great and glorious future?'

He reached out and held her face with a tender sort of melancholy. He was like a poet in her eyes, but a poet she didn't understand.

'Don't be sad, Pete. You can't be sad for us, can you?'

'I'm sad for all of us, Martha,' and he swung his arm wide as if embracing the whole of the city that lay at their backs and the broadening sweep of the docks and the river before them, even the shores beyond.

Then he switched mood and turned back to her.

'More to the point, with things as bad as they are I think you should be in touch with your mother and father.'

She looked blank. Back in Sibling Rivalry the code of the house was that Martha had some bitter and ongoing row with her parents and no one was to remind her of it. It was too painful. Pete was breaking that code. He watched her. Almost daring her to be angry or outraged, to break down in tearful explanation or whining self-justification. She did none of those things. She simply looked at him steadily, then nodded quietly.

'Yes. Yes, I think I will.' The postcard she posted that night carried the address of the milk bar.

Chapter 33

She hadn't expected them to turn up in person. It was deeply embarrassing. She had just made ham and mustard sandwiches for a crowd of young schoolgirls when, half looking up, she saw two middle-aged people over by the door, waving gently towards her. Customers like them might not be used to the style of the place but she was not going to let them jump the queue simply because they didn't fit in. She kept her head averted in the hope they would go somewhere more suitable for older people. There was a Kardomah along the street. She took the cash from the ringleader among the girls and, half distracted, made some small talk about that night's concert over at Litherland Town Hall. The awkward couple were moving closer.

'Hello, Martha!'

It was said with a smile in the voice, a smile she recognised when she finally looked up.

'Oh, Dad! Dad, oh ... ' Her voice trailed away as she

realised who was with him. A woman with porcelain skin and softly waved hair. Her mother. She was wearing a dark tailored coat with a large collar of black fur; she had a trim little Tam o'Shanter of the same fur. The fur, inappropriate in the milk bar and the mild autumn weather, none the less commanding respect.

'Oh, Mum, you as well –' and more slowly, as all sorts of realisations were dawning – 'you look … well, you look really smart.' Then, as customers behind began to tut at having to wait, 'Why not sit down, and I'll come across in a moment.'

Her parents turned, moving towards a small empty table looking out of the large plate-glass window. They took refuge there. Martha looked and saw with surprise two ordinary people doing as she suggested. They raised no objection, made no qualifying remark, simply accepted her authority. As she busied herself at the counter she kept snatching glimpses of them, seeking to recalibrate the relationships she had once found so precious and so harrowing.

The postcard could only have arrived the previous day and they had come at once. And here they were, mild and unobtrusive, in no way the dominating figures she had battled with so long. Her father, though not seeming as tall, was still handsome, his limp still marked. But she noticed an air of resilience about him that was new: his shoulders were less hunched, his brow clear and open. Her mother was conventionally smart in the way you would expect of women shopping in Kendal Milne and taking tea there with friends. They sat together with the easiness of the long married, talking in a desultory way to one another, showing no excitement, not even any particular interest in what was being said. I hope Pete and I never come to that, Martha thought, feeling smug about the eagerness with which the two of them talked, the closeness of their locked eyes, even to their petty squabbles.

Eventually she was able to come across and speak to them.

'This job is only temporary . . . I'm filling in here while I decide what I really want to do.'

They hadn't asked but she had found herself offering an explanation.

'Your dad's got a new job.'

'Good, oh good.'

Had they come this far to tell her their own news rather than ask about her? Well, there was a relief in that, even if it came tinged with a certain regret at no longer being the centre of their world.

'Yes, I had seen the Grande was closing.'

Her mother's lips hardened into a disapproving line.

'Yes, we saw that you'd been!'

Ah, that was better, the old familiar criticism. She felt safe knowing she was on home ground. A sliver of defiance – familiar within her – squeaked into being.

'I tried to be in touch, to make up for missing Christmas really . . . I still have the key, by the way.'

'Oh, that's all right, Martha. It's just so good to see you.'

Her father, suddenly expansive and fond, splayed his long legs, almost tripping a couple of girls arriving and needing service. Martha returned to the counter to make their cups of tea.

Don't go back, don't pick up the old ways; she whispered her resolve. Don't fall into the trap, you're free of them, remember. And in gratitude for that freedom she was suddenly suffused with fondness.

Bruno with whom she shared café duties offered to cope alone while she sat with her parents. Everyone knew about parents. They had to be dealt with. He understood.

'Now tell me about this new job, and about everyone else. I'm dying to know.'

Eddie had heard on the grapevine of the great new building that Granada Television had recently opened in Manchester's Quay Street. Granada was being hailed as the most prestigious of all the independent television companies. Its programmes were the subject of talk in every shop and pub he went into. It was a youthful new enterprise rich with promises and opportunities. He began to abandon the sneering contempt with which he spoke of television. There was no good protesting for ever that it was a cheap and vulgar upstart, forcing cinemas to close. The Grande had gone, he needed to be realistic. He needed a job. Someone in the same union told him there was a vacancy for a cinema projectionist. He took the bus into Manchester Piccadilly and walked the rest of the way; there was a fine mist drifting on the wind and he drew his trench coat closer. It hadn't occurred to him to try to look smart. The thought only occurred when he saw the grandeur of the place. He entered the big glass doors into the spacious foyer and talked to a trim woman at a desk. Behind her a great splashy modern painting the size of an entire wall set the tone of somewhere spanking new and defiant. The taste wasn't his; he could see he'd need to shake off the cobwebby ways he had grown into at the Grande. He waited briefly, drinking in the neat efficiency of it all. There was a youthful casualness about the place where everyone seemed sure of who they were and what they were doing. He began to feel it would be good to be part of it. The feeling grew when he went along to see someone called Joe and was startled to find such a young man in charge. Joe was pleasant and to the point – neither lordly nor craven, treating Eddie as someone like himself, someone who knew his job. It all felt strangely exhilarating. Television was certainly where young people wanted to work. In the new building they rushed along bright corridors, calling to each other like frenzied parrots. He watched them with curiosity, almost envy. They dressed easily and gaily, the girls stalked past leggy and crisp, and boys without ties pushed in groups through the swing doors. The people he thought of as boys turned out to be producers: confident graduates, many of them, but others from the theatre with cravats and velvet cuffs. The older generation – people like himself – had jobs in the vast workshops and building the studio sets. Chippies, scenery painters, people who already had crafts at their fingertips. Eddie would come to see that they mattered as much to the success of programmes as many of the people with clipboards and desks. Certainly there was an air of involvement on everybody's part he hadn't known for years, and he was hoping to join in. He was only in his forties, after all. His life needed shaking up. News of the new job brought him approval from Beattie. Granada was where they made *Coronation Street* and in the two years since it began she had become addicted, following the stories of women she believed somehow to be like herself, or like those she knew. Ena Sharples was a scarcely exaggerated version of her own grandmother, long gone; Annie Walker had the forced charm of an old aunt who had cheered her on when she enrolled at the factory; and Elsie Tanner had just the sort of breezy glamour she had fancied she had long ago. Women across the north of England were recognising themselves and their dreams and following each episode to see how their fictional selves might behave. The idea of Eddie moving within the same orbit stirred her into something like enthusiasm. All this he told Martha in the milk bar. What he didn't tell her was how it had come about that Beattie was with him.

Beattie had returned in thoughtful mood from the outing with Derek. She had decided there and then it would be their last outing together. She couldn't risk any further claims on her past, and such an absurd one as this. Derek had been totally deluded years ago and was still deluded. Now she was almost afraid of him and the fact he so insistently followed a dream. She returned home in silence, a particular kind of silence, bemused and self-doubting. She needed to unburden herself to someone. Eddie was hardly the right one. She sat at the table and opened the red leather correspondence case.

'Dear Muriel, You remember what you were saying

about Derek ... ' Her pen gathered pace, skimming across the frail blue airmail paper, updating Muriel on their latest sidecar outing. She came to Derek's confession and hardly hesitated. On she went, relating the circumstances almost with relish: her sitting beside him on the country wall, the cows browsing in the field opposite, his sudden diffidence towards her and nosiness about Martha. Out it spilled as though she were talking to herself ... her sense of shock, her utter rejection of such a notion, and even, as the writing itself calmed her, the whole idiocy of the idea. She ended with a flourish and sat back, purged.

Later, they sat talking together over the debris of their meal – the fat from the grilled sausages congealing on the plates, and Eddie pressing a slice of bread into the thickening but tasty mess.

'Yes, I shall have to give up the bike and catch the bus from the corner of Chapel Street, and it'll take me longer to get to work. Something like three-quarters of an hour ... of course, I'll be on different hours from before, but just as awkward. You'll manage OK, won't you?'

Beattie paused without answering. She was wondering in what way his travel arrangements would call for her to manage; she had managed their lives together long enough. How odd that he should enquire.

Ever since the strange intimacy of her birthday weekend they had sustained a tentative tenderness for each other. They were more thoughtful than had been their habit. They took occasion to remark on the other's well-being, and even appearance. It was a sort of truce in their implied war. But it was a fragile truce, constantly at risk of Beattie's sudden bad temper. Perhaps along with the new life came a new assessment of how things should be between them. Well that was fair enough, Beattie thought. It had become a mess, over the years, and none of it her doing. Yes, it was good that he was giving some thought to her. The idea of the job would have to wait.

'Oh, yes, I'll be fine. Right as rain. Don't you worry about me.' Though privately she was pleased. 'I'll just wash the pots,' and she got up abruptly, stacked the dirty dishes high and carried them into the kitchen.

Eddie heard her running the tap into the sink. He took out his pipe and, reaching across to the smaller table for an ashtray, saw Beattie's letter to Muriel lying open on the red leather writing case.

It was with a sense they were coming closer that he did the unthinkable and went over and smoothed the pages of her letter. He stood over the space where she wrote, tamped the tobacco down and read the letter. It was like reading the diary of a young girl. Beattie was clearly imagining romantic situations for herself and inventing stories about her life. He was startled to find no mention of himself, and instead an entire episode with Derek taking a central role, cast as both clumsy and deluded lover. He read on: meeting, excursion in the sidecar, talks in inglenooks and pub gardens . . . all of it innocent and childlike. When it came, the story that Derek thought he might be Martha's father either proved he was barmy or was some crazy fantasy of Beattie's. If there was one thing of which he was sure, it was Martha.

She was said to look like him, her speech had his lilt. Put the palms of their hands together and they were identical. Beattie wrote in an excited girlish hand, the long looping writing crawling across the pages with its own eagerness to be read. He was glad not to be mentioned: he could only have appeared as the villain and he was thankful to be absent. He left the pages as he found them, moved to the armchair and waited for her to bring the cups of instant coffee for them both. The clatter of dishes and pans in the kitchen had fallen silent. She would be in, any minute. He struggled to decide what to do: to ignore the letter, to confess that he had read it, to make a scene about its contents, to make no scene, to wait and see. He waited.

The moment Beattie thrust the tray of coffee before her into the room she felt a sense of the letter lying open on her writing case. She glanced towards Eddie. He was sitting back smoking, tapping his pipe a little keenly into the small brass ashtray. He had not risen to help her bring the tray into the room, as he had taken to doing. Her hands began to shiver and the tray to shake. Milky coffee slopped into the flowered saucers.

'What's up, love?' He didn't look at her, turning his eyes towards the window as though suddenly preoccupied with their meagre garden. 'Something wrong?'

'You know how it is. I write to Muriel quite often ... it's like I was young again, gassing away to a friend I never see ...'

He turned quickly and faced her. 'Is it true?'

'What? Is what true?'

291

She dumped the tray of coffee on top of the open red leather correspondence case. She knew the letter would never be sent. She sat opposite him and looked him in the eye.

'What do you mean? Is it true?'

'Your story to Muriel ... the yarn you're spinning about Derek and, you know, about Martha.'

Beattie felt herself swamped by contradictions; feeling defensive, feeling annoyed.

'Well, I have been out in Derek's sidecar. That's true. I got bored, Eddie, you can understand that, and he was so sad.'

'Why didn't you say so, then? I thought since your birthday—'

'Well, that was special, I'll give you that. But we don't, do we? We don't ... talk much. That's our way, that's how it's become ... hasn't it?'

'Well, you talk to Derek. You talk to Muriel. And you make me look a fool!'

Beattie was stung by what sounded like an accusation. 'And you talk to Martha. Oh yes, Martha, Martha. The love of your life. I sometimes think you're married to her, not to me! How do you think that makes me look?'

'Well, I'm not any more, am I? She's gone, hasn't she? She's left me!'

'And what about me? I'm her mother. Why doesn't she—' Beattie was surprised to find she had a lump in her throat. She swallowed hard. This was no time to collapse. They were talking, finally telling the truth. 'What d'you mean, "She's left me"? She's not dead, she's left home and that's all. It's what they're all doing nowadays. It's not so terrible.'

The pause between them was so painful she relented and handed a cup of tepid coffee across to him. He still needed looking after.

'And Derek, what's he up to, eh? Why did you see him? All this nonsense about Martha: what's that about?' He gulped at the coffee and grimaced at the taste.

'Oh, yes, yes, I think he's mad, he's gone quite mad. I've never heard him say such things before.'

'He may be mad, Beattie, but I need to know . . . '

'Well, yes, he did ask me, that much is true. As I told Muriel, he did suggest – that idea about Martha. I think he even hoped.'

A shadow of hesitancy in her breath caught Eddie's ear.

'Was there anything . . . at all about the two of you?' Eddie frowned suddenly. Why was he going over the past like this? He had been away at the war, fighting, being wounded. He felt a sudden exhaustion. Did it give him the right to control what people at home got up to. He hadn't cared then. Did he really care now? He couldn't clearly remember whether he had locked Beattie into the loyalty that went with a ring on the third finger. He rather thought that came later with his return home. Of course it had, yes. He had been lying all strapped up in the local hospital and asked a nurse to go out and buy one for him. The matron had thought it very odd, but the nurses had gathered round to see and were sure it helped his recovery. When Beattie came to visit he had slipped it on her finger and the ward had raised a cheer to them both.

293

Beattie watched the changing moods across his face. She feared to say the wrong thing, whether it was true or not.

Funny that what mattered was not some 'yes' or 'no' about long ago, but being all right with the other person: being right together. It suddenly mattered a great deal.

By the time the postcard arrived at number 26, it was natural they would both want to come.

Chapter 34

Eddie settled comfortably into work at Granada Television. He found the job he had to do wasn't all that different from the Grande. It was a matter of working with familiar machines and being part of a company sending out a world of stories to an ever-widening public. But the place was entirely different. Granada was the creation of two brothers – Mr Sidney and Mr Cecil Bernstein, impresarios whose panache left the Vernons looking feeble and insipid. It was their idea to hang an engraving of the American impresario P. T. Barnum in every office, setting the tone of boisterous show business they hoped their staff would copy. Mr Sidney was the big chief, always immaculately groomed, arriving in his grand chauffeur-driven car early in the morning, or even taking his own plane from London and staying overnight in the penthouse flat at the top of the Granada building. Once on duty, he moved through the building taking an interest in every little thing, coming up all the time with new ideas and notions for making things better. On his regular rounds with a flock of managers in tow, no speck of dust, no painting hanging askew on the white walls went unnoticed. The Film Operations Department knew to keep the preview theatres neat and tidy, most especially the main preview theatre in the basement, which was Mr Sidney's private cinema. Eddie warmed to the sight of its cinema curtains, the lights that dimmed, just as they did at the Grande. One day it might be Eddie's turn to attend on Mr Sidney there.

Most welcoming of all was the pay: Eddie was offered a good deal more than he had earned at the Grande. Although he had never been consciously greedy for money and promotion, Eddie felt the pleasures that a rise in income at any level brings with it. It meant he could be more generous with the housekeeping allowance he gave to Beattie every week. He could buy a magazine on impulse, or begin to think of saving for a car. He had a sense of relaxing into an easier life. There had been something constrained and shabby about his former job that had conveyed itself to his home. It even infected his attitudes to people; he saw now that in recent years he had been quick to disapprove and to judge, ungenerous with his encouragement, guarding his affections close, reserving the best of them for Martha. Now with the security of work and more money in his pocket, his moods were less jaundiced, he could even imagine himself being indulgent. The black gloves had been a success. Perhaps he and Beattie might have a holiday abroad.

As the year went by he became more aware of the affairs of the world. Granada was a company regularly accused of political bias by the Authority that ran the independent companies. It was an allegation officially denied by its cultivated director of programmes, who remonstrated grandly with the top men in London. At the same time he was urging his army of aggressive young journalists to make bold and challenging programmes. He wanted to show audiences things that mattered, make them think for themselves once a programme was over. It was the pioneering spirit he had brought with him from serving in the government's surprisingly adventurous Central Office of Information.

Eddie felt he was being jolted from the lush pastures of cinema films into the more hectic waters of the world around him. He began to notice that things were shaping up badly in the Cold War. He had always held himself apart from concerns about international threats. He reckoned he'd done his bit, and bad headlines made his old wound twitch. At least his generation wouldn't have to go there again. By 'there' he meant 'the front', 'the battlefield' wherever the enemy struck. But now things were looking as though there was no actual front any more, no places where men with guns faced up to others like themselves. The Cold War had shifted the parameters. Both East and West had the biggest weapons man had ever made and it seemed to him the battlefield tactics he'd known were gone for ever. The problem was they would do away with everything else as well – with ceasefires and truces, with negotiations and trade-offs. That seemed to be how things stood, with America and Russia daring each other to be the first to press the button and incinerate the world. This seemed so ludicrous a prospect that Eddie had simply assumed that those whose business was dealing with such things had them well in hand. It was beginning to seem that they didn't. He had been alarmed when he read about Americans building nuclear shelters in the basements of their cities. He was not reassured by Civil Defence advice given in Britain about how to respond to a nuclear attack. Apparently you had four minutes to get under a table and put your head in a paper bag. Or some such rubbish. Surely world powers who had jostled for supremacy ever since the division of Germany in 1945 had the sense not to go too far. But did they? And how far was too far?

Eddie had never bothered with such things before. But in the world of television he was brushing shoulders with young newsmen who seemed to be full of facts no one had told him. They were worth listening to. He would overhear them in the canteen, a place where everyone converged: stage crew mixed with telecine operators, make-up girls chatted with actors. Even programme directors would queue with the rest talking intensively about the company's newest projects. A new quiz show had just begun that pitted different university teams against each other. There was concern it might not get enough viewers. Others were getting all steamed up about the current affairs programmes that attacked things that were wrong or corrupt, and in so doing offended many of those who had the power to hit back. More and more people were watching ITV and Eddie as a small part of it was pleased to see the stuffy old BBC outpaced by these noisy, assertive Granada reporters. Most particularly he was impressed by a tall forceful Australian who had an opinion about everything in the world and let everyone share it.

Eddie took his lunch tray to the table next to his. Tim – that was his name – was telling all about his recent series about Cuba.

'They held me in custody, the bastards, for five hours the day before we were due to leave. That gave me a bad fright, I can tell you. Cuba's a bastard and that's a fact. Still it was fascinating ... the revolution was long overdue, no doubt about it. They'd been outrageously exploited by the Americans ... Cuba probably needs its heavy dose of Marxism.'

Eddie kept his head down, quietly slicing his toad-in-the-hole and picking up what he could of the conversation. Was Cuba a good thing then? He had no way of working out what to think.

Things got instantly worse in mid-October. By the twenty-first, Soviet ships were steaming across the Atlantic, ostensibly, they said, to defend Cuba from American aggression. The buzz went round the Granada building that NBC news's Walter Cronkite had made a statement full of foreboding. Apparently Americans were beginning to stockpile food; there had been a bigger than usual attendance at church the following Sunday. Then on the twenty-second President Kennedy made an important speech to the American people more or less setting out that they were on the brink of nuclear war. Could it really be happening? Could it be that serious? The answer seemed to be agreed. There was a hush in telecine when the news was carried in Britain. The usually buoyancy of the news crews and the technical staff, the talk in the offices, the rehearsals in the studios were subdued and thoughtful. The talk prattled on but there was a tinny quality to it, and half-hearted attempts to be normal. When people went off duty that night many of them let their fears show.

'See you tomorrow.'

'Well, let's hope so, eh?'

'What's going on, Eddie, what's happening—'

Beattie scarcely waited for him to get through the door. She'd heard people talking in the grocer's and was bewildered by what they said. Surely if any nuclear bombs were dropped they would all feel it, wouldn't they? No one would be safe at all. Some were even angry with the Americans.

'You mark my words, the moment they have nuclear shelters to keep them safe, they'll take the risk!' It all seemed so preposterous.

'They say it's really bad, this could be it. Could it, Eddie?'

But no one knew what 'it' was ... some science fiction future of global destruction now being talked of as a date in the diary, today or tomorrow ... or any minute now.

'I don't know much. The blokes at Granada say it's really serious between America and Russia: the Soviet ships are still sailing across the Atlantic.' Then with a sigh: 'We can't do anything, Beattie. Panic won't help. Best thing is to get on with supper and watch the news on the telly later.'

And privately he worried what Martha was making of it all: where was she? She was in as much danger as all of them. What was she thinking? She must be frantic that the CND campaign didn't seem to have done much good.

*

While the world held its breath it also went on turning. Work had to be done and people went about their daily routines in a haze of apprehension. At Granada the bright young men and women were constantly under pressure to have new ideas. They held brain-storming sessions. Eddie liked the sound of that but was at the same time aware it was well beyond his range. He was a part of the theatre team who dubbed the commentaries and sound effects on to the final edit. He knew his limitations. A young producer called Jeremy – he wore jeans and a loose shaggy sweater and looked little more than a student – was trying out a new format designed to appeal to teenagers. Eddie had spoken with pride of his daughter more than once and Jeremy, who was casting around looking for intelligent young people with opinions, asked whether Martha might like to appear on the programme's panel.

Eddie made a show of hesitation but it was soon agreed she should be approached. Martha had been happy enough the evening Jeremy had come over from Manchester to Sibling Rivalry to meet her and assess her suitability for the programme. He clearly warmed to the quirky set-up of the household, lumbering round the house with the uninhibited inquisitiveness of media folk. Duncan hadn't minded; after all, they were about the same age and they were soon gossiping together about friends they had in common. Jeremy met the others, too. Jake raised a languid hand in greeting as he passed through collecting a mug of coffee. Cassie and Monica stayed to talk, curious and even hopeful about opportunities to be seen on television. Pete was away on CND business. But Martha had come up to the mark – the right age, a pert presence and enough fluency to express her opinions without turning strident. Yes, Jeremy would be in touch.

She felt a quick thrill of excitement at being asked her opinions. She had never thought before that her own ideas might matter.

Chapter 35

In Sibling Rivalry Duncan presided over a long and chaotic supper. He was being urged by several voices to pull what strings he could to get tickets for the Little Richard concert at the Empire. The American legend had been a sensation at New Brighton recently and Brian Epstein had persuaded him to come back. Liverpool was agog to be there. Pete was shrinking inside his tweed jacket, cowering away from the mayhem. He looked at each of them with sad eyes, finally turning towards Martha with a smile of pained regret that he could see wrenched her heart.

'How can they all think about music and concerts, at a time like this?'

He spoke beneath his breath, aware that his intervention would call down mockery from the others. 'There's no let-up in sight. The latest news is the Russian ships are nearing the American blockade ... and all the fuss is about Little Richard.'

Jake caught the last remark. 'Oh, but he's just a great performer: terrific style, energy –' and he gave himself up to his own rendering of 'Tutti Frutti'. Others grinned and tapped its rhythm out on the table.

'Don't be such a killjoy, Pete, sitting sulking there.' This from Cassie who had cooked the meal and needed help. 'Give us a hand if you can't join the fun.' Then, as he stumbled willingly to his feet: 'He and The Beatles on the same bill ... you've got to admit it's historic.'

Pete smiled at that. 'Yes, of course, it is.' And then with a sudden lurch of goodwill, 'I'd really like to hear them myself, I really would!'

He turned to Martha and smiled, more brightly this time. He must shake off this sense of doom. It had haunted him too long. He loved the fellowship of the house and hated to see himself cast as a wet blanket. He shook his shoulders hard as though he could throw off his mood like discarding a heavy cape. Then he joined Cassie at the sink and began to wash out the clogged saucepans.

'I know you worry a lot, Pete, but there's little any of us can do.'

She spoke under the clatter of the washing-up.

'You'd probably have to go into politics to make any sort of difference, and think what a useless lot they are.'

Pete pulled a grim smile. He wasn't going to disagree.

'We made them listen to CND, didn't we ... for a while at least?'

He said this without believing it. It was a solace, a consolation as he watched the world rushing to its own destruction. He had done all he could as a moral being to have some influence in the world: others had joined him, churchmen and poets, thinkers and, yes, politicians. But Britain still had the bomb. So it was useless, futile. His efforts were a pitiable joke, his cries of rage echoing out into the void a tiny echo of all he had once felt might be achieved.

He turned with the tea towel in his hands, wiping dripping bubbles from chipped plates, and looked back at the table. Martha was smiling at some remark made by Monica. Everyone was hacking lumps off a large yellow block of cheese and biting into it. They were all smiling, together, enjoying the remark, enjoying the same things in life. And Martha was one of them. Pete felt he was looking in on this happy scene as though through a separating window. Except there was no window, no glass. Just his own self, his very being, was making him feel this way. Nothing about him gave off any clues.

He turned smiling towards Cassie, and listened to her.

'I'm sure Duncan'll get us those tickets, you know. He has friends at the Empire. You'll come then, won't you?'

Pete grinned at the prospect, reassuring her that he was one with them all. But he had decided in that moment that he would not be going.

That night he lay with Martha in their wide cool bed. They lay beside each other, loving but not wanting to make love. He held her close, feeling her aliveness as a sort of magic bestowed on her. She was what it meant to be fully human, full of energy and enthusiasm for things, yet calm in her gentle caring for him. He propped himself on an elbow watching her. 'You go to sleep, go on ... I'll keep vigil. I'll watch over you, my love. My heart: you deserve a long and happy life. We all do.' She reached out a hand and held it to his cheek then turned her body into the bedclothes and nestled down like a small animal.

When she woke he had gone. It often happened like that. He would follow his own routine, which was to have no routine. She was up and off to the milk bar where she was working out a week's notice. She had asked Jen at the bookshop to look out for a job with more zing to it, something with some purpose. There was talk of converting the cinema at Hope Hall into a theatre: there might be a job there one day, but it was no more than a rumour. And there was the possibility of this interview on Granada. She was both excited and afraid. And that felt good. Now she was leaving, she felt fond of the milk bar. She would miss Bruno, who had made a point of being nice to her parents. She even felt fond of her parents, now they were safely back home and reconciled to her leading her own life.

It was Pete who had done all this, who had given her such confidence, who had listened to her ideas and confronted her miseries. But the miseries had steadily lifted. And as that happened other choices arrived. She wasn't sure which came first, whether things happening apparently at random improved her mood, or whether the changes in her mood somehow conjured up new choices. Perhaps they interacted one with the other and right now were improving together. Was this how the world worked? If so, she was grateful for it. She bestowed a reward on herself, a foaming cream slice from the milk bar display.

Chapter 36

Beattie was cooling towards her American friend. Muriel's letters were growing frantic: there was an urgent distress about them that hinted at derangement. Her voice shrieked off the pages of the airmail letters that arrived sometimes as often as twice a week. It seemed that Gus's business was failing; he was just not making the sales that were expected of him. Their income was threatened and with it the tenancy of their home and the future of college for the children. What to do, what to do. The great American dream seemed to be crumbling. All this might just be bearable, they could get by with help from the local church and such. But there was something much worse. Rather late in the day and tipped off by an anonymous letter, she learned that he had been neglecting his sales visits in favour of rendezvous with a string of women. 'Just imagine,' Muriel's letter screamed. 'The cheap hussies preying on a helpless lonely man like that?' Beattie recalled a capable assertive man who knew very well what he wanted in the world. She sent tentative consolations in neutral language, but the hissing grew stronger. 'The two-faced bastard, I can tell you, I'm not taking this lying down.' Beattie backed away from sympathy, musing it was the other women who were taking it lying down. The little joke made her smile, which she didn't do very often. Her life was easing up just as Muriel's was falling apart. 'He dares to come home and expect me, the ideal wife, to be waiting all smiles and apple pie ... but not any more. This place is a battleground, I can tell you. I've got plenty of neighbours telling me all he's been up to over the years. Jeez, Beattie, one even told me she'd had an abortion. "Cripes," I said, "why should that have anything to do with Gus?" And then she told me all the details ... cheap scent, phony furs and more. Grisly stuff. I'm taking it all down and making it over to the lawyer ... or I will be doing when I can get myself together.' Beattie knew what that meant: Muriel's writing had become a tangled mess of letters and blots. And the blots might not always be ink: tears, thought Beattie at first, and then perhaps gin. She wrote briefly suggesting Muriel see a doctor. She hesitated to say psychiatrist because she wasn't sure what they did, but Americans were keen on such things, weren't they? As she cautiously withdrew from the correspondence she folded Muriel's letters away, zipped up the red leather case and put it aside.

As she did so she remembered another clutch of letters, the faded pack she had once tied up with ribbon and an elastic band and kept at the back of her underwear drawer. She hadn't thought about them for ages.

She went looking and was only mildly surprised to find they weren't where she supposed. Like much of her past they had gone missing. She felt a pang of loss: they were her collected love letters ... the sum total of all the declared passion she had ever enjoyed. Some rather abrupt notes from Eddie away at war, an urgent invitation she had totally ignored from a married supervisor at the factory, a whole bunch of mawkish letters from Derek with the sort of words they used in birthday cards ... ardour, devotion. Not words anyone would ever speak. That's why she had kept them. They were the only tangible evidence she had ever engaged someone's passion. And sometimes through the years she had needed to know they were there. She had tucked them away secretly as though they were the passionate declarations of a poet. It had been her fancy to pretend as much.

Martha had come across them when she was tidying her room in Sibling Rivalry. She and Pete had agreed to share a room together, an act of bonding that sent a whisper of disapproval around the other inhabitants of the house. Theirs was after all meant to be an experiment in living, and pairing off like this was the first crack in their unity of purpose. But Martha was again breaking with the past and moving on. It was a time for sorting things out and throwing away anything she would no longer need in her life with Pete. The tattered pack of letters she had stolen from Galton Road seemed to come from an ancient time; they had lost the poison of excitement that stealing them had bestowed. They were remnants merely of a life long left behind. She could give them back to her mother, but anything to do with Derek filled her with loathing. She didn't want Derek's letters to lie next to her father's. She knew it wasn't really her decision but she made it anyway. She decided she would make a ritual of their disposal.

Taking the ferry across the Mersey she slowly shredded the letters into the churning foam. Returning on the same crossing she faced the waterfront of the city, her city. She was seeing a new world born and was eager to be part of it. None of them yet knew what it would be. They only knew it would be different from what had gone before. The house was curiously still when she arrived back at Sefton Park. She walked up the drive expecting to catch the drift of music from within, or glimpse the shadow activity from one of the big bay windows. It stood its ground, solid and prosperous, its double-fronted red-brick presence usually radiating a welcome by tiny hints of activity. But right now there were none.

Her eyes roamed the windows. Duncan often stood reading where he could see out into the street, watchful for new arrivals and old friends. But he was not there. She jangled her clutch of keys and turned the appropriate one in the side door, making towards the big family room. 'Hellooooa!' Her voice had an edge of expectation. It might on another day have been anxiety but she was in too good a mood for that. There was little sound but she had a sense of people being near. Hefting her bag on to her shoulder she moved eagerly to open the door. They were all there, except for Pete.

Duncan was standing by the sink and looking towards the door. She saw him first: his look was direct and steady, conveying nothing. Some were sitting round the table and staring towards the place where she came in. They didn't speak or smile: they were frozen as if in terror and panic. Only Cassie was moving, heaped on the red sofa. She looked up, agony on her tear-stained face.

'What? What is it? What?' Martha dropped her bag and searched out an answer in every face.

Finally Duncan. 'Martha – it's Pete ... '

'Yes, of course, it's Pete. But what? Tell me what's happened?'

'He's been found ... '

'Is he hurt? Tell me. Spell it out! Tell me!'

Duncan made a move towards her, intending some kind of tenderness. Martha put out her hands to fend off any generous gesture.

'Just tell me. Is he ... OK? Just tell me.'

'No, Martha. Pete is ... dead.'

She looked from one to another: each of them was reluctant to have it be their own voice that broke her heart.

Cassie snuffled away, curled into her own misery.

'Oh, God ...'

'They think, Martha, they think he committed suicide ... they pulled his body from the Mersey.' Something strange was happening inside her head. It felt as though the bones of her skull were lifting off and her brain was flying away. She felt a sort of giddiness, a rush of euphoria. Looking round the room the colours were all strong – red and blues she'd never noticed; Jake had a new purple

311

scarf; Monica was pulling a thread from her cardigan. It was all in vivid sharp focus: like a dream, like a nightmare.

'Well … he always said the world would end … how funny is it? He was right. He knew he was right. The world has ended, it has.' She was shouting at them, crying into their faces.

Chapter 37

In the days after Pete's death Martha tried hard to be on her own. But she found herself caught up in a circle of mourners who devoured her in their grief. Her own grief was like no other. It was laced with a furious anger. Two days after Pete had despaired of the future, the Cuba Crisis, as it came to be known, had been resolved. Russia's ships had turned back, the missiles would be dismantled. Whatever had gone on between the leaders had turned the threat of nuclear war aside. No one would ever know; no leaders would ever reveal exactly what had happened. But the world still turned, the sun still shone. Yet for Pete there was no return. He had lost faith – in her and in himself. Her rage was uncontainable.

She seized a coat, rushed out to the local park and sat slumped among autumn leaves, beating her fists on the ground until they ached. Pete's parents arrived pale with shock and treated her with a tenderness that made her want to scream. She sat meekly with them on the old sofa, screwing her tangled black hair and biting her lips.

'He wrote to tell us about you: he said you were his true love.'

Martha raised an eyebrow at his confiding such thoughts. She searched their faces and found traces of Pete's features: his high wide brow, and the curious twist to his nose, just like his father's. His mother's speech had something of the same dark lilt, her thick chestnut hair had the same texture as his own. Their being with her, reminding her of how he looked and spoke, gave a strange reality to Pete's existence. They who had created him, had borne him into the world, had lived to see his life completed. Their lengthening years enfolded his. They spoke gently of his achievements, his dedication, his joy at having found happiness with her. She listened, unblinking. She felt helpless, gutted, without substance, as light as thistledown and as likely to float away.

The telephone call had been uneasy. Martha said she wondered whether Beattie would like to perhaps have a coffee with her – or, 'Well, more likely a cup of tea, eh?' Beattie had hidden any surprise at the call, speaking rather in tones that suspected some kind of trap. But yes she would be in Staveley the following afternoon and would make time for her daughter. Quite how much time wasn't clear to either of them. But Beattie had in mind no more than half an hour. She had to be gone by four o'clock.

Martha began to think it might be a mistake on the

way over on the train. She was still in a limbo of grief. With plans for the funeral made by Pete's parents, she had two days to wait until she went over to their home in the Wirral for the service. Her mind was filled with thoughts of what it might be like. How she wanted to shape and phrase her final farewell. Flowers? What did Quakers go in for? It wasn't at all clear why the impulse to meet her mother had arisen and now it had begun she was bewildered.

'And how are you, Martha? How's life at the milk bar?'

Beattie, who had never seemed to Martha in the least bit jaunty, was jaunty now. Her stride had a good deal more confidence about it. She was trim and neat with a swinging jacket of bright green and Cuban-heeled shoes in brown and white. She was almost modern. For Martha the idea of giving any thought to how you might look belonged to another world. She had wrapped herself in a big navy overcoat of Cassie's and tethered a dirty red scarf around her unruly hair. They had met on the corner by the bus station, in sight of the Grande, now dressed in garish posters declaring 'Bingo Nights For All': neither of them referred to it.

'We could go to Aldo's coffee bar, would you like that?' Martha had been tentative.

'Which one did you mean? There are three of them now ... they're the coming thing, aren't they? But there's a nice café opened too. I've been there with friends and it's, well, as I said, nice.'

Martha let the remark about friends lie between them, unchallenged. They settled in at a window table with a pot of tea and a plate of Kunzle cakes.

'I've left the milk bar now: I'm hoping to get a job in some kind of theatre set-up ... there's lots happening in Liverpool. I'm hoping there might be a place for me there.'

Without Pete, Martha was indifferent to her future. The strange anticipation of nuclear war that had seized them with its terrors had left everyone but her blank with relief when it was suddenly over. Khrushchev had blinked first, it seemed, and the world had been saved. If that was international politics then Martha didn't think much of it. She had rowed with Duncan about it and fled in tears from the room.

' ... I was just wondering how you were. I know Dad's got a new job and likes it too. Do you think it's a good thing?'

'Well, it's bringing in a bit more money. That's a relief, I can tell you.'

'And you?'

'Yes, well, I've got some news too.'

Beattie braced her shoulders with a flash of pride. It wasn't much, given the dash and daring of her daughter's flight from home.

'I've branched out myself. I'm following your example, Martha. I've signed up for a pottery class at the same college. In fact, I'm on my way there now. It was lucky I could fit you in.'

Martha cut her small cake in half, playing for time.

'You've what? Really? Tell me about it.'

'Pauline Johnson and I go every week. We have to take overalls 'cos we get very messy. The clay gets everywhere you know.'

Martha recognised the family priorities. 'Well, that's just great. Just great!' And for the first time in days, Martha smiled. Her mother's announcement gave her the push she needed. She took a deep breath.

'I think I told you about Pete, didn't I?'

'Mmm? Oh, one of the crowd at that house you're in ... some sort of commune, don't they call it?'

'No, we don't call it that. Not at all. In fact we call it Sibling Rivalry.' The idea of further explanation defeated her. 'Yes, Pete was one of them. But rather different from the rest ... '

Her mother's appetite for the Kunzle cakes filled the silence.

'He and I had ... well ... ' None of the clichés would do and yet that was all she had. 'He and I had become close. Very close ... '

Beattie paused among the crumbs and looked at her.

'Yes, we were serious!'

Martha managed a bleak smile as tears pricked behind her eyes.

'Are you saying you're thinking of becoming engaged, Martha, because you must realise you're far too young for such things. Dear girl, you're only seventeen; it's puppy love, that's what it is!'

The cliché hurt and Beattie, seeing her daughter wince, relented. 'But that's fine; fine by us. I'll break it to Eddie and make sure he takes it on board. So when can we meet him ... this Pete of yours.'

And then she told her mother.

Chapter 38

Pete's death hit the house hard. Autumn rains darkened the skies and kept everyone scurrying along pavements clogged with sodden leaves. The water skittered into roadside drains, setting up little eddies that splattered their clothing. The bushes in the front garden had the dark green of graveyard trees: everything reminded them of loss. Duncan had not held court for weeks: he claimed to be working up lectures for some future series in Liverpool and kept to his room. Once when he came out he had taken the papier mâché figure with its rampant erection, put it in the big drawing room and thrown a black curtain over it. Perhaps, he explained to the others, his grandma might arrive and claim her room back. They shrugged. He hadn't needed to explain.

Each of them – Jake, Cassie, Monica, Charlotte, Duncan – had grown more reticent, each wanting to speak of Pete in their own way, but fearful of distressing Martha. There were spates of sudden humour and jokes,

jokes, hardly funny, but prompting guffaws of laughter. The thought was growing that whatever had held them there had been fractured. It wasn't as though Pete had been the life and soul of the party. Far from it, with his doomy talk and earnest politicking. But there had been an invisible balance between them that kept them living in harmony. Without Pete the balance had shifted.

Meanwhile Martha's unobtrusive grieving choked the air. She moved among them like a sleepwalker, going about the daily routine unassumingly, seeking not to draw attention to herself but somehow making her presence incandescent with sorrow. Then suddenly she would erupt with odd notions in surprisingly breezy tones.

'Full breakfast fry-up everyone?' she had called out through the house one morning. In a matter of moments the kitchen was busy and noisy as though she had given them permission to be themselves. It was a euphoria born of the knowledge that something was slipping away. The plates heaped with delicious slabs of gammon, a dark mess of field mushrooms and the glistening yellow of egg yolks spread across the scrubbed table like some farewell banquet. Martha surveyed them all knowing it would soon be time to move on. She had gained so much from being there – confidence, style, daring, courage and true love. But it was time to go.

Jake talked of going travelling; Duncan mentioned quietly that a couple of new people would be moving in. One a supply teacher called Pamela. Then towards Christmas Cassie announced that she would be joining a theatre company touring round the country. Their particular dream was coming to an end. Martha had decided that, though she'd been accepted, she would not appear on *Let Youth Have Its Say*. She telephoned Jeremy and left a message with a secretary.

She made the announcement at supper round the scrubbed table.

'I've just decided not to: I don't want to. So that's that.'

She was messing a helping of ratatouille round on her plate. She had no appetite at all; only occasionally she yearned for something cloying and sweet and got Cassie to make pancakes for them all. Comfort food, they said.

'Oh, what a shame: have you said so already?' Cassie, Monica and Charlotte were each wondering whether Jeremy might consider them, but didn't want to seem pushy. Duncan was more thoughtful. 'What's the reason, Martha?'

'Do I need a reason? If so, the reason is I just don't feel like it.'

It was said without aggression or self-pity but with a sort of fading attention.

'I just don't want to do anything any more. Anything at all.'

'I had been thinking of the sort of thing you might have said. The ideas you might have had ... ' Duncan left the idea to hover.

Martha licked the fork; the trace of herbs was pleasing after all. 'Such as what ideas? My mind's given up on ideas.'

'Oh, just the things we all talked about ... Pete talked about.'

'I'm no crusader if that's what you're thinking.'

'No, no, of course not: but you could express your

doubts about the way politics is, the way things are. I've heard you talk about that often enough.'

'Have I really? I can hardly remember.'

She reached for a pear from the brimming fruit bowl in the centre of the table. The juice ran down her chin as she bit into it. They all laughed and Jake handed her a handkerchief.

'Oh, I'm such a mess ... look at me.'

'You're not a mess, Martha. Not at all. You're the essence of sane.'

Duncan got on with his meal. Jake and Monica talked of concerts they were going to. Cassie took out a script and began scribbling.

'So what could I say, d'you think?' Martha had moved to the leather armchair and was gazing through the window. The garden was full of winter's approach. The garden she and Pete had watched through the seasons was now patched with fallen leaves and black branches. She felt the heaviness of time on her hands.

'I suppose I might ... '

'Oh, you could talk about the things we discuss round this table ... the things Pete was so anxious about. You could speak up for him. People worry that young people don't have sensible things to say: but we do, don't we? You do, I know that. Pete certainly did.'

Martha got up and went out into the garden. The grass was overgrown from neglect and recent rain left wet strands brushing against her long skirt. She looked up to the top floor window of the room they had shared and talked to Pete's shadow. Gently they arrived at a decision.

*

Let Youth Have Its Say was to launch three weeks before Christmas. Eddie tried not to be excited. He had arrived that morning through the car park, through the cavernous spaces of the studios among the familiar clatter of hammering as programme sets were being put together. There were chippies and electricians, men with ladders and paint pots; some hoisted bright strips of carpet where an eager young designer in oversized spectacles was commanding operations. Others were standing ready with ranks of seating waiting to be put in place. There were people weighing up the lighting rig over their heads and still others preoccupied with microphones and an abundance of wiring snaking across the floor. Everyone seemed to know what they were about, and how that meshed with what others were doing.

There was a mood of concentrated energy under pressure as people shouted instructions, cursed problems, and then stood back to judge their handiwork. It was as near as Eddie had ever been to a film set and his heart had lifted. And now Martha was getting her chance. He felt content with his life.

'Good evening and welcome to *Let Youth Have Its Say*.' The presenter was tall and well groomed. He bounced on polished shoes nodding towards his guests then back to the camera. There was a tension about him that transferred into a chilly smile. He was not her friend; he was a cipher. Martha felt she could say anything to him without fear of contradiction. She took strength from his shallowness.

'We live in changing times: times of international

disputes and domestic crises. But this is a time like no other. Young people as never before are making themselves heard and seen in our society. We notice them, don't we, with their daring clothes, and different ways: we welcome their new music and outspoken opinions. Tonight we have a chance to hear what they really think: are they going to change the world? Are they the forerunners of a new kind of Britain? How will their new values and attitudes shape the future of this country of ours?'

At this he gave a knowing look to the camera, reassuring to older viewers, complicit with the young. Martha despised him.

' . . . and so Martha, you are eighteen years old, born in the last year of the war with no memories of the hard times your parents' generation went through. Do you feel at your age you have enough experience to understand the world . . .?'

And Martha spoke.

Acknowledgements

I have been greatly helped in writing this story by many people in the north of England who remember the times of which I write, or know and love the city of Liverpool. I offer my thanks to Alan Bleasdale, Billy Butler, Sylvia Hikins, Sam Leach, Shawn Levy, Spencer Leigh, Mick Orde and Ken Pye. Others have given expert advice about cinema and television history: Alan Ashton, Nigel Anderton, David Blake, Ted Doan, Ernie Eban, Philip French, Clyde Jeavons, Donald Mackenzie, Gary Trinder and Nigel Wolland.

I am, as always, hugely indebted to my editors at Virago, Lennie Goodings and Vivien Redman, and also to my agent, Ed Victor.

virago

If you have enjoyed this book, you can find
out more about Virago Modern Classics and
Virago Press, our authors and titles, events
and book club forum on our websites

www.viragobooks.net

www.virago.co.uk

and follow us on Twitter

Twitter.com/@ViragoBooks

Also by Joan Bakewell

ALL THE NICE GIRLS

It is 1942 and the war is not going well. The Ashworth
Grammar School for Girls signs up for the Merchant Navy's
Ship Adoption Scheme. The headmistress, Cynthia Maitland,
who lost her lover in the First World War, believes the idea
will broaden the horizons of her girls, especially Polly and Jen,
bright sixth formers eager to live and love despite it all.

All is as it should be in the line of duty until Captain Josh
Percival and his officers of the SS *Treverran* visit Ashworth . . .
The choices that follow will disrupt all their lives,
reverberating even to the next generation, when, decades later,
life and love are on the line again.

'Marvellously exciting and heartbreaking . . . poignant,
romantic and deeply satisfying' *Daily Express*

**You can order other Virago titles through our website: *www.virago.co.uk*
or by using the order form below**

☐ All the Nice Girls   Joan Bakewell   £8.99

*The price shown above is correct at time of going to press. However, the publishers
reserve the right to increase prices on covers from those previously advertised, without
further notice.*

Please allow for postage and packing: **Free UK delivery.**
Europe: add 25% of retail price; Rest of World: 45% of retail price.

To order any of the above or any other Virago titles, please call our credit
card orderline or fill in this coupon and send/fax it to:

Virago, PO Box 121, Kettering, Northants NN14 4ZQ
Fax: 01832 733076   Tel: 01832 737526
Email: aspenhouse@FSBDial.co.uk

☐ I enclose a UK bank cheque made payable to Virago for £ . . . .
☐ Please charge £ . . . . . . to my Visa/Delta/Maestro

Expiry Date ☐☐☐☐   Maestro Issue No. ☐☐

NAME (BLOCK LETTERS please) . . . .

ADDRESS . . . .

. . . .

. . . .

Postcode . . . . Telephone . . . .

Signature . . . .

Please allow 28 days for delivery within the UK. Offer subject to price and availability.